BLACKOUT

BLACKOUT

marco carocari

First published by Level Best Books 2021

First edition

ISBN: 978-1-953789-09-9

Cover art by Mark Gutkowski (Revolver based on licensed Shutterstock image)

This book was professionally typeset on Reedsy.
Find out more at reedsy.com

For Alfredo, Mauro, Andi

And for Mark, who, it turns out, is the answer to everything.

Praise for BLACKOUT

"New York's crime world and gay scene converge in this compulsively plotted mystery, where long-held secrets refuse to stay buried. Carocari delivers a strong debut that's equal parts thrilling and heart-felt." — Edwin Hill, author of *Watch Her*

"BLACKOUT is a gripping debut from an exciting new author to watch. Carocari had me turning pages long into the night—prepare for an electric read." — P. J. Vernon, author of *Bath Haus* and *When You Find Me*

"*Blackout* is *Rear Window* meets the dating app. Marco Carocari's impressive debut gives readers an unrelenting thriller, with twists and turns you won't see. A fearless and unflinching portrait of corruption, past and present, and a poignant journey of a son trying to understand the father he never knew. Turn on the lights and read *Blackout* into the night." — Gabriel Valjan, Agatha and Anthony-nominated author of *The Naming Game*

"In a stunning debut from Marco Carocari, dark secrets from the past envelope Franco DiMaso after witnessing a murder. He goes from unreliable witness to prime suspect and nothing is as it seems. A gripping, well-plotted, page turning read." —James L'Etoile, author of *At What Cost, Bury the Past,* and *Black Label* (2021)

Lower Manhattan, 1977

Wednesday, July 13, 9:16 pm

Francesco DiMaso steered his old, blue Ford LTD down 5th Avenue in the waning evening light, woefully unaware he was about to have his ticket punched in less than seven minutes—six, if traffic was good.

He turned onto 8th Street, barely noticing the scantily clad mobs of people roaming the streets, everyone trying to escape the brutal heatwave holding the city hostage, their laughter mixing with noise from bars flashing colorful neon signs, and the growl of pulsating traffic.

Thick, muggy air pushed in through the car's open window, carrying the stench from rotting garbage bags lining the streets, and exhaust fumes pushing through gullies. He caught a glimpse of his bruised face in the rearview mirror, sweat trickling down his busted left brow. The Door's "Riders on the Storm" played softly on the car's radio, ironically fitting, considering recent events. His conscience was heavy with lies he'd told Julie, his pregnant wife, to keep her from worrying.

But his hadn't been the worst. Disappointment, anger, and dread tightened his chest and twisted his insides.

He glanced at the passenger seat, where his four-year-old son, Franco, sat crumpled in a pile on the dull, tan leather, dead to the world.

From somewhere deep within, a faint smile pushed through. Julie would kill him if she knew about all the junk he'd let him eat, not to mention riding shotgun. But today he couldn't refuse his kid a single wish. Today, he wasn't a cop, just *Frank*, father of soon to be two, trying his damndest to spend a few hours without a care in the world.

Tomorrow all secrets would end, whatever the consequences. It would break his family, the only way for the healing to begin.

He stopped at a red light and ran a hand through his son's tousled, blond hair, envied his innocence. He'd done his best to protect him from the evil in the world and teach him right from wrong.

By the time he turned onto Mulberry Street, he'd left the crowds behind, and barely spotted a soul. He found an open space under a bright street lamp, half a block from home, and switched off the engine. He sat and rubbed his eyes. Little Franco's soft, even breathing and a TV blaring somewhere in the distance were the only sounds in the dusky neighborhood. After catching all of six hours of sleep over the last two days, exhaustion took over, and all Frank wanted was to lie down and tune out the world.

He exited the car, made his way to the passenger side, and opened the door. He leaned over to pick up his son when the first bullet hit him in the lower back. The crack of the gun registered before shock and pain did. He jerked hard, his body twisting around, then two more bullets tore into his chest. His legs gave out and he crashed to the ground, banging his head. Everything turned black.

Wedged between the Ford's cabin and its open door, the possibility of death never occurred to him. He was too busy processing his situation and trying to regain control of this temporary setback.

A hooded man kneeling over him roughly searched his pockets, panting hard. His intense body odor made Frank think bum or junkie. But at such close proximity a perfectly executed head butt or knee jerk to the nuts would send his attacker flying.

In theory, anyway, because his arms and legs pushed feebly at the ground in weak, uncoordinated slow-motion. Panic gripped him. Why couldn't he move?

The backup gun strapped to his ankle miles away, he could no longer deny a serious disadvantage. The bright street lamp above stung his eyes, preventing him from seeing the junkie's face. His attempt to reason with the man ended in wet grunts. A coppery taste filled his mouth and warm streaks dribbled down his chin.

Frank shifted his stinging eyes until they fell on a pair of unmoving, skinny white legs with tiny feet in brown leather sandals, resting on the car's seat.

The robber choked out sobs, muttering to himself, and Frank felt his head lifting as the man pulled on his golden necklace with the cross. The chain snapped and the back of his skull slammed against the passenger door. Everything around him slowed down.

Tufts of blond hair emerged over the seat's edge as his boy leaned forward, hair disheveled, eyes wide, his tiny mouth hanging open.

Sit still, don't say a word.

The warning remained trapped in Frank's mind, the words glued to his tongue. He strained his blurring vision, but the image of his son grew dimmer, the sky darker. The street lamp shining on his face caved in on itself, the sobbing above him ceased, and weight lifted off his chest. Retreating footsteps and squealing car tires echoed, but he never took his eyes off Franco, never gave up hope. Ninety-seven seconds after the first bullet hit, his heartbeat stopped.

Down the street a radio blared through a window, and through another up the block a couple argued heatedly over the wails of an infant. Minutes ticked away, then the street lamp above the Ford fizzled out with a buzzing sound.

The boy's breath caught in his throat and his body stiffened, his small fingers clutched the edge of the seat. Like a rolling wave, every light and electronic appliance in the neighborhood ceased to function, and a blanket of darkness descended over Manhattan. In one heartbeat the city fell eerily silent. Then all hell broke loose.

Chapter One

Manhattan, 2016

Friday, July 22, 12:09 am

Franco couldn't deny it any longer. This had been a mistake. "I'm sorry…hold on a second," he said, gripping the rooftop's metal railing to keep his balance, his blue gym shorts around his ankles. All around him low hanging pinkish clouds held back SoHo's city lights, dousing the neighborhood in a muted glow.

The half-naked man behind him grunted and stepped back. "Dude, this isn't working for me."

Franco detected frustration in his voice, but found it hard to care. Wiping sweat from his forehead, he scratched the blond stubble on his cheek, his naked skin damp from the sultry air. "Sorry, I…need a moment. I don't feel so hot," he said over his shoulder, straightening up. He spat on the ground, but the strange metallic taste lingered in his dry mouth. He swayed and saw double. "What the hell was *in* that thing?"

He got no answer and glanced at his bare chested hunk of a date standing there, zipping up.

Okay, considering this had barely taken ten minutes, *date* was probably grossly overstated. Franco eyed the ripped, olive-skinned stud who went by Pitcher9 on the MeatUp app, but whose real name he'd already forgotten. Pressed, he'd go with *Hey* since that was as intimate an introduction the situation warranted. A fading, crudely drawn mermaid tattoo on the man's left oblique, possibly a blast from his youthful past, only increased his bad boy vibe.

"You're not used to smoking weed is all," Pitcher said with an edge to his tone. "Tense as you are, you needed it…not that it made a difference."

Seriously, criticism from the guy playing *whack-a-hole* for the past ten minutes? Vampires were staked with more finesse. Franco bit his tongue and massaged his throbbing temples. He'd only experienced weed once, years ago, to a surprisingly aphrodisiacal effect; tonight, not so much.

He pulled up his shorts, the motion oddly uncoordinated and detached. Five stories below, Wooster Street turned into pieces in a kaleidoscope. He shut his eyes, his throat burning from the nasty coughing fit earlier, and spat again. "I'm sorry, but this didn't taste like anything I've ever—"

"You gotta learn to loosen up a bit, daddy. It's all good."

Franco stiffened and clenched his teeth. All right, his face sported a fair amount of wrinkles, and his short, dirty-blond hair had thinned at the temples—he was a forty-three-year-old photographer slash waiter slash bartender still waiting for his big break—but he'd never been more popular, *thank you very much.* Besides, this prick was, what, four, five years his junior? Fuck him.

He snatched his black tank top off the ground and almost tipped over. Pulling it over his head in an awkward motion, he noticed light inside an apartment on the fourth floor across the street. The brownstone was still undergoing renovations, but recently a few tenants had moved into the grossly overpriced studios and one-bedroom units.

He began turning away when two shapes stumbled into view, slamming into the window with such force he heard a heavy thump. A pair of blinds were nearly ripped from the sill as the two men grappled with one another, their bodies writhing, twisting, and tripping backwards into the room. The one with shoulder-length, dark hair had the other guy's neck in a tight chokehold, clamping one hand over his nose and mouth. The victim bucked wildly, clawing at the arm around his throat. The whole scene was a blurry melee of heads and limbs until a sharp jerking motion froze everything for a second. Then both men slumped forward and disappeared from view.

Franco inhaled sharply and reeled back. "Shit, did you see that?" Adrenaline rushed through him as he spun around. Everything tumbled out of focus and he steadied himself against the railing. "He's killing that guy."

Pitcher was crouched on the ground, tying his sneaker. "What?"

Franco grabbed him by the arm and pulled him up, pointing at the window. The apartment lay in total darkness.

Pitcher shook loose. "Fuck are you talking about? You trippin'?"

"I…where'd they go? I'm serious, he killed that guy. We gotta do…" Why did his tongue feel so heavy? He turned back to the building across the way.

A figure stood at the window, staring straight at him.

"Oh, shit." Franco flinched hard, bumping into Pitcher. "Over there, see him now?"

Busted blinds hung lopsided in an otherwise dark and empty window.

"Seriously, dude, chill the fuck out," Pitcher said with a low growl. "If you can't handle drugs, don't do them."

"I swear…I'm not making this up." Franco's voice sounded tinny in his ears. With fingers like putty he fumbled for the iPhone in the pocket of his shorts, but it slipped from his grasp and clattered against the ground. "Shit. We gotta…call the cops, or something…he needs help." And a hearse, most likely.

"There's nothing there, all right? You're high as a kite and you wanna call the cops? Good luck with that."

Franco picked up his phone, his perception skewed, like he wasn't inside his skin. He stared at the building across the street, then at the pavement five stories below. Blinked. Climbing over the guardrail would get him to the street the fastest, with time being of the essence, and all. He stood and stared, thoughts in his brain splitting like atoms, until a surprisingly insistent internal voice pushed through, and convinced him taking the stairs would be more beneficial to his health in the long run.

He sighed, turned around, and opened his mouth. Weird. Hadn't someone just been there moments ago? And why was his mouth open?

Oh right, *help*. Someone needed…

Gently, an invisible wave washed over him, like sliding under the water surface in a bathtub and gazing at it from below. He entered another dimension, his legs on autopilot.

Chapter Two

"Sir, are you all right?"

Franco woke with a start to a firm hand shaking his shoulder. Confused, his stomach churning, he blinked at red and blue lights bouncing across the cobblestoned street. His left temple throbbed painfully, and a hard surface pressed against his back and the palm of his hands. He glanced down.

Why the hell was he sitting on the sidewalk, propped up against the wall of the flower shop in his building in nothing but skimpy gym shorts, a tank top, and flip-flops? He raised his head in slow motion at the uniformed police officer looming over him. Asian guy, maybe early thirties, his eyes pinched, the face with the huge green fro warping in and out of focus. Oh, wait, not a fro, just the maple tree growing outside The Green Thumb.

"Are you all right, sir?" the police officer repeated more forcefully, his tone more suspicious than concerned. Franco didn't blame him, he had a few questions himself…maybe once the spinning stopped. He realized his mouth was hanging open, and he closed it, feeling self-conscious. Some fifteen feet away another officer stood next to a white and blue patrol car, talking to someone over a cackling radio.

"Yes, I am…okay," Franco said through a mouth like cotton, a bitter taste biting the back of his throat. He caught a whiff of urine and checked himself, relieved not to find himself sitting in a puddle. Hopefully, just the lingering scent from the wall's encounter with a territorial dog.

Another patrol car pulled up behind the first one and two more uniformed officers got out, joining the one talking on the radio.

"Are you hurt?" the cop asked, and Franco pushed himself up, his thighs burning like he'd run a marathon. His vision rippled, his entire left side throbbed, and a sharp sting shot up his left elbow. He pressed his lips together and winced.

"Sir?" The officer, whose name tag read HAHN, sounded impatient, staring at him expectantly.

"I'm…fine," Franco said with a strained half-smile, feeling like shit.

"Did you call 911?"

"Um, what?"

"*911,* did you report an assault?"

The hair on Franco's arms bristled. The brutal attack, the stranger's face in the window…the botched, random midnight hookup.

"Yes…I called." Not about the last thing, though.

His pulse quickened, and a chill prickled his damp skin. "Please hurry, someone murdered a guy up there."

"Name?"

How the hell should he know, he'd never met—*oh...*

"Franco…DiMaso." Pointing at the building across the street to a spot several flights up, it took every effort to push the words from his mouth. "He's on the fourth floor…second window from the left."

Apart from dull amber light pushing through curtains of a second-story window, the building lay in darkness. Goosebumps sprouted on his arms, and Franco rubbed them vigorously.

Jesus fucking Christ, he'd witnessed a murder. How could he pass out on the street? How late was it? He squeezed his eyes shut to focus, but words and scenes tumbled through his brain like balls in a gravity pick lottery machine—every time he thought he recognized a number in the dancing, white flurry, it spit out a different one.

An Emergency Service Unit vehicle rolled up and Hahn said, "Wait here." He joined his colleagues and Franco's eyes slowly traveled up his apartment building's facade, a contemporary, eggshell colored walk-up.

The dense clouds from earlier had lifted, turning the night several shades darker. He stared past lights from his landlords' apartment to the rooftop where he'd been standing only moments ago. He *had* been standing there moments ago, right? Yeah, sure, with the smoking hot...prick.

What happened to Pitcher, or whatever the hell his name was? One moment he'd been right next to him on the roof, berating him, something about drugs and kites and cops, and then...*nada*, one big blank.

He craned his neck, but couldn't see him anywhere. Franco rubbed his temple and squeezed his eyes shut as a thousand needles skewered his skull. What the hell had they smoked?

He'd meant to say no when Pitcher shoved the fat doobie in his face. But then his friend Gino's voice popped into his head, taunting, "*Merda!* Stop being so damn boring and live a little," perfectly underscored by the 80s hit "Try it Out." And he thought, hell, if disco compelled him to do it, what could possibly go wrong?

Yeah, well...

Talking with his colleagues, Officer Hahn pointed at him, and Franco heard the words *asleep* and *loopy*. He crossed his arms over his chest, puzzled at the unexpected pain. He couldn't say why, but something told him to play it cool and resist the urge to rub his throbbing side.

The poor dead guy took precedence. Besides, wasn't like he could explain his discomfort...or shake the feeling he'd screwed up, somehow. His chest tightened.

Three of the cops made their way to the building across the street with flashlights jaggedly painting the path before them. Hahn blocked his view. "Mr. DiMaso, got an ID on you?"

"Upstairs." Could Hahn smell the weed on him? He resisted the urge to take a step back, but apparently only barely.

Hahn's forehead pinched together. "You okay?"

"Um, yeah, sure, why?" Too loud and clipped.

"Your pupils are dilated. Are you under the influence?"

Franco forced a tight-lipped smile. "No, I'm not."

Hahn didn't look convinced, but let it go. "Is this where you witnessed the crime?"

"No, I was on the roof."

"Can you show me, please?"

Franco opened the thick glass door to his building, motioning for Hahn to follow. A sting made him flinch, earning him a questioning stare.

"Tripped on my way down," he said. Probably true, but best to omit any reference to that part of the evening. Hahn seemed wary enough.

"This building have a security system?" He pointed at the dated camera hanging from the far left corner.

"Not really. It's old, from when they redid this building…I don't know, ten years ago? Only covers the entrance, same for the one inside The Green Thumb. Nothing on the outside, or upstairs."

"Who else lives here?" he asked when they passed a double door on the second floor.

"Just my landlords, Bob Owens and Tony Prentice…but they're in the Hamptons," Franco said. "Bob organizes high profile fundraisers, and this is his office. They live one flight up."

"And the flower shop?"

"The Grangers opened The Green Thumb four years ago, but live somewhere over in Hell's Kitchen." The more he focused on everyday things, the more details of the evening solidified. Except nap time on the sidewalk—that scene had ended up on the cutting room floor, and someone had wiped their filthy shoes on it.

On the fourth floor, Franco pointed at a double door ahead. "This is me, one sec." He entered the dark, open floor plan apartment without turning on any lights and retrieved the wallet from his computer desk. When he returned, Hahn craned his neck, peering past him at ghostly outlines of lighting equipment standing near the window front. "You a photographer?"

"Yes."

"Fashion?" sounded almost accusatory, the way he said it, but maybe Franco's hearing was off.

He handed over his driver's license. "Sometimes."

Hahn pulled out a pad and pen and wrote down the information, returning the ID.

They climbed the last flight up to a metal door that opened out to the roof with a soft creak. Franco flipped a switch and small bistro lights wrapped around trees and plants softly illuminated the space with its lush garden and sitting area for alfresco dining. It had been his favorite place for years, but now, approaching the roof's guardrail, the hair on his neck pricked up.

His hand recoiled at the touch of the cool metal rail, and the street below seemed to rush toward him, flipping his insides upside down and sideways. Holy shit, had he seriously been standing here, considering a one-step shortcut to the street? What the actual fuck?

His heart stuttered, and he hid his trembling hand behind his back, stealing a glance at Hahn. The cop stared across the street where his colleagues had turned the light on inside the apartment with the crooked blinds.

"Is this where you were standing?" Hahn asked, pulling out a small notebook.

"Yes." Sort of.

"Then what happened?"

"Um, okay," he said, folding his arms across the chest. "I…noticed an unusual light in the apartment—"

"Unusual how?"

"Um, they've been renovating the building…I think only a handful of units are rented." He took a deep breath. "Anyway…first, I thought maybe new tenants had moved in, but then two men appeared behind the window, fighting each other. One grabbed the other in some sort of chokehold…and the other guy, the victim, was struggling really hard. The whole thing only lasted a few seconds, really, then there was this terrible…jerking motion, and the whole place went dark." He rubbed his left temple.

"You sure you're okay?"

"Migraines."

"And when did this happen?"

"I don't know, half an hour ago? Just after midnight."

Hahn stopped scribbling and looked at Franco, his eyes probing. "What is it, half an hour or midnight?"

"What?" Franco pulled out his phone. 1:23 a.m.

He could have sworn he and Pitcher had come up here right before midnight, and were there for less than fifteen minutes. This made no sense. Feeling queasy, Franco took hold of the guardrail again. "Um…I…I guess about twenty minutes ago—thirty, maybe." Maybe he had the time wrong? Increasingly frustrated with Hahn *and* himself, he swore inwardly. Nothing added up.

The cop leaned over the rail and squinted his eyes. "Didn't you say your neighbors were gone? I see light in their apartment."

"Their lights are timed."

Hahn scribbled on his pad. "Was anyone with you when the attack happened?"

"Yes, um…a friend, but he's gone." Not surprised by Hahn's puzzled expression, Franco quickly added, "He didn't see what I saw, and left." Hahn just stared, and Franco's cheeks prickled warmly. "All right, so he wasn't exactly a friend, more like a date. We were up here…talking. When I saw the attack, he was sitting on the ground over there. He insisted he didn't see anything and left."

Hahn's radio squawked. He held up a hand and walked a few steps away to talk to the person on the other end in short, clipped sentences.

Franco lowered his head, feeling his energy evaporate with every breath.

Behind him, Hahn said "right" a few times, and ended the conversation. The cop studied him for several seconds. "Mr. DiMaso, there's no crime scene or body over there."

Franco's jaw dropped. "What? That's…impossible. I don't understand."

"The apartment is practically empty, and there are no signs of a forced entry. My colleagues talked to a couple on the second floor, but they didn't see or hear anything, and don't know who occupies the unit. Any chance you got it wrong?"

"I…*no,* this is the apartment, I guarantee it."

Hahn scanned the ground with his flashlight until it came to rest on a crumpled condom, lying there almost mockingly. Franco closed his eyes, listening to the figurative thud of his dignity hitting bottom.

"This yours?"

"Ahh…"

"What about this?" Hahn picked up the remnants of the joint and held it between his fingers.

Franco considered feigning total ignorance, but really, at this point, who was he kidding? "No, my date's."

Hahn turned the flashlight on him. "I'm getting the impression you've had several hits yourself."

"One, I barely felt it." Franco sidestepped the beam and balled his fists, angry and embarrassed. Could this damn night get any worse? Why hadn't he just, literally, taken matters into his own hands, and gone to bed, instead of trolling for tricks on that frigging app? His head pounded dully. "I know what this looks like, but I'm telling you the truth."

"Okay."

"You don't believe me."

"We are canvassing the area and looking for witnesses, but I gotta say, so far, there's nothing here corroborating your story. My guess, the blunt hit you harder than you think."

"Shit, I just told you I only took two hits. I know what I saw."

"So, we're up to two now?"

Franco's cheeks burned.

"Maybe we should have the medics check you out." Hahn placed the stub on the metal rail.

"Thanks, not necessary." Feeling silly and humiliated, he stared defiantly at Hahn.

The cop sighed. "I think you had a rough night and need some rest. We'll take it from here, and contact you if we have more questions."

Franco threw up his arms. "Fine, whatever. You got my statement, do with it what you want." He resented the notion he'd dreamt it all up. Embarrassed, but too exhausted to argue or care anymore, he only wanted to pull a sheet over his head, and forget everyone and everything.

Hahn handed him a business card and said goodbye, then talked to someone over his radio as he left.

Franco felt defeated. With a last glance across the street, he picked up the joint stub and made his way to the door, tail between his legs. He switched off the roof lights, locked up, and descended the stairs back down to his apartment.

He closed the door and leaned against it in the dark. Through sheer white curtains cascading over massive windows on his right, pulsating emergency lights from the street illuminated the familiar shapes in the generous space before him—a computer desk with a Mac to his left, the vintage Saarinen table with the matching chairs by the cooking area, across the room, and several strobes and backdrops against the wall by the door.

He sighed and closed his eyes. That guy in the window, he'd not hallucinated him.

And yet, he barely remembered anything about him…and little more about the attack.

He raised his eyes to the ceiling with a frustrated growl and kicked off his flip-flops. Staggering into the bedroom, he shut the sliding door behind him, as if to put a protective layer between himself and the outside world. He stepped into the bathroom, opened the toilet lid, and flushed the joint.

Back in the bedroom, he plumped down on the queen sized bed and pulled out his phone. A hairline crack cut across the top of the phone's screen.

"Aw shit," he muttered. Five years old or not, the damn thing better hold together. He was too broke to replace it.

1:35 am.

Calling Gino and Carmine was out. The restaurant had closed hours ago and they would be asleep. And though Vince was likely not, closing up at the club, Franco's call went straight to voicemail.

He hung up and fired off a *Please, text me, urgent!!* to Pitcher in Meat-Up, but the profile was offline.

He plopped on his back and gazed at the ceiling fan, slowly churning the warm air. Gravity dragged down his lids and faces and word fragments with little meaning jitterbugged through his mind. He gently probed his throbbing ribcage, his motion sluggish, strained.

Gotta get up...check the damage.

He was out before he finished the thought.

Chapter Three

Strange, wet noises surround him...it takes him a moment to recognize the inside of his dad's car, though he's seen it a million times before. Something smells sharp and rotten, and he crinkles his nose. His hands and legs are smaller than he remembers, and somewhere someone is sobbing. He turns his head, looks out the open door. A single light from the sky like a spotlight shines upon a hooded figure, kneeling close to him. He instantly senses danger and violence coming from...that thing. It mumbles as it rifles through the pockets of someone lying on the sidewalk. He lowers his gaze and sees his dad staring at him, wide eyed and motionless.

He tries to swallow but has no spit in his throat, and a chill grips his insides. The thing in the hood snaps its head around and glares at him. It's a man with dirty skin and hair, and crazy yellow eyes.

His heart pounds against his chest, and a warm wetness runs down his legs, spreading across the old leather seat beneath him. The hooded man lets out a strangled cry, jerks back, and...dissolves like dust into thin air.

Trembling, he searches his father's eyes, but then everything around him turns pitch black. His breath catches and his body turns ice cold. No sound comes across his lips, he's frozen in place. A face he's never seen before materializes in front of him, like an apparition, in a darkness so vast it threatens to swallow him. The mouth opens wide, a piercing sound cutting through...

Franco jolted awake, pain shooting up his left side. A shrill car horn blared outside. He blinked, and his mind cleared, leaving him with nothing but a sense of dread. He rubbed his stinging side, stumped to find himself still dressed in last night's clothes. He felt a vibration against his hand and realized it came from his phone. The locked screen notified him of two missed calls from Vince, and claimed it was 4:21. In the afternoon, judging by the bright light flooding his bedroom through the window behind him, the city's constant murmurs permeating the walls.

When had he last slept eight hours uninterrupted, let alone...*fourteen*?

He didn't feel particularly refreshed, more like a truck had rolled over him, then took the time to back up several times.

Shit, what a night. What happened in that apartment? Scratch that, what the hell happened to him? He raised his thrumming head, but the closed sliding door kept him from seeing into the main space. He pulled up the websites of several news outlets and scrolled through them, but none mentioned anything about the murder. Instead, they all reported a tragic accident that had occurred after midnight, several blocks away on 6th Avenue. A drunk truck driver had lost control of his rig, ran a red light, and plowed into several cars, killing eight.

Thursday night had been a nightmare all around, but unlike some, he got to wake up.

He glanced at the framed original 1977 *Star Wars* poster hanging to his right, and the '79 ad of a naked guy stepping into his *Studio 54* jeans, prized possessions he'd snatched up at a yard sale years ago. Below them, dust on the packed walnut bookshelf along the wall reminded him his place could use, at the very least, a thorough dusting.

He tried Vince but only got his voicemail again.

Catching a whiff of himself, Franco grimaced, then pushed himself off the mattress and peeled off his clothes. The tank top stuck to the skin above his lower left back tore open a roughly three-inch cut covered in a bloody crust. Another, smaller cut and several scrapes graced his hip.

What the hell?

He grunted in frustration and headed into the ensuite bathroom where he switched on the light and observed himself in the double wide mirror above the sink. A red welt on his left temple, and the circles under his dark blue eyes were noticeable, and a thin white crown around his pupils were like coronas during a full eclipse. He'd never checked last night, but they weren't dilated now. He cleaned the wounds with a washcloth, carefully scrutinizing the athletic body he spent countless hours slaving away at the gym for.

Daddy, my ass.

But fresh anger and embarrassment replaced his sense of accomplishment. How could he have been so stupid? Pitchers' joint had to have been spiked. He didn't do drugs, drank in moderation, and never lost control, something his friends teased him about incessantly. Nearly overdosing on sleeping pills at age eighteen cured him of any desires for chemically induced states of mind. A desperate act, at the time, and stupid, yes, but it had left a lasting impression.

Last night he'd longed for the comfort of someone else's touch because it had been ages since he'd last had sex.

Okay, five months, but still. There were times he remembered when five hours felt like a lifetime. In fact, after a slew of random hookups and one nighters, he'd slowed down quite a bit, wanting more. Except, *more* remained elusive, and so, feeling like unwinding with someone other than his right hand, he'd jumped back into the game. And tripped, hard.

Franco returned to the bedroom and checked his phone for a reply from Pitcher. Nothing. He tried re-sending the message, but the app's automated service notified him the user had blocked him.

He snorted angrily and tossed the phone on the sheets. Unable to shake a strange pull he couldn't explain, he opened the sliding door and advanced to the large windows across the room, the cement floor cool against his bare feet.

Below on the street people walked past, dressed in light and colorful summer clothes, and a cyclist rang his bell at a couple blocking his path. Workers across the street walked in and out of the building, but nothing indicated a late night tragedy, or that cops were ever there. He glanced at the apartment with the broken shade, but nothing moved inside.

He closed his eyes to a jumble of blurred faces, hectic motion, and arms and hands, flailing and clawing...and something else, staying out of reach.

He rubbed his eyes, returned to the bathroom, and brushed his teeth. When he stepped into the spacious glass shower, he grimaced as water pelted his wounds. Turning it as cold as he could stand, he felt more awake and refreshed when he emerged a few minutes later.

After he dried off, he applied antiseptic and bandages to the cuts, and returned to the bedroom where he slipped into long, dark blue jeans and a white dress shirt, as formal as his shift at Gino's required.

He padded barefoot into the kitchen and grabbed a small water bottle from the refrigerator, emptying it in four gulps. Rolling up his sleeves, he took in the space's bare white walls. Sometimes he photographed his subjects against them, using the window front's natural light, but today he wished the space provided more warmth, felt more nurturing.

Time to paint a wall or two, maybe, and hang some of his work to give it a more homey feel. Someday he'd be able to afford a few more nice pieces of furniture, though he didn't expect it to happen anytime soon, considering his perpetually low bank account balance and less than stellar networking skills. Despite being well liked, and having a solid body of work, many of the well-funded projects he applied for frequently went to people with bigger egos, bigger mouths, and better agents. Well, not better, just *agent*—something else he needed to get his hands on.

After all, he didn't plan to keep working three jobs simultaneously for the rest of his life to make ends meet. At forty-fucking-three he should be at the top of his game, not barely scraping by. But lately he'd struggled to find the drive.

Truth was, he could only, barely, afford to live at his loft-like SoHo pad by combining workspace and home, and because Bob and Tony were wonderful, generous people. They placed more value on having a trusted tenant to keep an eye on the building when they were gone, which was often, than making a killing renting at market value. Wasn't like they needed it, loaded as they were, but still.

He returned to the bedroom, picked a pair of black leather sneakers, grabbed his keys and backpack from his desk, and sprinted out the door, slamming it shut behind him.

He stopped in his tracks and eyed the staircase to the rooftop, then stomped down the stairs. For once, he was glad about Bob and Tony's return this weekend. The thrill and freedom of enjoying an undisturbed late night dalliance in the building had lost all appeal.

On the sidewalk he blinked in the bright sunlight as humid air thick enough to slice smacked him in the face. An uncomfortable tingle ran down his back, and he felt exposed. People and cars passed him, and he half expected to find someone watching him. But in true Manhattan fashion, no one gave two shits, hustling by without so much as a glance his way.

Great, now he was getting paranoid. Clenching his teeth, he turned and briskly marched north on his short walk to work.

Chapter Four

Franco reached Gino's on Prince Street a mere six minutes later. The cozy Italian restaurant's foldable window front stood open and a handful of guests occupied the small patio on the sidewalk, intently staring at their mobile devices. He spotted their part-time day waiter, Tom, inside, standing behind the old oak bar, serving a customer sitting on a stool. No sign of Carmine. In less than an hour the small place would be hopping, their eleven tables booked until closing.

Feeling clammy from the short walk, Franco fanned himself with his hand, envying everyone dressed in shorts and T-shirts. He calculated he had about twenty minutes before his shift. Gino would be upstairs, still recuperating from the nasty stomach flu that had put him flat on his back, almost three weeks ago.

He entered the eggplant colored, five story building's entrance to the restaurant's right and sprinted four flights up the creaking wooden stairs two steps at a time. He arrived breathless on the top floor where the brothers had converted two small, opposing apartments into one comfortable space with separate entrances by eliminating the shared living room wall.

He knocked once and entered through Carmine's side without waiting for an answer. "Yo, anyone home?"

He turned left into the expanded living room with windows facing Prince Street. Fashion magazines and a *New York Times* lay strewn about the heavy oakwood dining table, and a gray wool blanket hung off the black leather couch. The image of some color period movie was frozen mid-scene on the TV.

"Over here, *amore*." Gino's voice sounded from the hallway around the corner. "How are you?"

"Man, you'll never believe what happened to me last—" Franco stopped and stared.

Dressed in surprisingly loose fitting sweatpants and T-shirt, Gino emitted a tired chuckle. "That's what nearly three weeks of uncontrollable crapping will do to you."

He kissed Franco on the cheek and sat on the sofa, covering himself with the blanket. He ran his hand over the salt-and-pepper stubble on his scalp. His round face was pale and thinner, and his thick, untrimmed black beard was spotted with gray patches.

"Damn, how much weight did you lose? Carmine didn't say a word." Franco sat down beside Gino, who'd been pushing two-twenty at five foot nine, last he saw him. They'd only spoken over the phone, with Carmine as the go-between for anything else.

"Eighteen pounds and counting."

"Isn't that dangerous?"

"It's not ideal, but the doctor said as long as I'm feeling okay, I should be fine. He'll run more tests tomorrow. I just feel drained. All I've managed to keep down for the past three weeks is soup and crackers, and Mama's special home remedy she swears will put hair on my chest."

"Not where you need it."

Gino chuckled, pulling down his collar to reveal a jungle of black, curly hair.

"Well, if you didn't look so chewed up, you'd look amazing."

"Gee, thanks."

"No, seriously, when's the last time any of your diets ever worked?"

"Yeah, well," Gino said, patting his gut. "Would be nice to get down to one-eighty again, minus the virus, obviously. The last few weeks have been pure agony, running to the crapper every five minutes, and my poor ass—"

"Yeah, thanks, got it," Franco said, waving his hand. "But you're feeling better, no headaches or nausea?"

"Not until you got here. Let's just call this is a welcome side effect to a truly horrific few weeks. If not for Mama and Carmine, we likely could have shut our doors for good."

"I bet she imagined retirement differently."

"And I'm sure she'll never let me forget it, either." He rolled his eyes. "I appreciate her help, but having her practically move in for two full weeks has been...a challenge. She's leaving tomorrow, back to Brooklyn, *finalmente*."

Franco knew Gino loved his mother, whose doting on him hand and foot he enjoyed well enough, as long as it came without the nagging and complaining over the lack of grandkids. Filomena and Carlo Esposito solidly ignored the fact their oldest son was gay, handling the sore topic like other uncomfortable family issues that emerged over the years: don't speak of it and it doesn't exist.

"So you're back to work?"

"Monday or Tuesday, at the latest. I'm going stir crazy in here."

"I'm not real busy with clients and can cover all week if you need me. Just won't be of much use in the kitchen."

"Truer words have not been spoken, my culinarily challenged friend," Gino said, patting Franco on the cheek. "But you do a wonderful job taking care of the guests, and I am grateful."

"Hey, you're paying."

"So, what's new?"

Franco slapped his forehead. "Shit, I almost forgot. I think I witnessed a murder last night."

"Say what?"

"I know it sounds crazy, but I swear I'm not making this up."

Franco unburdened himself for a full five minutes in what seemed like one endless, winding sentence devoid of pause or punctuation.

When he was done, Gino quietly eyed him for a good moment, his cocked brow ripe with attitude. "*Imbecille.*" He shook his head. "What the fuck are you doing getting high with strangers? The prick probably laced it with coke, or LSD, or something...people get creative when they want to push their highs. I hope you learned your lesson."

"Well, technically, this is *your* fault. You're always on my ass about loosening up and trying new things."

"*Ma vaffanculo!*" Gino said, throwing up his hands. "I meant socializing in different circles, exposing yourself to the arts, yarn bombing, if you must. Not getting fucked up with the cheap tricks you hook up with through those stupid apps. I'll never understand how anyone can waste their time on that garbage. Who orders sex like take out? *Common.*"

"Don't call me by my middle name," Franco quipped half-heartedly. Now who was being uptight?

"Excuse me, *dear*, Common is your first name, you just choose to go by Franco."

"It's just so frustrating. Images, words...everything is all jumbled, like echoes in my mind."

"Yeah, going, *idiot...idiot...idiot...,*" Gino said, cupping a hand around his mouth.

"Your empathy warms my heart."

He touched Franco's arm. "Look, I'm sorry, all right? What happened to you was terrible, but let's face it, by your own admission, you weren't all there, half the time." Franco opened his mouth, but Gino held up a finger. "*Calmati*, relax, there has to be a logical explanation for this. Did you call the cops for an update?"

"No, they said they'd be in touch, and there's nothing about it on the news. I'm telling you, something bad went down over there." He groaned in frustration. "Shit, I don't know anymore, all right? I close my eyes and it's like staring through fog."

"Something probably did happen, just not what you think," Gino said. "I do believe whatever you saw deeply upset you, but you were high, agreed?"

Franco nodded.

"Maybe try and keep an open mind?"

"This is *so* embarrassing. Oh, here." Franco lifted his shirt, exposing his bandaged injuries. "And don't ask, I don't know."

"Ouch, is it bad?"

"My ego's taken the bigger hit."

"Yeah, well, don't be so hard on yourself, happens to the best of us. Back in the 90s I dropped acid once, then spent the entire night smelling rocks. You can always call the cops tomorrow and check in with them."

Franco shrugged and nodded.

"You gonna be okay?"

"Sure."

Gino clicked the remote and the movie on the screen jumped to life. Actors dressed as Roman soldiers with bushy headgear and red capes lit a pyre in front of a massive staircase, surrounded by throngs of wailing people. Flames shot up and the howls and cries rose in pitch.

"What's this?" Franco asked.

"*Cleopatra*."

"Never saw it."

"You kidding me?" Gino shook his head and flicked his wrist, his fingertips pinched together. "It's Elizabeth Taylor, for Christ's sake, have you been living under a rock? It's the part after they murder Caesar and burn his body."

Franco couldn't tell whether the highly agitated crowd was mourning or celebrating the event as they tossed torches, chairs, tables, and entire wooden chests onto the flames. "What's with all the furniture?"

Gino shrugged. "No Tuesday pick up?"

Chapter Five

Three minutes to six, Franco entered the small restaurant with its dark hardwood floors, stained concrete walls, and worn 60s furniture. A hint of garlic and basil lingered in the air, and his stomach growled. Maybe there'd be time to grab a bite before it got crazy.

He didn't see Tom, who had probably already left, but Carmine, dressed in his purple Paisley Park T-shirt over loose fitting, black cotton pants, was flirting with a pretty, dark-skinned woman on the patio, judging by his tilted head and hearty chuckle. They exchanged a few words during which she put her hand on his, then she got up with a smile and left.

Carmine watched her with a goofy grin, then he turned and spotted Franco, and came inside.

"Hey, man," he barked in a sonorous voice people could hear one block over. He resembled his older brother even more now that Gino lost all the weight, right down to the build, beard, and bald, shiny dome.

Franco suppressed a smirk. "What'd I tell you about turning tricks at the restaurant?"

Carmine chuckled. "I'm telling you, it's a chick magnet. Works better than a dog. How you doing?"

Before Franco could answer, the swinging doors to the kitchen opened and Carmine's aunt, Pina, a short, round woman in her late sixties, peeked out and motioned for them to follow.

"We'll talk later," Franco said, grabbing a clean, white half-apron from behind the old wooden bar near the kitchen, and tied it around his waist. The aroma of fresh herbs and spices hit Franco's nose as he walked into the small, modern state-of-the-art kitchen, and his mouth watered.

"*Buona sera, signore*," he called out, pretty much the only Italian words he knew, apart from the various swear words he'd picked up listening to the brothers over the years. Unlike them, he didn't have anyone to teach him growing up, and they, considering his name and heritage, jokingly christened him 'la vergogna della nazione', the national disgrace. But, in truth, few from the more recent Italian-American generations spoke their ancestral language anymore.

"Ah Franco, *sei arrivato. Benissimo*." Filomena Esposito put a tray with fresh crostini on the large steel table in front of her. When Carmine snatched one, Franco copied him with a sheepish smile.

"*Smettetela*," she said, meaning *cut it out*, but her pleased eyes belied her commanding tone. Despite her small size, the busty woman oozed authority, and Franco never entirely relaxed around her. How she and her husband Sal, immigrants who'd worked in factories since arriving from Naples, Italy, in the late 60s ever managed to put away nearly half million bucks to gift their sons to finance Gino's still puzzled him. "I guess all those years with the mob really paid off," he'd quipped one night, garnering such disconcerting stares from the elderly couple, he half expected to wake up with a horse's head in his bed.

Pina headed to a table farther back, where she continued stuffing fresh ravioli, and Filomena took him by the arm.

She explained the evening's specials, *lasagne all'emiliana*, and *agnello alla romana*, in broken, heavily accented English as if she'd gotten off the boat yesterday, but in reality had taken her decades to master. Spending most of her life around other immigrants at the factory, she simply never showed much interest in perfecting her English, adamant her sons learn her native tongue growing up.

After she finished, she turned to Carmine and continued in Italian, her appearance and gestures like some character straight out of *The Godfather*. Franco tried picturing her with a fedora, dark overcoat, and piano wire, but just couldn't see it, biting the inside of his cheek to keep from chuckling.

Talking to his mother, Carmine absentmindedly grabbed one of his

Japanese knives, and Franco instinctively took a step back. With the family's habit of animated gestures when operating kitchen utensils, wide berths came highly recommended. Carmine cut a slab of meat on the chopping block, but Filomena pushed his large frame out of the way as if he were a rag doll.

"No, no, no! Ma che fai? Levati!" Clearly, she disapproved of his way, yanking the blade from his hand to show him how it was properly done. And just like that, Franco suddenly could see it.

* * *

Sitting at the bar inside the closed restaurant at ten past eleven, Omar's "Simplify" playing in the background, Franco wrapped up retelling his adventure, then watched Carmine empty his glass of single malt with one gulp.

"Rough night across SoHo," he said, shaking his head. "First the accident on 6th, now you." He refilled his glass.

Franco sipped his ginger ale. "I read about that accident earlier. Frigging crazy." Maybe that's was why the cops hadn't shown up sooner, not that it mattered anymore. So much death, tragedy, and unanswered questions. He didn't want to talk about it anymore and changed the topic. "Two more weeks until your new life. Excited?"

"Cautiously optimistic." Carmine flashed a lopsided smile. After fifteen years, he'd quit his job at the insurance company, opting to work from home, managing private clients, so he could support Gino better at the restaurant.

"It's risky, we need the regular income to pay off our debts. But if Gino has another...episode, or falls sick again for weeks, we're fucked."

Gino's nervous breakdown the previous year made him reevaluate his life and priorities. After years of preparing lavish meals for their friends at their home, opening their own restaurant seemed like the logical next step, the brothers' lifelong dream. Slowly emerging from a severe six-month depression, the project turned into Gino's salvation. What if it became his destruction?

Franco said, "Wouldn't your uncle be somewhat sympathetic if something happened to you guys?"

The song changed to Cameo, singing about the "Single Life," and Carmine shrugged. He studied his whiskey before draining the glass in one gulp. "Maybe...probably, but business is business. He could have sold this property to anyone. If anything, it makes it tougher because we're family. He'll still expect payment on time." He waved a hand. "Eh, we'll be all right, I'm just nervous."

Franco suppressed a yawn and Carmine patted him on the back. "Go on, go home, I'll finish up here. Are you gonna talk to the cops tomorrow?"

"I don't know. Maybe last night really was only..." He flashed an embarrassed grin and softly shook his head. They hugged, and he headed out.

A warm breeze blew in his face as he walked east, the air as thick as the night before. Talking about other people's problems had temporarily muted his own, but now his mind began spinning again, no closer to answers.

He turned onto his street a few moments later, detecting a woman's sweet perfume in the air, probably from the couple talking and walking half a block ahead of him. Someone passed him on a bike, the ticking of spokes echoing through the night.

As he approached his building, everything around him was quiet, normal. He chided himself for blowing the whole thing out of proportion. He unlocked the main door and rushed up the stairs two steps at a time. It didn't escape him that he entered his home without turning on lights, ignoring the house across the street completely.

He stripped naked, brushed his teeth, and climbed into bed. Exhaustion pulled him under, and he fell asleep almost as soon as his head hit the pillow.

Chapter Six

Saturday, July 23

Remnants of another bad dream dissolved, and Franco blinked his eyes open, a tightness inside his gut. It took him a moment to situate himself, a stale taste clinging to the back of his throat. He rolled out of bed and headed to the bathroom.

He checked the time, saw it was ten after eight, and decided to hit the gym to clear his mind. Within minutes he'd dressed in workout gear, stuffed his backpack with a change of fresh clothes, and headed downstairs. He unlocked the race bike he kept under the stairs in the lobby and stepped outside. Though the surrounding buildings provided some morning shade, the sun already promised to fry sidewalks by noon. Without so much as a glance across the street, he took off, his eyes leveled at the road.

He reached Crunch'n'Punch south of Canal a few minutes later, greeted Brian behind the check-in desk, and entered the workout room. Only a handful of people sweated away at the machines. Saturdays, people tended to come in late.

He put on earphones, streamed DJ Osmose's "Pitchdown Disco Boogie" on SoundCloud, and got busy amidst the mellow edits of 70s and 80s tracks. He frequently cheated on leg days by cutting the workout short, but pushed himself for nearly ninety minutes, until he could barely stand. He still felt sore from Thursday, but the bruises were healing.

After a quick shower, he dressed in beige shorts and a green polo shirt, put his earphones back in, and left as a throng of people filled the gym. His thighs and calves burned fiercely. They'd hurt worse tomorrow.

Navigating past slow moving traffic on Canal Street, he barely avoided a collision with tourists mindlessly swinging their selfie sticks left and right. He wondered if any of them gave a crap about Green Street's historic, cast iron buildings, or if they were just bargain hunting at the countless designer boutiques which had replaced the old neighborhood stores.

It was crazy how rapidly Lower Manhattan had changed in recent years, with rents soaring past the astronomical. If his photography business didn't pick up some bigger jobs soon, he wouldn't be able to afford to live there much longer. Worse, only a few months ago Bob and Tony dropped another remark about maybe selling and moving upstate for good.

Turning into his street, he noticed a U-Haul parked in front of the building across from his. He stopped, his eyes resting on the window on the fourth floor. An invisible pull urged him to ease his mind once and for all, and his heartbeat quickened.

Before he could change his mind, he chained his bike to the tree in front of The Green Thumb and crossed the street. He kept the earplugs in, but lowered the volume to a mere whisper. Jean Carne, telling him not to let it go to his head, calmed his nerves as he entered the wide open door. Disembodied voices hollered from somewhere above, probably from whoever was moving in. Scanning the dark hallway, he carefully approached the stairs leading to the upper floors, an ineffable force pulling him along. The air smelled of paint and glue, and he experienced an increasing sense of familiarity as he climbed the stairs.

On the fourth floor, light shone through a medium sized window facing the back alley, and a long corridor extended past several apartment doors on his right. Down the hallway, a sliver of light announced an open door, and he swallowed hard, the sound amplified in his head. The blood pounded in his ears and he thought he heard his name, a low, urgent hiss, as if the room beckoned him. He shuddered, taking a shaky breath, and pushed the door open, knowing what he'd find inside before he saw it.

Fingers dug into his shoulder and he yelled out, smashing into the door frame. He fell over and landed hard on his ass, earbuds dangling around his neck. He raised his eyes, holding a protective hand over his head against the figure towering over him in jeans and a faded yellow West End Records T-shirt stretched over a small belly.

"I'm sorry, I'm sorry," Vince laughed, blushing under his short-cropped beard.

"*What the hell?*" Franco hissed, his heart in his throat. "Are you nuts?"

"I called your name like three times, didn't you hear me?" Vince held out his hand and Franco pulled himself up.

"Does it *look* like I heard you? You almost made me piss myself."

"Sorry," Vince chuckled, "I guess that would be rather awkward, you trying to explain the puddle all over the crime scene if the cops came back to check."

Seemingly incapable of wiping the smirk off his face, Franco was tempted to do it for him. "What the hell are you doing here?"

"Shouldn't that be my line? I ran by Gino's this morning, heard the news, and figured I'd swing by to see how you're doing. I called, didn't you get my message?"

Franco pulled out his phone and saw notifications for two missed calls and a voicemail.

Vince moved past him into the unit, the gray eyes above his thick nose curious. "This it?"

Franco nodded. Doused in bright sunlight, the tiny one bedroom featured an open kitchenette by the entrance and a small bathroom at the far end. A chair with metal legs lay toppled over on the floor, next to a twin-size blow up mattress. No other personal items.

Vince said, "Who the hell lives like this?"

Franco dry swallowed. "I was in here, Thursday night."

"What?"

Franco threw Vince a flustered glance. "I remember standing right here... sometime after the attack, I guess, looking for whoever was hurt...or dead." Putting himself in harm's way wasn't like him at all, and the thought of blindly rushing into a dangerous situation made the hairs on his neck prick up.

"How'd you even get in?"

Franco opened his mouth and closed it, shrugged. "Beats me, but I see the door standing wide open all the time. Not sure the workers lock up at night."

"No, I meant up here."

He shrugged. "Wasn't locked, either, that much I know. The room was dark, and I remember tripping over something, and...pain, probably from the chair. *That's* why I'm all banged up."

"You're saying you managed to trample all over the crime scene *before* the cops showed up?"

Franco groaned, but Vince waved a hand. "Oh relax, I'm messing with you. You came here to help, and besides, from everything Gino told me, I doubt the cops will spend a lot of time and resources on this. I mean, no corpse last we checked, right?"

"No." Franco crossed the space and stood by the window. He recalled standing there and looking at the roof top, but only barely, like trying to see through cheesecloth.

The tangled blinds likely caused the deep indentations on the drywalled window frame during the struggle. A thin cable hung from a tiny hole in the wall, and a two-by-two inch white plastic plate with a broken off stem lay on its side, double sided tape attached to the bottom.

"Security camera system?" Vince said next to him. Whatever it came from was gone.

Franco pulled out his phone, tapped the screen a few times, then showed it to Vince. "See, I was right. Pitcher messaged me in the MeatUp app at 11:52 pm to say he'd arrived downstairs."

Vince chuckled. "MeatUp? Who comes up with these names?"

"If you think that's bad, you should see some of the usernames."

"Why, what's yours?"

*"Anyway...*he arrived before midnight and we went straight up to the roof. Fast forward about ten, fifteen minutes to me tripping from that damn joint. But I'm sure the attack happened right after midnight, like I always said, except the cops didn't show until fifteen past one."

"An hour you can't remember?"

Franco shrugged weakly, waving a hand at the empty apartment. "Some of it, but at a glacial pace. I watched this place from the roof one moment and then stood here the next." He shook his head, letting his eyes wander around the place.

"Wrong apartment, maybe?"

"No, this is it." Franco pointed at the blinds. "I must have gone downstairs afterwards…I guess. Weird thing is, when the cop told me no one was up here, I didn't believe him. But it's true…the door was unlocked and the place empty when I got here." He studied his phone's call log. "Don't really remember that part, either, but apparently I dialed 911 at 12:22 a.m."

Vince pointed at three red entries, missed calls. "They called you back."

"But why? And what's up with my damn phone? It doesn't ring or vibrate half the time, just goes straight to voicemail. I guess I dropped it, and now my screen's cracked."

"Maybe something came loose. Shouldn't cost you more than a hundred and fifty to replace the screen."

"Great." Franco sighed in frustration. "This is ridiculous. You know me, I *never* get wasted. Never. Okay, once, during my first high school reunion, after a few of us were drinking into the wee hours at the hotel we stayed at, and I woke up massively hungover in Grace Cunningham's room with her sobbing in the locked bathroom."

"Did you show up in the same dress?"

Franco shot him a look. "No…actually…I woke up naked in her bed."

"So she cried because you didn't know where to put it." Vince smirked, clearly enjoying himself.

"Trust me, I'd come out to her years earlier—she knew exactly where I like to put it. That was the first and last time the movie just sort of stopped midway, and it's been fourteen years since." He scanned the room, chewing his lip. "Should I call the cops again?" He closed his eyes, the same scene playing out in his head: hands fumbling, bodies twisting, an arm grabbing the collar moments before they all went down.

"And tell them what? You still don't remember anything relevant, and—"

Franco's eyes popped open. What arm?

Vince's eyes narrowed. "What?"

"There was someone else. I...I keep seeing the same scene, over and over, but for a moment, right before the lights went out, someone grabbed the victim's collar. As in, another person."

Another trick of his mind? Vince's creased forehead also expressed skepticism.

"Look, I don't know what to tell you," Franco said, spreading his fingers. "It's all bits and pieces. A snippet of a memory here, then nothing for the next ten minutes, then another one there."

"Sounds like everything's still—"

A door slammed shut somewhere below them, the sound reverberating through the building, and Franco jumped. "Let's get the hell out of here."

Vince nodded, and they crossed the room. Franco grabbed the door handle through the hem of his polo. Probably a bit late, but he wiped down the metal before closing the door, anyway. He came here hoping for closure, but felt more unsettled than ever.

Back on the street, the sun's heat bounced off the cobblestones, turning Franco's skin damp.

"So what now?" Vince said.

Franco shrugged. "I thought about maybe calling Uncle Sal, see if any of his old contacts at the precinct heard anything."

"You guys talking again?"

Franco bit his lower lip. "We never not talked...just not like we used to. The Nick thing kind of put a dent in it."

"Ridiculous, it's been, what, almost two years, and you guys dated for all of two seconds—"

"Four months."

"—I'd have thought Sal got over that by now."

So had Franco. His dad's older brother had always been the closest thing he'd known to a father figure. He and Aunt Angela were a major part of their life, helping out when Franco's mom worked her shifts at Bergdorf Goodman.

But with his old world breeder views the gay thing was a challenge, to say the least. And though Sal learned to deal with the topic better, over time, he instantly disliked Nick, the handsome, self-centered and highly opinionated man Franco had been nuts over. The feelings were entirely mutual. The few times Sal and Nick met, their attitudes were frosty, at best. They didn't agree on anything, and the situation only deteriorated after heated social and political arguments over one too many drinks turned ugly, and words had been exchanged.

Sal demanded Franco never bring 'that arrogant piece of shit' around anymore, and Nick threatened to bust the 'ignorant old fart's' lip. Franco's mom tried to smooth the waters, but he, in his infinite wisdom, and blinded by lust, sided with Nick, telling his uncle to back the fuck off, and stay out of his damn business. Good times.

Franco sighed. "Yeah, well, clearly he wasn't all wrong about Nick, but ever since then he's kept his distance, like he wants nothing to do with this part of my life. And I don't tell him anything anymore because if he can't be happy for me, it's none of his business, anyway. Not that there's ever anything *to* tell."

"In fairness, we all shared his opinion of Nick."

"The man had other qualities. Point is, Sal might still have some contacts, even though he quit the force in '85. Not sure I want Mom to know, though." He checked the time on his phone. "Shit, I gotta get cracking. I'm taking her to the airport at two."

"Oh, right, the Caribbean cruise with her gal pals. I'm sure Julie will have a blast."

"She better. Damn trip nearly wiped me out."

"I thought your sister was gonna pay for it."

"Yeah, like I'd let her. We did a fifty-fifty. Mom gave up so much for us, it's only fair we do something nice for her every now and then. I'll manage."

Vince patted him on the shoulder. "If you want extra shifts at the club, let me know."

"Will do. See you tonight."

Chapter Seven

The swaying C train's slumbrous effects were rudely interrupted whenever the car rocked violently, and the screeching wheels yanked Franco back to the present, Joni Mitchell's "Help Me" playing softly in his earbuds. He rubbed his eyes and checked his phone for the time. 6:30 pm.

Stifling a yawn, he stared at the empty seats across from him, then out the window at dark tunnel walls streaking by.

He thought of his mom and smiled.

She'd been excited and ready for adventure when he'd picked her up at her one-bedroom condo in Park Slope, shortly after two. Dressed in yellow and white summer dress, which nicely hugged her five-foot five frame, and freshly cut and colored auburn hair, she looked none of her sixty-five years.

He and his sister, Andrea, surprised her with a cruise when they got together on the anniversary of their father's death, a few weeks back. The tradition was a chance to spend time together, just the three of them, and celebrate their bond, rather than mourn the tragedy which changed their lives.

Coping with his father's death had grown easier over the years, but the murder had devastated his mother. And yet she never gave up, doing an amazing job raising them, with the help of Uncle Sal and his wife Angela.

Franco massaged his neck and stretched his arms. He didn't tell her anything about Thursday night. Why worry her for nothing? Because it was nothing but a stupid, not to mention thoroughly embarrassing mistake... right?

The train pulled into Spring Street and Franco was relieved to escape its lingering smell of sweat and unwashed people, only to be hit by a gust of baked urine and week-old garbage, the moment he stepped onto the platform.

He grimaced and held his breath. Manhattan in the summer was his favorite time of year, but the pungent odors the heat frequently unearthed made him want to send the city off to the showers.

"Aw, shit, are you fucking kidding me? You filthy pig," a voice thundered somewhere ahead of him. Franco reached the stairs to the street where a young man with a furious expression held a kindergarten age boy by the hand. He yelled obscenities at a homeless man, who sat a few steps up, his legs spread and pants undone, taking a piss.

The little boy appeared terrified, his eyes glued to Tourette's Dad, whose face colored as spittle and profanities flew from his mouth. Franco's heart went out to the little boy and he had a gnawing suspicion that seeing a somewhat scary looking bum pee in public was likely the least of the poor kid's problems.

Skipping several steps to bypass the bum's steady stream, Franco reached the sidewalk where a small group of Asian tourists stood frozen, staring wide-eyed and open mouthed at the scene before them, city maps clutched to their chests like protective shields.

Suppressing a smile, he tipped an imaginary hat at them. "Welcome to New York City."

He left them behind and walked down Spring Street, selecting Chaka Khan's '78 debut album from his phone. It always put him in a good mood, the songs a perfect underscore for the setting sun, which bathed everything in the neighborhood in a glorious, amber hue. Every now and again he stopped at a window display, and by the time he turned the corner to his street Chaka's rendition of "Love Has Fallen on Me" blasted through his earphones, every wail and perfectly placed high note sending exquisite chills down his spine.

His eyes fell on the police sedan parked next to an ambulance in front of his building, their lights flashing silently amidst a small gathering of gawkers.

His smile flatlined, and he stopped dead in his tracks. What the—?

He pulled the buds from his ears and trotted, then sprinted towards the scene, pushing through the group of people.

His neighbor, Tony, stood by the ambulance, tall and lanky, his large hand across his mouth as he watched paramedics lift Bob into the ambulance, an oxygen mask strapped to his face. Blood clotted his short, gray hair, and stained the collar of his shirt.

Tony noticed Franco and reached out to grab his hand. "Franco, thank God!"

"What happened?" Franco said as they hugged.

Tony ran his hands over his ashen face and bald head. "Someone broke into our apartment and attacked Bob."

"*What?* Is he okay?" What the hell was up with this damn neighborhood?

"I don't know, they're taking him to New York Presbyterian. He was bleeding all over the place when I found him."

A stocky man in casual business clothes approached them. "Mr. Prentice, may we please finish your statement?" The detective's attire and appearance were so masculine, Franco didn't realize she was a woman until she spoke.

"Yes, I'm sorry, Detective. This is my neighbor, Franco DiMaso."

She nodded a greeting, her round face expressionless.

"As I said, we returned home from our trip and I briefly stopped in the office downstairs while Bob went ahead with our luggage," Tony said, glancing at the ESU van. "A moment later I heard shouts and commotion from the apartment and ran upstairs. When I made it to our door, a man in a hoodie and a cap charged me and pushed me out of the way. I fell down a few steps, and by the time I recovered he'd bolted."

"Can you describe the man?"

Tony shook his head and exhaled deeply. "I already told the patrol officer, and the camera got him."

"The entrance cam only shows a man with a gray hoodie and a blue baseball cap, keeping his head low, and face hidden. By the time he entered your home, he wore a bandana over nose and mouth. I was hoping you got a better glimpse of him."

He shook his head in frustration. "It happened so fast. Over six feet tall, maybe a few inches shorter than myself, and strong. Definitely younger, but that's more of a feeling. I wasn't wearing my glasses." He sighed. "This is awful. First thing tomorrow, I'll have the entire place outfitted with a brand new security system."

Franco questioned how far he'd get on a Sunday, but this was probably not the time to point that out.

"Can we go over everything one more time, and check your apartment, see if anything's missing?" the detective said. "The more information we have now, the better the chance of finding who did this to your partner."

One of the paramedics stuck his head out of the back of the van. "Sir, if you'd like to ride along, we're leaving."

"I'm coming," Tony said. "Detective Reynolds, is there any way we can have this conversation later? I don't care if he took stuff, it can be replaced. I just want to be there for Bob."

Franco's pulse quickened, and he temporarily tuned out the pair. Two incidents within days, right across the street from each other? No coincidence. Except officially, of course, no crime had been committed on Thursday, other than him getting wasted, and flushing tax payers' precious dollars down the crapper.

Had he watched two queens role-playing, mistaking their admittedly unusual take on auto-erotic asphyxiation as something more sinister? Hell, he'd watched enough online porn and spent enough time on dating apps. There were some crazy kids out there...what did he know about what got who off behind closed doors? He did possess a vivid imagination, no argument there, and last time he managed to come across like a bat-shit crazy tweaker. Maybe once a week was enough?

The detective exchanged business cards with Tony, who promised to reach out as soon as Bob was okay.

"I'll call from the hospital," Tony said, touching Franco's shoulder. He climbed into the back of the van.

They took off with flashing lights but no sirens, and the small crowd began thinning out.

"Before we check out your place, I'd like you to take a look at the security footage, see if you recognize the man," Detective Reynolds said. Franco nodded, an uncomfortable tingle spreading through his intestines.

When they reached Bob and Tony's apartment, a technician wearing gloves and glasses was dusting the door. The footage she showed him on the computer in Bob's tiny home office didn't trigger anything. The one from the entry cam was grainy, and the spy cam only covered the living room. Franco cringed, watching Bob enter the place roughly five minutes after the intruder, but fortunately the attack happened off camera. The man kept his face hidden, and his choice of clothes disguised any body features, including the length of his hair.

Next, Reynolds examined the locks on his apartment door, but didn't detect any signs of tampering. Franco opened up and flipped the light switch, turning on the floor lamp near the Saarinen table.

Reynolds asked him to wait by the door while she flicked on a flashlight and entered the space.

"There's another light above the sink, and one by the bed."

"No problem," Reynolds said, slowly moving about, shining a flashlight ahead of her. "Anything seem out of the ordinary to you?"

"Not that I can see."

"What about in here?" She motioned for Franco to join her, pointing the flashlight at the rumpled bedsheets and the clothes strewn about the floor.

Franco blushed. "Um…hectic morning."

"You're okay, then."

Franco sighed. Again, he considered mentioning Thursday, but realized this would require explaining how he'd ended up decorating the apartment across the street with his fingerprints. He settled for "What happens now?"

"We're talking to neighbors, see if anyone witnessed the break-in. Any idea how he got into the building?"

"The door sometimes doesn't lock properly unless you pull it all the way shut. Plus, the flower shop buzzes people in all the time. All he had to do was wave through the window, pretend he was a courier." The thought unsettled him. "You should ask Cody, the owner."

"My colleague is talking with her now. All right, thank you," she said, and they shook hands. "We'll notify you when we're done, downstairs."

Reynolds left, and Franco began pacing in his apartment, agitated and spooked. He stashed the dirty clothes in the hamper, then packed an overnight bag. No way he'd stay here by himself after this, especially with Bob and Tony at the hospital.

His shift at the club didn't start until nine, but Vince would be home, and Franco could shower and change there. The rest he'd improvise.

Thirty minutes later he went to check on the cops, but they had left without notifying him. He returned upstairs, grabbed his bag, and headed out, making sure the glass door to the building locked properly. A weird prickle in his neck made him turn his head and observe his surroundings, but nobody acknowledged him. Why couldn't he shake the feeling of being watched?

His jaw tight, he hurried up the street, the brisk walk turning into a full sprint the moment he rounded the corner.

Chapter Eight

"Gotta say, I'm freaking out here a little." Franco sat on the black leather sectional in Vince's massive loft, a coffee table covered in books and still wrapped CD's between them. Vince, sitting to his right, took a bite of his ham sandwich. Franco said, "What if the two incidents are connected? What if the guy from Thursday thinks I can identify him?"

"All right, deep cleansing breaths," Vince said between bites. "I get it's not been a good week for you, but they broke into Bob and Tony's place, not yours."

Franco's eyes widened. "He was on the wrong floor."

"What?"

Adrenaline turned his body into a bustling anthill. "There were no lights on anywhere in the entire building, except Bob and Tony's place, because they're on a timer. What if he thought whoever was up on the roof lived there?" He buried his face in his hands. "Shit, it's my fault Bob was attacked."

"Okay, stop." Vince turned his hand in a calming gesture. "You don't know that. You're shook up, and I would be, too. But these incidents...they are most likely unfortunate coincidences, nothing more. Let's face it, you still can't say for sure what actually happened."

Franco opened his mouth to protest, but Vince held up a hand. "Uh-uh, hear me out. Most days you're this level-headed person with a 'nothing's ever black and white' attitude, almost clinically dissecting problems from every angle with surgical precision. But sometimes something happens and you turn into this rabid dog with a bone, blind to any answer other than what's already locked in your head, logical or not."

Franco sighed and dropped his shoulders. "How can I be so sure of something and be so wrong?"

"Believe me, in nearly thirty years of club life I've seen a thing or two, and this isn't close to the worst. People experience the weirdest shit when they're high."

Franco dropped his head between his hands. "I'm exhausted…and my nightmares are back."

"How long since the last time?"

"Four years, maybe five. Every time they return, I'm back thinking things would have been different if I'd run for help."

"You were four. It wasn't your fault."

"Yeah, well, when I sleep my subconscious tends to disagree. I'm four again, and everything's happening right this instant, in 3D and Technicolor. I swear, every time I wake, the first thing I do is check for a puddle. The blackout…I didn't sleep in the dark for two years."

Vince nodded. "Can't imagine what things must have been like for you. We were blissfully unaware of what was going on Uptown, or over in Brooklyn. Once our system got fried, we sat around our living room with flashlights and told ghost stories into the middle of the night." His lips almost cracked a smile. Almost. Vince never mentioned his family or childhood, and Franco's ears pricked up as he quietly watched him, seemingly lost in the memory.

He'd met Vince through Gino some twelve years ago. The two had been best friends since high school, exploring Manhattan's club scene together in the late 80s, and hanging out at The Pyramid, Boy Bar, or The Palladium—fully equipped with raging hormones and a pair of fake IDs, back in the days when Vince still had a last name. He never elaborated, but Franco assumed he'd dumped it to cut ties with his past and his family. Considering Vince and Gino were only three years his senior, they'd lived vastly different lives, becoming part of a club scene Franco wasn't even aware existed until his twenties, and then often found too intimidating to explore.

Vince left home before his nineteenth birthday and spent years living with Barry, a man twice his age, who ran the nightclub Friction in the Meatpacking District for nearly two decades before it closed in the early 2000s. When he died, eight years ago, Barry bequeathed the old warehouse to Vince, who reopened the club to new success a few years later.

"Maybe your dreams would end if the police ever caught the guy," he said, finishing his sandwich.

Franco snorted a humorless chuckle. "I've stopped holding my breath." After the cops discovered his dad's alleged secret locker, the fifty K, and enough coke to keep every broker on Wall Street awake for an entire year, their interest in clearing his name quickly waned. They couldn't prove his guilt, but his dad's once solid reputation remained tainted.

His mom and Uncle Sal remained convinced of a setup, that the NYPD had turned their back on one of their own, and chosen to sweep the affair under the carpet to avoid another scandal. Sal kept investigating on his own, even after he quit and joined the fire department, but he never got anywhere, either.

Over the years Franco often wondered, though never out loud, and certainly not to his mother, if the allegations held any truth. Did his dad do it...and why? But that kind of thinking never got him anywhere, other than feeling like a traitor to his father's memory.

From below, a muted bass and bottles clanking against one another permeated the floor.

"Sounds like Ben and Jerry are here." Vince got up, checking the time on his phone. "Are you gonna be okay to work tonight?"

"Yeah, sure, I'll just jump in the shower and make myself a double espresso. Don't worry."

"You know where the towels are." An odd, melancholic expression flitted across Vince's face. "Try not to drive yourself crazy. You can't change the past, only how you choose to live in the now. Sometimes you have to burn down what came before so you can move on...don't give bad memories the power to destroy you."

Franco nodded wordlessly. He let that happen once, and it nearly cost him his life.

* * *

1 a.m. found Friction in full swing, with Vince behind the turntables. Franco handed him a cold Corona and returned to the old, thirty foot oak bar, squeezing past a throng of sweaty people bumping and grinding on the dance floor, Zalmac's "What's In It For Me?" blasting through the speakers. The large disco ball twirled high above the animated, mixed crowd, dousing everything in a bouncing sea of colored lights. Saturday's *Vince Wants You* had become an insider tip for anyone who loved funky 70s and 80s grooves mixed with contemporary electronic music, and the small club always filled at capacity.

Ben and Jerry stripped out of their tight T-shirts, exposing impressive, sculpted torsos to an appreciative crowd, and Franco felt downright skinny standing next to them. He'd photographed Jerry, a farm grown Utah native, a few weeks ago for his thirtieth birthday. That man had it all, top to bottom, back to front, and Ben...well, Franco could only hope to be in as great a shape when he turned fifty-eight. He'd met him a decade earlier at another club in town, where Ben, after closing, served up a stiff one of a different kind in the storage room. Good times.

While he emptied the dishwasher, a bouncy new edit of The Jacksons "Everybody" turned into a looped version of Melba Moore's "Love's Comin' at Ya" and Franco loved every minute. His fascination with all things 70s rivaled Vince's, and he appreciated the myriad of talented DJs who continuously awarded these tracks with newfound glory. Tonight, it helped put his mind at ease, and leave the troubled week behind.

Ben and Jerry were doing shots with a customer, so Franco kept to the other end of the bar, before getting roped into joining them. After Thursday he wanted to keep a clear head, perfectly content to sip from his chilled water bottle.

A young guy at the bar got Franco's attention and waved him over. The sexy, shirtless twenty-something with the hairy chest flirted like crazy before disappearing into the crowd with his drinks, leaving a twenty-dollar tip with his business card. Franco didn't get it: he could score all day with guys young enough to be his kids, but couldn't for the life of him meet someone remotely age appropriate that took an interest in him.

During "Pull Up to the Bumper" Jerry playfully grabbed Franco by the waist, grinding his crotch against his. Franco's skin tingled as Jerry's hard pecs pressed against his chest until a sudden cold spray of water made him gasp. Ben winked from a few feet away, cocking the soda dispenser nozzle like a gun. People at the bar cheered and threw dollar bills at them, and Jerry pulled Franco out of his shirt.

"Feeling better?" he shouted over the music.

Wiping water from his face, Franco laughed and stuffed the shirt into the waistband of his jeans. "I can't imagine what must be going through Ben's mind right now."

"He sent me with his best wishes, told me to cheer you up."

On cue, Ben hugged Franco from behind, planting a quick peck on his neck. "You all right, buddy? Just wanna make sure you're okay."

"I am now."

A red light blinked behind the counter, indicating someone had opened the emergency exit out in the hall, probably trying to sneak a smoke on the stairs.

"My turn to kick some idiot's ass," Jerry said, rolling his eyes, as he headed out.

Ben raised a suggestive brow. "If you don't feel like going home tonight...
"

Franco had planned to crash on Vince's couch, but didn't have to think twice. "You're on."

Lower Manhattan, 1977

Thursday, July 14, 10:47 am

New York City fell into darkness, and destruction followed. That's what the man on the news said this morning, though the boy with the unruly black hair didn't know what this meant, not really. Maybe it had to do with all the lights going out everywhere last night.

The house was quiet as the boy sat on the Oriental rug in his father's study, hidden behind a large armchair. The sunlight falling through the big window warmed his bare legs as he played with his Micronauts action figures he'd received on his last birthday. The batteries in the Biotron didn't work, but it would have to do until his older brother, Antonio, kept his promise, bringing him the coveted Star Wars action figures which were sold out all across town.

His father forbade him to play in here, where he conducted his business, but the boy favored no other space in the entire house. It made him feel closer to his dad when he wasn't there.

As if on cue, the door on the far end of the spacious room opened, and he froze. He heard his father talking to someone, and didn't dare move, his breathing shallow, afraid of catching a spanking.

"Yes, it's done," a man's voice he didn't recognize said.

"Good," the boy's father said. "There's a lot riding on this operation. It's in both our best interests nothing like this ever happens again."

The boy recognized that tone, and shivered.

"I understand."

"Make sure they all understand," his father said.

"What about—?"

"I will handle him...we have an understanding."

"I guarantee you, nothing like this will ever happen again, Mr. Lombardi."

"And I will hold you to it. *Arrivederci*, Detective."

A moment later the boy heard a door open and close, but he waited, afraid to move.

"Domenico, *vieni qui*," his father said, and Domenico's heart nearly stopped. He still didn't move.

"I won't tell you again."

Domenico rose, blushing furiously. "I'm sorry, *papà*." He didn't look at his father, readying himself for the impending punishment.

"You know it's not polite to eavesdrop."

Domenico began to shake his head in denial, but when he raised his head, his father's stern expression stopped him.

"I'm sorry," he said instead, drooping his shoulders. He approached his father, who sat on the edge of his desk in a suit, his salt and pepper hair slicked back.

"Sit down."

Domenico scrambled onto the chair, his eyes nervously darting from his father to a family picture on the large mahogany desk of himself, his parents, and his two older brothers, who already had families of their own.

His father studied him quietly. Perhaps he wouldn't get in trouble after all.

"You know you are not to play in here. This is not a safe place for you, understand?"

Domenico simply nodded, his eyes cast down.

"Good. But you were wise not to lie to me."

Domenico waited, but his father didn't smack him, or take him over his knee, and he relaxed a little. "Who was that man?" he quietly asked.

"Police." Domenico's eyes widened in surprise, and his father added, "He works for me."

Domenico found this strange, and thought about it for a moment. "You can buy the police?"

"I can."

Domenico thought his father must be very powerful to be able to do that, and it filled him with pride. "Does he have a gun?"

"He does, to make sure nothing goes wrong."

"Like what?"

"People trying to steal from us, taking things which don't belong to them. People trying to hurt us. He makes sure that doesn't happen."

Domenico thought about this. "He is your friend?"

"No."

"Why did he come here?"

"He and his friends made a mess of things, and he came to tell me they cleaned it up. And someone lost his life because of it."

Domenico's eyes opened in fear, and his father patted him on the head. "It's all right now. But there is a lesson I want you to remember: all lies have consequences, son, never forget that. Make sure they're worth it."

Chapter Nine

Manhattan, 2016

Monday, July 25, 10:37pm

"I wasn't gonna say anything..." Gino said, letting the phrase linger in the air—translate, he'd been jonesing to pounce all night—and Franco, busy wiping down the bar's sticky countertop, cocked a brow at him. The restaurant's lights were dimmed and the private dinner group they'd hosted on their usually closed Monday had left half an hour ago.

"You going somewhere with this, or am I supposed to guess?"

"Rumor has it you went home with Ben and Jerry the other night." Gino's smug expression read *try and deny it.* Feeling lightheaded and a tad sick from five rounds of melon shots the dinner group insisted he, Carmine, and Gino partake in, Franco rolled his eyes, but the corner of his mouth twitched up.

"Mhm," Gino said with a satisfied nod. "A, you're a whore, and B, *spill.*" He took off his apron and discarded it on a chair, then straightened his striped T-shirt.

"Nothing to tell." Franco fanned himself against the humidity lingering inside the restaurant, courtesy of the massive thunderstorm which had pelted down over all five boroughs earlier, flooding several streets and subway stations in the process. The booze plowing through his system didn't help, either. He unbuttoned the top of his dress shirt. "We just spent some time together, quite harmless."

"Bull-*shit*," Gino said, dropping ice cubes into a clean tumbler with each syllable. He grabbed a bottle of Grey Goose from the shelf behind the bar.

"Let's just say we enjoyed hanging out—"

"I bet."

"And had a really nice time. We cooked together, and then the three of us chilled on the couch, watching movies. I stayed all Sunday and made it home this morning, and I gotta say it was quite…unexpected."

And the sex had been pretty damn spectacular, but, far better, for a sliver in time the guys made him feel like part of their relationship. Of course he had no illusions about it, and no expectations, but he'd loved experiencing a kind of safety he hadn't in a long while. He craved feeling this way with someone special again, someday, but somehow things always imploded way before reaching that level.

Gino's eyes bore into him as he took a sip of his drink. "So, this gonna be a thing now?"

"Nah, but after last week I feel I deserved something good coming my way. And it did…three times, as a matter of fact."

"Yuck." Gino grimaced theatrically, but then they both laughed.

Franco had been feeling more at ease again, the past two days. Who knew, maybe things were looking up. He meant to text Ben and Jerry earlier and thank them again, but realized he'd forgotten his phone between rushing home from the gym to change, and the security company crew buzzing around, installing the new camera system in their building.

Carmine emerged from the kitchen and joined them, and the brothers talked him into one last drink for the road. Considering recent events, Franco felt he deserved to take a load off with his besties. Settling on a vodka with ginger ale, which Carmine served with a heavy pour, he sat with them as they talked about friends, the week ahead, and commented on pictures of the double rainbow over Manhattan after the storm that people had been plastering all over social media.

Mtume's "So You Wanna Be a Star?" came through the speakers and Franco moved his shoulders to the music, sipping the last of his drink, and feeling pretty light on his feet. He'd likely regret it tomorrow, but, fuck it, it had been a fun night with great tips, and if it turned out he was too hung over in the morning, he'd allow himself to skip the gym and sleep in.

Twenty-five minutes later they said goodnight, and Franco half-walked, half-floated home in the muggy air, heat roaring through him and pushing out his pores. Pathetic, what a lightweight he was.

He reached his building and fumbled with his keys a good moment before he finally managed to open the door. The crew hadn't finished, and cables, tools, and cameras were stored next to his bike under the stairs.

He collected his mail, which consisted mostly of bills, and leaned with his back against the wall to keep the stairs from swaying. When everything had settled again, he stomped up to his apartment using the wall and banister for balance. He opened the door, but the handle slipped from his grasp and banged against the wall. He winced, hoping it wouldn't rouse Bob and Tony, and flipped the switch by the door for the dining area lamp across the room. Given the heat plowing through him, he was surprised not to see steam shooting from his pores. He'd officially been over-served.

Time for a cool shower, or he'd never sleep. He swayed over to the kitchen where he'd left his phone on the table, but the screen remained dark when he tapped it. Great, no juice.

It took him three attempts to get the plug in to recharge it, and he glanced out the window. There were lights in a few of the apartments across the street, but the one on the fourth floor positively glowed. He creased his forehead. The broken blinds were gone.

"Franco, you're home."

"Oh, shit." He jumped at Tony's voice coming from somewhere behind him. Swirling around, he bumped hard against the table. He'd not closed the door fully, and Tony stood in its frame with a concerned frown.

"Sorry, I didn't mean to startle you," he said, taking a tentative step forward. "Are you all right? We were worried. I called you several times, but it always went to voicemail, and the last two times, not even that."

"Yeah, sorry," Franco half slurred, slowly moving his way. "Forgot my phone and now the butter's dead...um, *battery* is dead." His mouth tasted of stale melon, and he repeatedly scraped his tongue against his teeth to get rid of it. Tony studied him with a quizzical expression, and Franco realized he probably looked like a regurgitating cow, and stopped.

"Detectives were looking for you," Tony said. "One wanted to see the rooftop and asked all sorts of questions about you. What's going on?"

"What?" Everything in his brain settled at half speed. He gaped at the apartment across the street where a backlit figure now stood in the window, staring back at him.

He flinched, and his heart started break-dancing.

"Franco, are you in trouble?"

He shook his head. "No, I—"

The buzzer for the building's main entrance sounded, and he hit the intercom. "What? I mean, yeah?"

"Police, Mr. DiMaso, please open the door."

You gotta be shitting me. The cops, now?

Tony's eyes crinkled and Franco realized he'd spoken out loud. Cheeks stinging, he pressed the buzzer and dropped his forehead against the wall, groaning loudly.

Worst. Timing. Ever. He could barely think straight and now the cops—again. He needed to keep cool. Worse, Bob and Tony would surely toss his ass out in the street if they felt he'd endangered their lives. No, not if, *when*. He eyed Tony sideways. "I'm so sorry, I think…it's probably got to do with the attack I saw last week."

Tony's eyes went wide. "The what?"

"Thursday." It came out *thirsty*. "You guys were…in the Hamptons, n'I think…no…*saw* someone get murdered inside an apartment across the street."

"What? Oh my God, Franco, why didn't you tell—"

Hot flashes potent enough to jump-start a small car pelted him left and right. "Look, the cops said it was nothing, said I had imagined it all, n'after a few days…" He shook his head and massaged his temple. "Hell, I thought, shit, maybe I did, you know? Imagine it, I mean. See, I met this guy, and he brought this joint and went up on the roof and things got all—"

"Slow down, what guy?"

Heavy footsteps thundered up the stairs. Franco turned his head to where a broad shouldered, slightly overweight man in an ill-fitting, dark gray suit emerged, his gut testing the elasticity of his white shirt.

Around sixty, and breathing from the climb, he flashed his ID at Franco. "Detective O'Shea, NYPD. You reported a homicide last Thursday, and I have a few questions," he said in a deep, raspy voice like he'd been smoking all his life, or drinking, if the red blotches and popped veins around his thick nose were an indication. He wore his choppy, gray hair short, and his pinched eyes appeared wary.

"Um, sure." Franco swallowed down an acid reflux, then took a deep breath. He immediately regretted it, his nose filling with the cop's sharp body odor and heavy cologne.

"Sir, if you don't mind," O'Shea said to Tony. Nothing about his tone said *request*.

"Oh, yeah, sure, sorry." Tony touched Franco's arm. "Come see us after."

Franco nodded, already dreading the moment.

"You're a hard man to find, Mr. DiMaso," O'Shea said. "We've been trying to track you down all evening. Something wrong with your phone?"

"Sorry, forgot it at home."

O'Shea nodded toward the door. "Mind if we do this inside?"

Put off by the detective's demeanor and gruff tone, Franco stepped aside and let O'Shea pass. He moved to close the door, but the cop shook his head. "My partner will join us in a minute." He scanned his surroundings, then his eyes settled on Franco. "So, where were you?"

"At work." Franco inched toward the computer desk, parking his butt against its ledge for balance.

"The restaurant or the night club?"

Franco pinched his eyes. How the hell'd he know? Also, he really, really needed to pee. "The restaurant. We're, um...not usually open on Mondays. Private party." He crossed his arms over his chest. "What's this about, did something happen?" He spoke slow enough not to trip over his tongue. "I already gave the other cop...sorry, police officer a statement, last week.

Officer Hahn?"

"So, you won't mind telling me again." O'Shea stood at the ready with a stoic expression, pen and pad in hand.

Franco took a deep breath and recounted his story, but O'Shea interrupted him every few moments with questions, breaking his already fragile concentration.

"Do you know who lives in the apartment?"

"No."

"Did you see anyone enter or exit the house before or after the incident?"

"No."

Franco kept his breathing shallow to avoid the cop's intrusive odor, but, getting antsy, he forgot himself and inhaled, catching the distinctive whiff of forty proof. He was pretty sure it didn't come from himself, but the combo created havoc with his olfactory senses. He tensed up, unaware of approaching footsteps until someone entered the doorframe to his right.

He turned his head, and everything froze in a perfect Kodak moment: mid to late thirties, intense eyes, a roman nose, dark designer stubble covering a square jaw line, and thick, wavy, black hair, casually styled, the athletic six-one frame clad in a snazzy beige suit.

The newcomer parted his full lips, revealing perfect, white teeth. "Detective Aidan Torrance, NYPD," he said in a modulated voice, extending his hand, and Franco took it absentmindedly, his mouth hanging open.

He wanted this one to ask the questions. Naked, preferably.

An uncomfortable silence percolated, and he realized he was staring, and still holding Torrance's hand. "Oh...sorry," he said, blushing, and let go, "Franco DiMaso."

"What about a description of the attacker you saw in the apartment?" O'Shea said, pulling Franco back into the now.

"He, um, he was tall and fit, in his thirties, maybe...like you," Franco said, addressing Torrance. "I think he wore a light shirt with dark sleeves...um, and he had dark, shoulder length hair. I'm not sure about the other."

"Other what?"

"Man. I'm not entirely sure, but I think there may have been two of them."

O'Shea threw him a glance. "Two attackers?"

Franco nodded. "I never saw him, only this, I don't know, spare arm, reaching for the victim...just out of sight. But then the place went dark, and..." He shrugged, and O'Shea shook his head in disbelief.

Franco side-eyed Torrance. "Did you...find anything?"

"We're investigating a homicide half a block from here," he said. "The body was discovered earlier today, and we're trying to establish if he is the man you saw getting attacked."

"I knew it," Franco said, way too elated, considering someone lost his life. But he couldn't help feeling vindicated—he *wasn't* crazy. Of course, that created a whole new problem, what with his drug-fueled field trip across the street. His body temperature dropped a few uncomfortable notches, and he grabbed his stomach.

Torrance said, "You all right?"

"I'm...yeah, sorry." Everything before his eyes came with duplicates.

O'Shea's eyes hardened. "Have you been drinking?"

"A few shots at work."

O'Shea looked smug. "And last week you were intoxicated when you spoke to our officers. Would it be fair to say you have a substance abuse problem?"

"What? No!" Franco's cheeks burned. "I had a few drinks with guests, is all. And last week...it's not who I am, ask anyone. I lacked good shush... *judgement,* and no one's sorrier'n me, okay? Shit, I mean, I did the right thing and called it in, didn't I?"

O'Shea mirrored his scowl. "Yes, glad you brought that up."

He pulled out his phone, fumbled with it for a moment, then tapped the screen with his thick thumb.

"Damn it, where'd he go? You gotta come quick, I know what I saw. Shit...crazy motherfucker killed him..."

Franco barely recognized his harsh, tinny whisper coming over the phone's speaker.

"Sir—"

"That was so intense...think he snapped his neck. When will you be here, you

gotta hurry...oh, shit, what if he saw me?"

Franco cringed. He sounded out of breath…and like a complete lunatic.

"Sir, please calm down and speak up. Can you tell me your name?"

"Franco. The idiot said he didn't see anything...makes no sense, all right? I know the guy's dead! Hell, dead doesn't even begin to...oops."

"Sir, I need your full name and location. Can you tell me where you are? Sir... Franco, are you still there? Hello?" Beep.

Franco held his breath. Though he heard it played back verbatim, he didn't remember a single word of the exchange.

O'Shea glowered. "Took them almost twenty minutes to locate your phone through cell towers. You have any idea how much time we lost because of you?"

"Because of me?" Franco balled his fists. "If it weren't for me, you wouldn't even have a body. Um, *what I meant,* I told those guys all along what happened…what they did with that has nothing to do with me." He trembled, and vodka took over. "I mean, seriously, what the fuck? I'm so sick of being treated like a…a nut job or a liar by you people. I called and told you exactly what happened. Don't blame me for your incompetence when it's clear *you* screwed up."

O'Shea's face darkened, but Torrance held up a calming hand. "We're not here to upset you, Mr. DiMaso. But we were hoping you might remember something new, something you hadn't mentioned before."

"Well, I don't, all right?" Franco noticed a scar underneath the detective's left eyebrow, and another along his right chin. Why snap at him? Torrance had been nice, so far. Franco exhaled sharply and dialed it down. "But, um… I should probably tell you I was over there, that night…you know, inside the apartment…after the attack. Before the cops got here."

"You what?" O'Shea barked.

"Sorry, I didn't know what I was doing…I guess I, I don't know, wanted to help?" He shrugged. "It's all bits and pieces. The place *was* empty, when I got there…but I couldn't remember until two days ago."

"And you never thought to mention this until now?" O'Shea snapped. "We'll have to get elimination prints from you."

"Hey, look, I already said I was sorry. Either way, I called like a good sit… *citizen*. Clearly, there was a body all along. I can't explain what happened, but last I checked that's your damn job." He stabbed an angry finger at them, his insides an out-of-control rollercoaster, his bladder protesting sharply.

O'Shea's phone rang, and he answered it with a sharp "What!"

"We are just trying to get a clearer picture of what happened," Torrance said, his tone level.

"A little late, you ask me." Franco tasted bile in the back of his throat.

"Are you sure you're okay?"

Franco grimaced and held up a finger. "One…moment." He rushed to the bathroom and locked the door. His heart pounded against his ribs and he grabbed onto the toilet's water tank. He sat down to pee, plopping his head into his hands.

Shit, shit, shit! He took deep breaths while rocking back and forth, waiting for the nausea to pass and the room to settle down. At the very least, please, no going full-tilt Linda Blair until *after* those two left.

What a disaster. Then again, what did he expect from the fucking cops? Like when they railroaded his dad, always blaming everyone but themselves. He wanted them out and gone, now.

He finished and turned on the faucet, drinking greedily from it. He splashed some water on his face, every motion an effort. After drying off, he took a deep breath, and headed back into the studio. Only Torrance stood there, half turned, taking in his surroundings.

"Feeling better?" he said when he saw Franco.

"Not really. So…what happens now?"

"Under the circumstances. I think we should try again after you…" *Sober up* seemed on his lips. "…have some rest. I'd like you to come down to the precinct, say ten a.m. tomorrow, so we can go over your statement, and take your prints."

Franco cringed, too tired to argue. Torrance handed him a business card, and he took it without enthusiasm.

The detective glanced at Franco's photo equipment. "What's your area of expertise?"

Fucking up. "Portraits, some interior design, architecture."

"A lucrative business."

"So I've heard." The comment, intended to be self-deprecating, came out rude and defensive.

"You seem to be doing all right, considering the neighborhood."

"Lucky, I guess." He blinked and sighed. Torrance wasn't the enemy, and *he* was being a prick. "My landlords...are generous people," he tried, more contrite. "Rent isn't cheap, but they could ask for double and get it...and I'd kill before giving up living here." He raised his hands in a calming gesture, eyes wide. "Figuratively speaking."

Torrance nodded. "All right, well, get some rest, and I'll see you tomorrow morning."

They said good night and Franco watched him go. He felt regret...for losing control, for being in this mess, and, definitely, for that last drink. But most of all, that someone lost his life, the poor bastard. Part of him hoped he'd only hallucinated it, no matter how bad it made him look. At least this would have meant no one died. Now it was real, and his heart went out to the victim.

He shuffled over to the door and locked it, then started up his phone to text Bob and Tony he was in no condition to talk, that things were all right, and he'd see them in the morning.

Without waiting for a reply, he switched off the lights, crawled into bed fully clothed, and let exhaustion knock him out.

Chapter Ten

Tuesday, July 26

Three minutes to ten the next morning, Franco found himself sitting in a bright interview room inside the First Precinct on Ericsson, a glass of water in his hand. The window behind him overlooked the street and a small park below, and the one across from him provided a clear view of the busy squad room. His left leg twitched, and he tapped the floor with his foot.

He'd overslept, of course, barely leaving time for a quick coffee and half a bowl of cereal to make it there on time. His stomach growled, still upset from last night. He postponed talking to Bob and Tony until later, the impending conversation only spiking his anxiety, and he distracted himself, watching the action in the squad room.

The dated precinct held little of the old world charm of police stations on TV shows. At some point the old and new had been merged to mixed results. Old filing cabinets and desks with modern computers and phones filled the squad room, which also housed an empty holding cell in the far corner. The stone columns holding up the tall ceiling belied the station's true age despite noticeable attempts at renovation, and fresh coats of paint here and there. Uniformed cops and plainclothes detectives worked at their stations or bustled about, talking on phones, their voices blending with the traffic outside.

A fresh surge of resentment gripped him. The callous way the cops had treated his father's murder soured Franco's opinion of the organization, and he remembered being glad when his uncle quit to join the New York Fire Department, where he remained until his retirement a decade ago.

Franco's stomach rumbled, followed by an acid reflux. The next person that brought up the idea of melon shots he'd pop in the mouth.

Five minutes past ten, Detectives O'Shea and Torrance entered the room together, carrying files. Torrance greeted him politely, but O'Shea only half grunted. He wore a suit as cheap and rumpled as its predecessor. Maybe he bought them that way in bulk. Torrance, on the other hand, wore stylish chinos and a shirt, and if anything, daylight only improved the view.

O'Shea took lead, grilling him over his testimony for twenty minutes in the same gruff manner as the previous night, growing increasingly frustrated over his spotty memory and lack of new information. Franco would have sympathized if the guy wasn't such a dick.

Torrance quietly took notes, but didn't look amused. Probably no cakewalk, with a jerk like O'Shea for a partner...unless he'd simply joined the growing number of cops discovering a profound dislike of *him*.

Either way, next time he'd think twice before calling the cops, not that he hoped there would be a next time.

As announced the night before, they fingerprinted him. Afterwards, Franco wiped his hands repeatedly on wet towels, and O'Shea said, "All right, next we want to speak to your...friend."

"He's not talking to me."

"Then try a little harder."

Grudgingly, Franco took out his phone and opened the dating app. He scanned for Pitcher's profile without success. "I think he deleted his account."

Torrance said, "If you give me the app's name and his handle, I'll contact the company for records. You have any photos?"

"Um...not of his face."

Torrance didn't move a muscle, but O'Shea grunted.

Franco gave Torrance the info, then cleared his throat. "I meant to tell you...we had a break in last weekend."

"Yes, your neighbors mentioned it yesterday. But your place wasn't hit?"

"No, but...I told you one of the attackers saw me on the roof. What if they thought I lived there?"

Torrance glanced at O'Shea as he mulled it over. "Did you notice anything unusual? Anyone who didn't belong, or followed you, the past few days?"

Only an eerie feeling of being watched, not that this counted as proof. "No."

"Likely just an unfortunate coincidence, but we are communicating with the detectives on the case."

O'Shea got up. "We're not getting anywhere. I'll go check in with the guys in robbery." He stomped out of the room, and Franco studied the back of his retreating head with a growing aversion. Had his hair been cut with a machete? Probably did it himself, the cheap bastard—that, or his barber was legally blind.

Franco folded his arms, the muscles in his jaw taut. "What the hell is his problem? It's not like I killed the guy."

"I apologize," Torrance said. "My partner is from a different breed and can be...a bit rough around the edges."

"My mother is from a different breed and still managed to teach me manners."

Torrance cocked a brow at him, remaining conspicuously quiet, as if the jury was still out on that one.

"There is one more thing I need to ask of you," he said, his expression softening. "I'd like you to come down to the morgue and take a look at the body."

Franco's eyes nearly popped out of his head. "No way, I already told you I never saw his face."

"I understand, but sometimes our brain stores away details until another encounter unlocks them."

"Don't you know who he is?"

"The victim was found without any identification. We are already exploring every avenue, but dental records take a day or two. And given the fact you actually saw him...well, it might trigger a memory. We found him several buildings from where you witnessed the attack, but might be able to establish he's indeed the person you saw Thursday night."

"Can't you check security cameras or something?"

"The building's system isn't yet operational, and the ones from the construction company were apparently vandalized last week. You lived next door from each other, maybe you crossed paths in the days before he died. Clearing a homicide decreases dramatically after forty-eight hours, and as it stands, we're racing against the clock." Torrance's green eyes locked on Franco's. "I have to warn you, though. The body spent several days out in the heat and is not in the best of conditions."

No shit. Franco grimaced, silently wrestling with himself.

"I wouldn't ask if it weren't important," Torrance said.

Of course he'd seen dead people before, starting with his father, and his grandparents, who'd insisted on open casket burials, but the prospect of looking at a dead stranger made him queasy. He met Torrance's eyes, and sighed. "Fine...let's get this over with."

He emptied the water glass in one gulp, set it down, and got up before he could change his mind.

* * *

Torrance drove them to Bellevue City Morgue on East 26th Street in an unmarked black Ford Taurus. He took two calls over an earbud, keeping him on the phone for most of the ride, and freeing Franco from forced small talk. He parked at the rear of the building, pulled the bud from his left ear, and killed the engine. "Does Pier 46 Enterprises mean anything to you?"

Franco lifted a brow. "Like the cruising area?"

"The what?"

"The old West Side Piers for the transatlantic luxury liners. They were built in the early 1900s, but by the '70s most of them were abandoned, and falling apart. They stood along what used to be the elevated West Side Highway before the city tore them down and created the new waterfront parks. Pier 46 was probably the most famous, or infamous, depending on how you look at it. Guys used to go there to sunbathe, party, and cruise for sex, and there's an excellent documentary…" He noticed Torrance's blank expression. "Never mind…no, what is it?"

"It's the name of the company who owns the apartment. The entire fourth floor, as a matter of fact."

"Never heard of them. Don't *they* have the victim's name?" Maybe he could still get out of this.

"So far, we've not been able to contact anyone there. Could be a shell company."

"Like, someone trying to hide money?"

Torrance half shrugged. "Always possible, though sometimes shell companies exist for the purpose of maintaining anonymity."

They got out of the car and entered the building in silence, descending a staircase to a hallway forking to the left, and ending in front of locked, frosted glass double doors. Goosebumps formed on Franco's arms, and he crossed them over his chest.

"Everything okay?"

"Yep." But he grew more uncomfortable by the second.

Torrance texted someone on his phone and pocketed the device. "I'm sorry you had a rough few days, and I appreciate you doing this." His eyes softened and Franco nodded, glad tensions between them seemed to loosen. "By the way, you do great work."

Franco threw him a surprised glance.

"Social media. And I saw your website, and the stuff you shot for the eyewear store near St. Marks."

For the past four years, the guys behind *The Eyes Have It* had hired him to create fun ad campaigns for their display windows and local magazines. The last one featured a series of nude couples of all genders, colors, and sizes tastefully shot in black and white, all claiming they felt naked without their glasses. Big hit, the pay covering two month's rent.

"Business is good?"

"I'm working several side jobs to keep afloat, so you tell me." He didn't mean to sound so damn defensive, and blamed his nerves, but Torrance unsettled him, *and* he was about to have a date with a decomposing popsicle.

"No shame in working hard to make your dreams come true," Torrance said, ignoring the remark. "You deserve success, your work speaks for itself."

Franco opened his mouth to thank him, and apologize, but the door opened and an attractive, petite woman in a white overcoat motioned for them to come in.

"Hello, Aidan, I hope you haven't been waiting long. I just got your text." She wore her brown hair pulled back and tied in a pony tail, smiling warmly as she shook Franco's hand. "Patricia Norton, Medical Examiner."

Franco stepped into the cool, dimly lit, medium sized room, his nose picking out several sharp odors he could have done without.

Norton walked over to a wall with two rows of metal doors, opened one, and pulled out a refrigerated slab containing a shape under a green sheet.

"Whenever you're ready," she said quietly. "Take your time."

He nodded, and she lifted the sheet, exposing the dead man's head. At least that's what he assumed he stared at. Franco inhaled sharply and immediately wished he hadn't.

"Fuck!" He recoiled, bumping into Torrance. "Half his face is missing." And what was left resembled a sandblasted tomato.

"I know this isn't easy, but please try to take another look."

He groaned, forcing his eyes toward the dead man, while fighting his growing nausea. They'd washed away most of the blood, revealing discolored, bruised, or torn skin and tendons. Teeth were missing, and the right side of the face caved in like a deflated football.

Franco lowered his eyes to below the left jaw where a distinctive purple scar ran all the way down the victim's neck. He felt a jolt, and his eyes grew wide. How the hell could that even...

He turned to face Torrance, but when he opened his mouth, a convulsion shook him. He bent over, his hand attempting to hold on to something, smacking against the detective's crotch, and vomited all over Torrance's leather shoes.

Chapter Eleven

"I'm so sorry," Franco apologized for the tenth time, five minutes later, wiping his mouth with paper tissues from a box Patricia Norton held for him.

"You have nothing to apologize for, don't beat yourself up about it."

He couldn't get the smell of decomposition and bile out of his nose. His head was spinning with millions of questions. Squatting in the hallway outside of the cooling chambers, he wished himself miles away, preferably to another solar system.

Torrance returned from the bathroom, his shoes marginally cleaner than moments ago, and handed Franco water in a paper cup. "Feeling better?"

Franco nodded, emptying the cup in two gulps, eager to cleanse his breath before daring to speak. "Again, I am truly sorry—"

"Don't worry about it, they were an old pair anyway."

"I may not be able to tell Gucci from Prada, but those shoes were new and I'll reimburse you for them."

"I appreciate it, but it's really not necessary. I've had worse things happen on the job."

Franco didn't want to know.

Patricia Norton said, "It's never easy to see a dead body, but especially one having sustained such severe trauma. The advanced decomposition in combination with the significant damage inflicted by—"

"I think I know him," Franco cut her off, before she got him hurling again. "I don't know how that's possible, it makes no sense."

Torrance perked up. "Who is he?"

Franco shook his head and fished out his phone. Zero bars. "I need a computer…please."

"You're welcome to use the one in my office," Norton said, pointing down the hall.

They followed her to a medium-sized nicely furnished room with a glass desk to one side, and a loveseat and chair facing it. With Torrance and Norton flanking him, Franco positioned himself behind her desk and hit the computer's keyboard, typing in a web address. He pulled up the main page of the Charles Prescott Foundation, then clicked on *About* and selected the profile of the CEO and founder.

A professional black and white portrait next to a brief biography showed a handsome, mature man of undetermined age with salt and pepper hair, and a winning smile. A prominent scar snaked down his left neck, a stark contrast to his otherwise groomed appearance.

A reminder of rougher days, he'd once said to Franco, remnants of a knife attack…down by the piers.

"That's him, Charles Prescott."

"So you *did* know the man who lived across from you," Torrance said.

"No, I knew, and barely at that, the millionaire philanthropist who lives on Central Park West, and owns several buildings in this city. I had no idea he kept a place across from my home. His foundation hired me over a year ago to photograph members of their team, and I haven't seen him in, I don't know, seven months, at least."

Torrance pulled out his phone and made a call. "I have a name for you. Charles Prescott of the Charles Prescott Foundation. Address is somewhere on Central Park West." He listened a few beats, and said, "Yes…yes…no, I'll have to call you back on that, just wanted to give you a heads up. Okay, later." He ended the call and said, "I need anything and everything you can tell me about Prescott."

Franco blinked at him.

"You can talk in here, if you like," Patricia Norton said. "I have an appointment in five minutes, my office is all yours."

"I need a minute," Franco said, overwhelmed. "Okay if I step out for a sec?"

She nodded. "Of course. I'm sorry for your loss."

Franco nodded, refraining from repeating he barely knew Prescott. Out in the hallway he leaned against the wall as a woman comforting a sobbing man passed by, walking toward the exit, and he felt a pang of guilt. He didn't mean to be a heartless prick, and regretted Prescott was dead, but even more getting dragged into this mess. Thing was, he'd swear he never saw Prescott anywhere near his house, nor recognized him through that window.

"—Blunt force trauma," he heard Patricia Norton say through the open door. He considered walking away, but something held him back. "The bruises are consistent with a chokehold, but it's not what killed him. The inside of the body bag showed blood, brain matter and bone traces on the head, and I'm certain he was still alive when he was put in."

"Which would explain the lack of blood spatter," Torrance said. "All we found—"

Two women in lab coats passed him, their conversation blocking out the rest. Half a minute later he heard Norton say, "The victim's body sustained a total of forty-four broken bones, consistent with a collision."

"We think he may have been dropped out the hallway window."

"That is another possibility, yes," Norton said. "The body bag is curious, suggests premeditation. An undamaged bag would have contained leakage and smells for a while."

Torrance said, "Yeah, we're not sure what to make of that. It's possible they had to change plans after they were seen. But I agree they came prepared. None of the cameras in the neighborhood caught anything, and more than a few were damaged."

"Listen, Aidan, I don't mean to put you on the spot, but body bags tend to stick out. Why wasn't he discovered sooner?"

"We fucked up. Nothing indicated a crime when the responding team arrived, and the witness was intoxicated and...difficult. Uniforms searched the area, but they must have walked right past him. Garbage collectors came across the bag in a container several buildings over from the crime scene, and called it in yesterday afternoon."

"Most unfortunate, to put it mildly."

Franco pushed off the wall and took a few steps down the hall. He needed a break from death, but his mind kept spinning. When had he last seen Charles? December...January? Prescott always treated him kindly, the few times they'd crossed paths. It just didn't make sense. And, considering his status, why didn't the news report him missing sooner?

"Are you ready?" Torrance said behind him, and Franco nodded. The detective's phone rang, and he answered it. Franco followed him back into the office. Patricia Norton said goodbye and headed out.

Torrance finished his call and motioned for Franco to sit on the sofa. "I'd like to record this conversation, if you don't mind."

"Yeah, okay, sure."

Torrance sat across from him, pulled out a notepad and pen, then set his phone on the square coffee table between them. "How long have you known Charles Prescott?"

"Year and a half, or so? He hired me...*actually,* Derek Brewster from his foundation did, to shoot new portraits of their team. The first time I met him was in February of last year, then a few times after that."

"Take your time and start at the beginning."

Franco nodded and took a deep breath.

Chapter Twelve

Central Park West, February 2015

Heavy rain pelted the windows to his left, drowning out the hum generated by his Broncolor strobes behind him. Chairs and tables in one of Prescott Foundation's spacious conference rooms had been pushed against the right hand wall. He parked his butt on the table holding his camera equipment and laptop, and checked his phone. Just after five. Three more people to photograph against the overlaying charcoal colored canvases he had custom-made for this job, and set up earlier. He stifled a yawn. He'd been here all day, shooting over thirty faces since morning, but his bank account was about to get a nice boost from the lucrative, two-day-gig, and he appreciated that.

The door opened and a tanned, mature, silver-haired man walked in. A significant scar marked the man's left neck, and he recognized him as the big boss from a portrait hanging in the reception area.

Charles Prescott greeted him with a firm handshake and a thin smile, but when Franco introduced himself, the CEO's expression froze. His eye twitched, then he held up a finger and pulled a phone from his pocket, excusing himself as he stepped away to answer a call. He spoke a few muffled words, ended the call, apologized, and said they'd have to reschedule. He shook Franco's hand and departed, leaving him completely clueless as to what had just happened.

A few beats later, Prescott's secretary entered, accompanied by the next person to be photographed, and informed Franco they'd rescheduled the CEO's slot for the end of the following day. He nodded—no time to think about it, with the next person already waiting—and resumed his work.

Charles Prescott returned to the conference room shortly before five the next afternoon, wearing a similar outfit as the day before. Still baffled by the previous encounter, Franco instantly felt self-conscious and nervous.

"I cannot apologize enough for the way we met yesterday," Prescott began, approaching him with a toothpaste ad smile. "I am afraid I had a bit of an odd day, and an unfortunate matter changed my plans at the last moment." He shook his hand, his watchful, probing eyes never leaving Franco's.

"That's okay, think nothing of it," Franco said, trying to decide whether the CEO was eccentric, or taking a dislike to him. "This will only take a moment." He waved a hand toward the chair in front of the backdrop and picked up his Canon.

"Everyone I spoke to from our team complimented you for your pleasant approach, and how comfortable you made them feel, sitting for you," Prescott said, remaining standing.

"Thank you."

"DiMaso is not a common name. It is Italian, is it not?"

"Yes," Franco said, lowering the camera. Maybe Prescott was nervous. Some bigwigs at major companies never got used to having their picture taken, no matter how often they stepped into the limelight. If chitchat helped him loosen up, Franco would gladly indulge him. "There aren't many in Manhattan, I think, at least not from my immediate family."

"Is that right? Your parents are from Italy?"

"Grandparents, but my mom's folks are from Virginia."

"Well, they must be proud to have a successful photographer as a son."

"Define successful," Franco said with a tart smile. "But yes, my mom's a big fan."

"Not your father?"

"He died when I was little." The camera was getting heavy in his hand and Franco set it on a chair near him.

A shadow flickered across Prescott's face. "I am very sorry for your loss."

"Thank you." An awkward silence followed, and Franco cleared his throat. "I don't mean to keep you, I'm sure you're busy."

"After rushing off like I did, I scheduled enough time to let you work your magic." Prescott's smile came across mechanical. "I fear I am not an ideal subject for such projects."

"I'm sure you'll do just fine." Franco picked up the camera again.

"The board decided it was time to get a makeover and spruce up our image. Apparently, some people are much more inclined to give when there's a certain *glamor* to the cause of their choice."

"Well, I've heard you've been very successful, and your foundation is highly regarded."

Prescott smiled genuinely now, a gleam in his eyes. "That we have, and that we are, indeed. It took a lot of work and I appreciate you saying so. We have treated thousands of young men and women suffering from addiction over the past twenty years. Placing them in stable living situations, helping them find jobs, and keeping them clean."

In preparation for this job, Franco had read that the Prescott's wealthy background and family history not only helped keep the organization afloat for years, it also opened doors to some of the most exclusive circles of New York's high society.

"All right, then, young man, shall we get on with it?"

Franco nodded and brought the camera up to his face. "Just be yourself and don't worry about anything. This will be over before you know it."

A few days after Franco delivered his finished work, he received a fancy envelope containing two invitations printed on expensive paper to the foundation's upcoming fundraiser. He called Prescott's secretary, and she informed him he'd requested to have the artist present, if at all possible, when they unveiled their new website and photographs in two weeks.

"The affair is *black tie,*" she said in a brittle tone, as if assuming his wardrobe consisted of nothing but jeans and T-shirts.

Spot on, but he still felt offended. Of course, he couldn't show up like he'd just rolled in off the street on the most glamorous event he'd been invited to in ages. And two weeks later, dressed in one of Gino's old Kiton suits he no longer fit into, Franco felt elated at how good he looked wearing the chic hand-me-down as he checked himself out in the mirror. Some minor alterations by Mama Esposito did wonders.

The invitation was for two, but Nick had dumped him a few weeks earlier. Franco's girlfriend, Terri, had collected a shiner the size of a grapefruit during one of her kickboxing sessions, and Gino, Carmine, and Vince all had plans. He was officially on his own.

It had snowed on and off all day, but the white flakes stopped falling by the time his Uber arrived at the party destination. The glass pavilion atop the foundation's beautiful seven-story building allowed for a spectacular view of Central Park, and Franco wandered through the stunningly decorated space, deeply impressed. Waiters offered appetizers and champagne on silver trays to the guests, many of whom he'd seen in magazines and newspapers. It was literally the perfect place to schmooze with New York's high society, and network the shit out of the crowd, but he felt awkward and out of place.

Five oversized prints, his black-and-white portraits of the foundation's head honchos, hung from a prominent wall, with roughly four dozen smaller sized prints of the remaining staff, many of them former addicts themselves, below it.

The crisp light he'd used framed his subjects beautifully and let their personalities shine through, wrinkles and all. Careful lighting and meticulous preparation before a shoot were key, and helped cut time spent in post-production. Franco enjoyed the warm, tingly feeling spreading through his body at seeing his work displayed so publicly.

He arrived purposefully late to guarantee the party would already be in full swing, allowing him to blend in without appearing more out of place than he felt. He spoke to a few people who recognized him from having their pictures taken, but spent most of the time by himself, not making any important new connections. An hour later he'd eaten enough hors d'oeuvres, and sipped enough champagne, and was ready to dash.

"Ah, there you are," a voice behind him said, and Franco turned. Charles Prescott stood a few feet away, dressed in an elegant black tuxedo.

"Mr. Prescott, I was afraid I wouldn't be able to thank you personally for a wonderful evening."

"Are you leaving us already? I hoped we could talk a moment."

"Of course. I was gonna get some fresh air."

"Perfect, then. We haven't had a chance to toast our successful collaboration." Prescott elegantly whisked two glasses of champagne off a passing waiter's tray, handed one to Franco, and led the way out to the patio where they were greeted by cool air.

They clinked their glasses and Franco smiled. "Thank you again for giving me this wonderful opportunity, Mr. Prescott."

"Nonsense, we are in *your* debt. And please, call me Charles. The portraits continue to receive the highest praise by everyone, and I am sure we will be working with you again very soon."

"That would be fantastic," Franco said. "Looks like your fundraiser is quite the success."

"Yes, indeed. We raised a nice sum for a new methadone program tonight, and I am happy so many guests donated so generously." Charles' expression changed from pride to concern. "These young people are in need of our help and attention. Not everyone is an immediate success story, and many suffer setbacks. Too many never make it at all, despite our best efforts."

"That must be hard," Franco said.

"Addiction is a tragedy." Charles gazed toward Central Park. "We try to educate about legal matters within our program. I'm not denying many drug users turn to crime, though it certainly doesn't apply to all of them. Many could be helped before they felt the needed to turn to illegal activities." He sighed. "I was born into a life of privilege, as you may well know, and had it all, as they say...yet I still succumbed to the lure of a constant high, to escape my personal...circumstances. Perhaps *because* I had it all." He shrugged, a sad smile scurrying across his lips. "It took nearly dying, and the intervention of my family, before I was able to break free. Most people are not blessed with my kind of resources. I was very lucky, it could have very well gone a different way. People underestimate the devastating damage drugs can cause—not just to the addicts, but the people who care about them." Charles lowered his eyes. "Fifty-nine years old, and I still find myself righting wrongs from a time I wish I could put to rest." He forced a nervous grin. "Listen to me babble on, I do apologize."

"Don't worry about it."

"This evening is about celebrating success, I did not intend to bend your ear with my depressing tales."

"Not at all. And you're living proof people can change their life for the better."

"You are very kind." Charles' upbeat expression faltered. "But I do not deserve your accolades."

A yawn crept up on Franco and he failed to hide it. "I am sorry, it's the alcohol. I didn't mean to be rude."

"Nonsense, you are perfectly *fine*." Charles' inflection and intimate smile suggested a double meaning. Was Prescott gay? He'd never mentioned family or a wife, but Franco had never given it a moment's thought.

"I had a wonderful evening," he said. "Thank you for letting me be a part of it."

"No, thank you for doing such a wonderful job, we'll gladly pass your name around."

Writing it on the bathroom wall should do it. Franco bit the inside of his cheek to keep from chuckling.

"How will you get home?" Charles asked.

"Uber, or a cab."

"I won't hear of it. My driver will get you home safely."

"Thank you, that's not necessary."

Charles shook his head. "Please, I insist."

They said their goodbyes, and twenty minutes later Charles' driver dropped Franco off in front of his building. He watched the limousine speed off into the night, then caught his reflection in The Green Thumb's window, pleased at how nicely he cleaned up in Gino's suit. The time on the clock inside the flower shop said two minutes past midnight.

And he hadn't turned into a pumpkin. Maybe things were looking up, after all.

Chapter Thirteen

Tuesday, July 26

By the time he finished, Franco had been talking for nearly eight minutes straight. The fact Torrance hadn't interrupted once suggested he had the patience of rocks, unlike the gang, who frequently threatened him with bodily harm if he didn't wrap up in thirty seconds or less.

"Was this the last time you saw Charles Prescott?" Torrance said, scribbling in his notepad.

"No, I contributed to a showcase, last winter. Saw him all of two minutes, but he bought three of my prints, two of them male nudes. The last time was in January, at a fundraiser my ex invited me to. Charles and I only spoke for five, six minutes, you know, the usual small talk, *how have you been*, and so on. He did say he wanted to speak to me over dinner, but had to take care of some things first."

"Did he say what about?"

"Nope, but I thought...well, *hoped* it was just about another project. I may be wrong but...I always felt he kind of liked me, from the way he looked at me, or said something. He was inquisitive, but respectful, and always very complimentary, but at the same time kept his distance. I liked him, just not *that* way, and I didn't want to hurt his feelings. So I wasn't too upset when he didn't call."

"You felt he initially took a dislike to you. Did he ever comment on the incident?"

"No." Franco shrugged awkwardly. "Sometimes I get intimidated, and… it's probably only my imagination." He shook his head. "I don't get it. He was kinda famous, why didn't someone identify his body sooner?"

"My partner spoke to his COO, Derek Brewster, and according to him Prescott frequently took personal days to unwind, without disclosing his whereabouts. But he never missed board meetings, and when he didn't show up yesterday, and no one could reach him, the foundation reported him missing earlier today."

"What was he doing in that apartment? Just makes no sense."

"Is it possible he could have been stalking you?"

"What? No." Franco shook his head. "I know what I said, earlier, I barely knew the man, but…I can't imagine that." But the thought unsettled him. He frequently walked around naked at home. Someone observing him from across the street by chance was one thing, but making a night of it with a glass of chardonnay and a plate of charcuterie quite another.

Torrance studied him silently, and Franco grew wary. "What?"

"When you were inside Prescott's apartment, did you notice cameras or recording devices?"

"No, just a loose cable." A thought struck him. "But if there were cameras you'll see I told you the truth," he said, excited. "Can't you access his cloud or something?"

"Working on it," Torrance said. His phone beeped, and he checked the message on his screen. "I'm afraid I have to wrap this up, but I appreciate your help and input."

"No problem." Franco cleared his throat. "And I'm sorry."

Torrance stood. "For?"

"Your shoes, for one. Last thing I need is to pile on to the negative impressions you already have of me."

"What makes you say that?"

"Well, we had a rocky start, and I didn't get the impression you could stand me much."

"True," Torrance said with the faintest of smiles.

Franco didn't get the chance to clarify which of his statements he agreed with. Torrance's phone rang, and he said goodbye before answering the call.

Now thoroughly self-conscious, Franco headed out, making his way back to the street where he let the city noise engulf him. Cars and buses thundered past, and he eagerly inhaled their exhaust fumes to cleanse his respiratory system from scents of decomp and formaldehyde.

He put in his earbuds and walked south, bypassing the subway stop.

Craving mellow sounds to soothe his nerves, he selected his Yacht Rock playlist, then briskly navigated through walls of pedestrians and congested traffic on First Avenue. "Give It Up for Love" gave way to "Who'll Be the Fool Tonight?" and "I Apologize" as he zigzagged his way downtown, eventually turning west on Houston. He thought of the few times he and Charles had met, and of Thursday's tragic event. By the time Terea sang about a "Pretty Bird" and he reached Wooster Street, he felt only marginally better.

In front of The Green Thumb, two security company vans blocked half the sidewalk. He squeezed behind workers and entered the building's open front door, emptied his mailbox, and climbed the stairs past electricians drilling holes, and attaching wires and cameras.

He heard classical music from inside Bob and Tony's apartment before he reached their landing.

Time's up, no delaying any further, much as he dreaded it. He knocked with a heavy heart, hoping to still have a roof over his head in about ten minutes.

Bob opened the door barefoot, wearing a pair of old sweatpants and a white T-shirt. "Hey slugger, here to get your new keys?" He smiled, holding a copy of the *New York Times* in his hand. Bandages covered the bruises on his temple, but he looked fresher than last Saturday.

Franco felt a pang of guilt. "That, too, I guess. How are you feeling?"

"Still hurts a bit, but I'll live. The fact someone broke in and attacked me really messed with my head, but I won't let some asshole make me feel unsafe in my own home. What a crazy couple of days, huh?"

Franco bit his lip and Bob stepped back to make room. "Come on in. *Tony, Franco's here!*"

He smelled pleasant hints of spices and cooked meat, and when Tony joined them in the living room, he wiped his wet hands on the apron covering his jeans.

His heart pounding furiously, Franco forced a smile. "I still owe you an explanation…but you might wanna sit down first."

Chapter Fourteen

Wednesday, July 27

Franco woke fully rested for the first time in a while. Not only did he still have a place to live, Bob and Tony were empathetic and understanding. Shocked, but supportive. They echoed everyone else's opinion that the two incidents were likely unfortunate coincidences and told him not to worry too much. That the cops would get to the root of things. He wished he shared their confidence.

He received new keys for the locks they'd had installed, complete with the verbal security code needed if an alarm went out, before an armed response team rained down on the building. Amazing what money could buy. At his last place, he'd waited three weeks just to get his toilet fixed.

He rolled out of bed, and, on a whim, scrolled through the MeatUp app. In a sea of anonymous, headless torsos which could have doubled as classifieds in Sleepy Hollow, he discovered a new profile with the same chest shot Pitcher9 had used last week. Except, he now called himself 9dwnurchute. Classy.

Franco resisted the urge to contact and possibly spook him, and forwarded his findings to Torrance via the email on his card. Thoughts of Charles began circling his brain, weighing him down, and he pushed them away. He had a new client showing up in less than half an hour, and needed to get in the right mindset.

He showered, then dressed in shorts and a T-shirt. After having a bowl of cereal and Greek yoghurt, he set up the strobes and backdrop for his ten o'clock. Howard arrived on time, and Franco put on his latest discovery, German DJ Supermarkt. Selecting the *Almost Summer* mix, mellow disco tracks and edits filled the space as they exchanged small talk, and Howard slipped into the formal attire his business portraits required.

Franco rearranged the strobes, a six foot Octabox for his main light with two twelve foot strips for fill, and adjusted them to Howard's height. He picked up his Canon with the attached wireless transmitter, snapped a few test frames, and together they evaluated light, position, and outfit on his computer screen before proceeding with the photoshoot.

Fifty minutes and two costume changes later, Howard left happy, and Franco pocketed the three hundred dollars with a mental note to deposit them in his bank before hitting Gino's. Tomorrow he'd work on a final selection and let his client choose the best five shots before editing those for print.

He flicked through his phone's music selection, put on Roy Ayer's "The Memory" and packed away his gear. When his phone vibrated, he answered cheerfully.

"Mr. DiMaso," the vaguely familiar voice on the other end said, "I hope I didn't catch you at a bad time. This is Derek Brewster."

Franco's eyes widened. "Mr. Brewster, how...are you?"

"We are all trying to cope." Charles Prescott's second in command sounded hollow. "This is such a major shock to all of us."

"I'm very sorry for your loss."

"Thank you. I apologize, but I just had to call you. The police...they say you were there?"

Aw, shit. "Yes, I was."

"May I ask...?"

Franco pictured the balding, homely, middle aged man at the other end of the line, struggling for words. He'd always liked the guy, and his heart went out to him. "I am afraid I don't have a lot of answers for you." He recounted his experience, leaving out any intimate, embarrassing, or gory details, making the story shockingly short. The guys would've been impressed.

"This is so…I have no words," Derek Brewster said. "I am…so sorry you had to witness this tragedy." They were silent for a few seconds.

"Do you know what Charles was doing there?" Franco said. "The police think he…owned the place?"

"He did, apparently. I found the documents in his safe. It appears he bought several units through a holding company he created sometime last year, but why, and without telling anyone, I do not know."

Join the club. But Franco said, "I was hoping *you* might have some answers."

Brewster sighed. "I'm as stumped as everyone else. Charles is…was a very private man, despite his outgoing personality. I'd like to think I knew him better than most. After all, we worked side by side for nearly two decades, and accomplished so much together. I considered him a close friend. But there were things he never spoke about, and I respected that. He was genuinely loved by everyone who met him, and I can't fathom why someone would want to hurt him, much less…"

Franco couldn't think of anything to say and remained quiet.

"I hope you don't mind I called you," Brewster continued. "I wanted to let you know Charles's service is set for Friday. I understand it's rather short notice. We're all scrambling to get everything done on time. Anyway, I understand if you'd rather not come, considering the circumstances, but he would have loved it if you could. He thought very highly of you."

Just how highly, exactly…and how off was Torrance's theory, really?

Franco sighed. "Of course, I'll be there. And thank you for reaching out to me."

Derek Brewster gave him the address, in case the invitation got lost, and they said goodbye. Franco empathized, glad not to be in his shoes, and continued unplugging his strobes and packing away his gear. From time to time his eyes fell on the building across the street, accompanied by a dip in his mood, and a fresh wave of uncertainty.

Ten minutes before noon the phone rang again, showing a number he didn't recognize.

"Franco DiMaso Photography, Franco speaking."

"Mr. DiMaso, this is Officer Williams with the NYPD," a female voice said. "The detectives on the Prescott homicide investigation would like to see you here at the precinct."

"But I was just there yesterday."

"It says here you identified the deceased?"

"Yes." Unfortunately.

"Your signatures are needed on a few documents. Just a formality, but necessary and urgent before we can release the body. Can you please swing by today?"

He raised his eyes toward the ceiling. "Fine, sure, I'll be there in fifteen minutes."

"Thank you, I appreciate it. Ask for me at the front desk."

Franco ended the call and shook his head, so ready for this to be over.

He left the remaining strobes for later, grabbed his keys and wallet, and walked downstairs. He unlocked his bike, stepped out, and made the short ride to the precinct.

Officer Williams, a petite, attractive Black woman in uniform escorted him upstairs, past the desks and interview rooms, and down a corridor with multiple doors. She opened one of them and showed Franco into a drab, windowless space with a single fluorescent light, and a table with three chairs. Franco's brows snapped together. Talk about a drastic downgrade in decor.

"The detective will be with you shortly," Officer Williams said, then closed the door behind her. He took a seat and waited for several minutes, listening to the muffled sounds outside, permeating the door.

Might be nice seeing Torrance again. The last encounter, embarrassing as it had been, cleared the air. Sort of. They would probably even hit it off over drinks, had they met under different circumstances.

The door opened, and he put on his best smile only to have it fizzle out half-cocked.

O'Shea entered with a grim expression, firmly shutting the door behind him. No Torrance. He slapped a bunch of folders on the table and opened one of them containing files and enlarged photographs of fingerprints.

"Well, then," O'Shea said, looking like a bloodhound, scenting prey. "Perhaps you'd like to explain why your DNA is all over my crime scene. The truth this time, if that word exists in your vocabulary."

Franco's skin prickled hot. "I told you the truth…I had an allergic reaction to the joint and suffered a blackout. I didn't remember being in the apartment, or what I was doing there until days later."

"Bullshit!" O'Shea slapped the palms of his hands on the table and leaned forward, invading Franco's personal space. He leaned back in his chair, unsuccessful in avoiding the cop's musty body odor. "Every time we talk your story changes, and I've had enough. You've consistently hindered this investigation by making false or incomplete statements, all serious felonies. This is your final chance to come clean before I throw your ass in jail."

Franco's ears pounded and his adrenaline spiked, but he held his ground, fists balled. "I told you everything I know. If you guys had done your job, you'd have found Charles immediately, not four days later."

"You mean the man you claimed you didn't know?"

Franco threw his hands up in frustration.

"I see right through you. Memory loss, very convenient. What was it, your sugar daddy disapproved of your promiscuous late night activities, and you guys fought it out, once and for all?"

"For the last time, Charles and I barely knew each other." Franco's legs twitched with anxiety. "He was a client, nothing more, and I had no idea—"

The door behind them opened and Torrance walked in with a puzzled expression. "What's going on?"

"It's okay, I got this," O'Shea said curtly.

"No, *really*." Torrance didn't budge and Franco wondered if he was indeed clueless, or if he'd ended up at the detectives' dress rehearsal for *good cop, bad cop*.

O'Shea shoved the folder with the photos at Torrance. "Our witness has left his DNA all over the crime scene—fingerprints, blood, you name it—while conveniently leaving out being in the victim's apartment at the time of his murder."

"I *told* you I was there, trying to help the victim," Franco said again, calmer.

"I probably tripped over the chair in the dark, that's why I was all banged up afterwards."

"After you disposed of the body, you mean."

"Are you crazy?" Franco half shouted, then pleaded to Torrance, "You *know* I have nothing to do with this. You were there when I identified Charles. You saw I was completely overwhelmed, and have the shoes to prove it."

O'Shea didn't let up. "The reporting officer said you repeatedly refused to have yourself checked out by the medical team on site. Sounds a lot like hiding something tying you to the crime. Wounds sustained in a fight, perhaps?"

"Oh, *Jesus*, here," Franco snapped, lifting his shirt and pulling down his pants enough to show the healing scrapes. "I was high, fell on my ass, and banged myself up. End of story."

"You certainly have an explanation for all the things you never bothered to mention before."

What if these ass-clowns really believed he murdered Charles? Or worse, if they simply needed someone to finger for it, and *tag*, he was it?

"Take a frigging sample, then. Why the hell would I call the cops if I was in any way involved? Charles was nearly a head taller than I, and heavier. What, I choked him standing on a stepladder, then hoisted him over my shoulder, out to wherever the hell you found him? I told you, I was on the roof, ask—" Shit, he still didn't know the asshole's name, "—my date from Thursday night. I sent you his information, he'll tell you."

Torrance gave no indication he'd received it.

"Maybe you worked together," O'Shea said, and Franco plumped back against the chair, exasperated.

Torrance said, "Can I talk to you for a moment?"

"Later." O'Shea turned his attention on Franco, but Torrance put a hand on his shoulder.

"Now."

O'Shea's face darkened, but he snatched up the folder and followed Torrance out the door, slamming it behind him.

Realizing he'd been holding his breath, Franco exhaled forcefully, his hands trembling. He was *so* beyond fucked.

If he could explain everything to Torrance, he'd surely see the truth, but O'Shea would never believe him. He shot up, fished his phone out of his jeans, and eyed the door. Time to call in the cavalry.

* * *

Aidan Torrance walked several steps away from the interrogation room where he waited until O'Shea joined him. He didn't bother to hide his anger, but kept his voice in check. "When were you going to tell me about this?"

"You were busy searching Prescott's mansion. I'd have told you eventually." O'Shea didn't sound convincing, and Aidan felt a prickle on his face. "Find anything useful?"

"Don't change the subject," Aidan snapped. "We're supposed to be a team, you don't go behind your partner's back with something like this. I don't know what's going on with you, lately, but I gotta tell you my patience is wearing thin."

"I don't know what you're talking about."

"Everyone can smell it on you, Aengus."

O'Shea scowled at him.

"If there's something going on with you, I'm here to talk. But I'm done covering. You show up late, paperwork doesn't get done, and you're even more irritable than usual, alienating everyone around you. Lay off the booze and get a grip on yourself, or I'll take it to the captain."

O'Shea's jaw worked silently, then he said, "Stay out of my business. Last I checked, we were trying to close a homicide, and you're keeping me from doing that."

"What is it with you and DiMaso? I was there when he identified Prescott, his shock seemed genuine."

"That doesn't exonerate him. He's a liar and has been hindering this investigation from the start. Every two seconds his story changes, and I know he's involved in this somehow. He's a fake, like his father."

"What the hell are you talking about?"

"Frank DiMaso, super cop, the righteous prick. A stickler for doing everything by the book, or so he made everyone think. Until he gets himself killed, and we find a locker with close to fifty grand and a shitload of drugs to his name. No, DiMaso was as corrupt a son of a bitch as they come, and an embarrassment to the force, and the apple rarely falls far from the tree."

Aidan shook his head. "Even if that's true, his father's actions don't make him a criminal. DiMaso may be a tweaker, and the epitome of an unreliable witness, but I don't think he's our guy."

O'Shea opened his mouth in protest, but Aidan cut him off. "If you're right and DiMaso is involved, we nail him by the book. No stunts, no antics. This case is already tainted. You said he left DNA at the crime scene?"

"Fingerprints."

"Which he already told us."

"Yeah, well after the fact. Norton sent her full report. She found traces of skin under Prescott's nails, and forensics pulled blood and skin samples from a chair leg. When they match it, I guarantee you, it'll be his. He and Prescott had history. Hell, you suspect he may have stalked DiMaso."

Aidan lowered his voice further, as two uniformed officers passed them. "All of it highly circumstantial, as I'm sure the DA will remind us if we present this to him without more hard evidence. I think you're barking up the wrong tree, *and* DiMaso just offered to provide DNA."

"Doesn't mean he's not involved, somehow."

Aidan shook his head. "Have you already combed through Prescott's financial and phone records?"

"Still working on it. Nothing so far, except a few cash withdrawals. A thousand here, a few hundred there. So, what did you find at Prescott's?"

Aidan sighed. "Nothing pointing at a motive, or relating to the pad he kept across from DiMaso. He owned two laptops. Brewster knew his password to the one at work, but I didn't see anything personal on it. Nothing mentions Pier 46 Enterprises, but techs are combing through it now, and I submitted warrants for his cloud. I suspect he kept his private affairs on a separate account, on the second laptop, but so far no luck with any passwords Brewster could guess. Might take forensics a while."

"Shit. We need the security footage from Prescott's pad."

"Provided there was any. Might already be gone if his killer got access to his phone. Bottom line," Aidan said, circling back to the original conversation O'Shea clearly tried steering away from, "if the DA gets wind you're hitting the sauce on the job he'll hand us our asses. You're on your way out, and may not give a shit anymore, but I won't let you drag me down with you. We're partners, like it or not, and I've had your back since day one. It's time you had mine."

O'Shea took a step back without responding. A young police officer approached them. "Aidan, Mr. Christopoulos is here, and the background check is on your desk."

"Thank you, Mike. Wait five minutes, then escort him to Interview Three, please." The officer left and he turned to O'Shea. "All right, this would be our elusive second witness. Let's go over his file before we introduce ourselves."

Chapter Fifteen

The groomed, olive-skinned man sitting inside the interrogation room did not look amused. He shot up from the table the moment Aidan and O'Shea entered. "Detectives, I strongly object to officers coming to my work and dragging me here without an explanation! What's the meaning of this?"

O'Shea waved a hand at one of the chairs. "Mr. Christopoulos, take a seat, this will take but a moment."

"I want to know why your officers dragged me here, it's unacceptable," the attractive man with the short, dark hair demanded, but he sat back down with his tailored suit and manicured fingers, one of them sporting a wedding ring with a discreet diamond.

"No one dragged you here, Mr. Christopoulos," O'Shea said, "you were given a choice."

"And have you people create an awkward situation in front of my employees? Do you have any idea how this looks?"

Before O'Shea could alienate him further, Aidan said, "We asked you here because we have a few questions regarding a crime that took place Thursday night, early Friday morning."

He and O'Shea took a seat opposite Christopoulos, who crossed his arms, avoiding their eyes. "So what's that got to do with me?"

"According to our information, you're a possible witness to a murder."

"Absolutely not, that's ridiculous."

The man's unwarranted defensiveness surprised Aidan. Something was definitely off here.

O'Shea said, "A Franco DiMaso claims you were with him on his building's rooftop when a man was killed in an apartment across the street."

Thanasis Christopoulos shook his head vigorously. "I don't know that name and have no idea what you're talking about."

O'Shea leaned forward. "People who have nothing to hide usually cooperate."

"I resent the insinuation. I told you I don't know anything about any crime, and you have the wrong person. This is beginning to feel like harassment."

"Mr. Christopoulos, we're not accusing you of anything. We need your help," Aidan said in a calm tone. "We have information placing you across from the house where the murder took place. You're not in trouble, but we want to know what happened."

"Well, whoever said I was there lied, Detective. It happens."

O'Shea didn't let up. "Especially when they're trying to hide a secret sex life."

"How dare you! Perhaps it's time I call my lawyer."

"You're certainly free to do so. In the meantime, we'll have a friendly chat with your wife." O'Shea scanned the file before him. "One Marianna Christopoulos, yes? And Konstantinos Dimitriadis, the Car Czar, is your father-in-law? They're aware of your rap sheet, yes?"

The color drained from Christopoulos' face. "You leave them out of this."

Aidan held up a hand. "Let's all calm down. You are not under arrest, our conversations are privileged, and there's no reason anyone outside this room needs to hear what you tell us in here," he said, calm but firm. "I'm sure we can clear this up, and you can be on your way."

Christopoulos eyed him warily.

Aidan said, "Detective O'Shea and I will be right back. Can we get you something to drink while you wait?"

"No." Christopoulos sulked with his head turned away, arms folded tightly across his chest. Aidan rose and pulled O'Shea with him. They stepped into the hallway and closed the door.

"What the fuck are you doing? This prick is lying, and if he doesn't cooperate this minute, I'll read him back his arrest record—"

Aidan exhaled sharply. "Calm down, I know that. He's extremely defensive, and given the wife, probably deep in the closet."

"So?"

"Time for Plan B."

* * *

After three failed attempts to reach either of the brothers or Vince, Franco was running out of options. Certain the cops would return any moment, he tapped in a number he knew by heart, though he rarely used it anymore. True, the doomed affair had only lasted months. Still, hard to forget a number ending in 6969.

"Nick Torelli, BTK Media Artists."

"Nick, I need your help."

"Franco?" he said, pleasantly surprised. "How are you, babe? It's been ages."

"I know. Listen, I'm sorry to bother you, but I need your help. I'm at a police station."

Nick chuckled. "Who'd you kill?"

"No one," Franco said excitedly, "but last week I witnessed a murder and I sorta ended up leaving my fingerprints at the crime scene, and now the cops think I did it."

"Oh...you weren't joking."

"Why the hell would I be joking? This is serious. I think I need a lawyer."

"All right, back up a bit. What happened?" Nick said in a calm voice, and Franco gave him the cliff notes.

"Wow, Little Miss Muffet got wasted? I have so many questions."

"Damn it, Nick, *focus.*"

"What exactly do they have on you?"

"Fingerprints and a DNA sample, they say. I fell over some damn chair and scratched myself, and now they claim I was in a struggle. Look, they'll be back any moment. You gotta know defense lawyers, with all the celebrities you represent."

"Hey! You make it sound like we run a criminal asylum," Nick said, defensively. "Well…I guess some *have* seen the inside of a courtroom… or two. Fine, I'll make some calls. Just stay put."

"Where the fuck am I gonna go? I'm in a goddamn interrogation room."

"All right, all right, chill. Unless they officially charge you, and I seriously doubt they will, you can leave anytime you want. Got it? Just be open and cooperative, tell them everything—"

"I already did, fifty-million times."

"—let them ask their questions, *don't interrupt—*"

"They won't listen!"

"And don't argue, for a change."

Franco sighed. "Too late."

"Shocker."

"*Hey,*" Franco snapped, tired of Nick's typical, nonchalant attitude. "I've been nothing but helpful, and this is the thanks I get. I'd like to see you stay calm if you were in my shoes."

"Oh, don't be so damn sensitive. You didn't do anything wrong and have nothing to worry about, all right? The cops don't arrest people willy-nilly and are generally very good at their jobs. So, sit tight and behave, and you'll be fine." As a successful talent agent with the reputation of being a rock in any crisis, he had a tendency to treat everyone around him like drama queens suffering various levels of hysteria. But Franco needed his help and swallowed his annoyance. "I'll get back to you as soon as I can. In the meantime, take deep breaths and stay calm. They're just trying to cover all bases. And when they arrest and Mirandize you stop talking and immediately ask for a lawyer."

"*When?*"

The door to the interrogation room opened and O'Shea poked his head in. "Okay, time to— Hey, no phones during interviews, hand it over."

"Gotta go." Franco ended the call, about to put the device back in his pocket, but O'Shea held out his hand.

"Give it up. Who the hell brought you in?"

Franco grudgingly handed him the phone and shrugged. If O'Shea wanted

Williams' name he could find out his damn self, Franco wasn't going to throw her under the bus. He followed him four doors down the hallway to another room. His eyes lit up when he recognized Pitcher, though he looked completely different from last week. Gone was the rough trade act, his conservative attire more suitable for a Republican convention.

Pitcher's eyes widened for an instant, but he recovered quickly, and turned his head away.

"Finally," Franco said.

"Franco DiMaso, Thanasis Christopoulos, though I believe introductions aren't necessary." O'Shea's voice dripped with sarcasm.

No wonder Franco couldn't remember the man's name, he'd never given it.

"I don't know this man," Christopoulos said.

Franco's jaw dropped. "Are you fucking kidding me?"

"Detectives, I've been patient and now I've had enough. I want to leave."

"That goes double for us, Mr. Christopoulos," O'Shea said. "We're trying to solve a homicide here, so we'd like a little more cooperation and a lot less attitude."

"Lawyer, *now*."

Torrance said, "We haven't read you your rights and you're not under arrest."

"Law-yer."

"I say we talk to the wife," O'Shea said.

Wife? Franco's mind spun. He needed the asshole to fess up and put an end to this now. "Listen, I don't know what your problem is, but you're not leaving until you tell the truth." He turned to O'Shea. "My phone."

"There are no phones during—"

"You want to end this farce, give me my damn phone."

Torrance nodded and O'Shea returned the device. Swiping across the screen, Franco opened the dating app, bringing up his and Pitchers' saved chat history. *There*, one of the x-rated photos Pitcher sent before meeting last week. It didn't show his face, only part of his chin, but his mermaid tattoo made him identifiable to anyone who knew him intimately, as did the wedding ring he must have forgotten to remove, prominently featured on the hand grabbing the hair of some bearded guy choking on his dick.

Franco held the screen so the cops couldn't see. "They think I had something to do with that murder, and you know that's not true. You were there and thanks to your spiked *spliff* I nearly jumped off the fucking roof. You saw the effect it had on me, and left me to fend for myself, you piece of shit. I could have died. So, either you tell the truth and it all ends here, or I swear I'll plaster your photos and texts all over the fucking web."

Christopoulos' blanched. He lowered his head, his face contorting. "I have your word, nothing I say here leaves this room? Under no circumstances will you contact my family?"

"Are you waiving your right to counsel? If you tell us the truth and didn't commit any crimes, I give you my word," Torrance said. "We don't care about the drugs."

Franco opened his mouth in protest, but Torrance's stare silenced him.

"Okay, yes, I waive my right to counsel. I was there...regrettably." Christopoulos sat up, and his arrogance returned. "I arrived around midnight and left twenty excruciating minutes later. We got a little baked, but I swear I didn't see anything or anyone suspicious. At no time did I witness or commit a crime, other than wasting my valuable time on a thoroughly unmemorable encounter."

Franco's jaw hurt from clenching his teeth, but he kept quiet.

"Mr. DiMaso says he told you about what he saw."

"I thought he was delusional. He kept babbling about suspicious people in an apartment across the street, but everything was dark. Far as I was concerned, he was just tripping. Whatever happened over there has nothing to do with me, and I can't put it to you any plainer: I did not see anything."

"Did anyone see you leave? Someone to confirm your whereabouts after you left?"

"You said you would keep this private."

Torrance said, "We have to corroborate your statement, but I promise we'll be discreet."

Christopoulos grimaced. "I don't think anyone saw me. I drove my car and arrived home around twelve-thirty. Our building's security cameras will have recorded it. My wife was already asleep, but she woke up briefly when I went to bed." His glare toward Franco suggested, given the chance, he'd kill him if they weren't already in a police station. "And as for my criminal record, Detectives, that happened nearly twenty years ago. I was a stupid kid and paid my dues. And if that's all I'd like to leave now."

"Mr. DiMaso says he suffered a blackout after smoking your joint, not common when smoking weed," Torrance said.

"The joint was a present from a friend who I will not name, and I assure you it was all perfectly harmless. For all I know he could have been high before I even got there."

Liar. But Franco clamped his mouth shut.

O'Shea rose. "You can leave once you've written down your formal statement." He walked out and motioned for Christopoulos to follow him.

"If any of this leaks to my wife or family, I'll sue your whole department." He leaned in close to Franco, hissing, "And fuck you for dragging me into this!" He got up and stomped out of the room.

Franco's knuckles hurt from balling his fists. He eyed Torrance, who collected the files on the table. "Am I under arrest?"

"No. But I'd still like to collect your DNA, like you offered."

Franco thought about it and nodded. Anything to prove his innocence. Torrance excused himself and returned moments later, swabbing Franco's mouth. After he signed a bunch of release forms, Franco said, "You *do* know I had nothing to do with this, right?"

Torrance pursed his lips and picked up the papers. "I regret the circumstances under which you were brought here, Mr. DiMaso. But you are free to go."

All formal, none of the empathy from the day before. He held out his hand and Franco shook it with a tired nod.

In the buzzing squad room, Thanasis Christopoulos sat at a desk, writing down his statement. A short distance behind him, two men stood near the captain's office, talking. One was Franco's height, with a balding head and glasses, the other one stood maybe a foot taller, wearing a pricey suit, and exuding the authority of a politician. They stopped talking and turned his way.

O'Shea approached him, blocking his view. "If you've got anything to do with this, I'll nail your lying ass, rest assured. You may fool my partner and think you're above the law, but you're every bit as dirty as your old man."

Franco grabbed his arm before realizing it. "What did you say?"

O'Shea pulled free and Franco stabbed a finger at his chest. "Who the hell do you think you are?"

People turned to stare, and Torrance put a firm hand on his shoulder, urging him to calm down. He angrily shook it off, adrenalin pumping through him with such intensity he felt lightheaded.

He glowered at O'Shea, his face hot. "Stay the hell away from me and don't *ever* talk about my father again, or I'll have your badge!"

He pushed past him before his wobbly legs could give way, hurrying past the two gentlemen watching him. Bolting down the stairs and out the door, he kept fighting the urge to keel over.

Chapter Sixteen

"O*r I'll have your badge?*" Gino cocked his brows and handed him a glass of water.

"Whatever, okay, it just slipped out." Franco sat at a table across from Terri and Carmine in the dimly lit restaurant, an hour after closing. "I was so livid I couldn't think straight, but trust me, I meant every damn word."

A seemingly never ending shift later, in which he'd screwed up three orders and managed to spill red wine on a guest, he was as pissed off as when he'd stormed out of the precinct.

"The guy sounds like a giant douche," Terri said, sitting in Carmine's lap, both of them sipping a glass of Old Pulteney. Between her real estate career and kickboxing, she didn't find much time to spend with them these past few months. Half an hour ago, she stopped by for a nightcap on her way home from training. A white wife-beater hugged her breasts, exposing several colorful tattoos of mostly birds and flowers on her arms and wrists, and she'd tied her long, black hair in a loose bun. "I'd have punched him."

"If I had, we'd be speaking through bars now. It almost seemed like he was baiting me into doing something stupid so he'd have a reason to lock my ass up. Clearly, he knew my father, and I want to know how."

"And prove what?" Carmine absentmindedly caressed Terri's exposed shoulder. The intimate exchanges between the two had caused many speculations over the years, but they just felt comfortable with each other, and never took their relationship past the platonic. In fact, between all of them, save Gino, none had been in a serious relationship in years.

"I don't know, maybe I could get him kicked off the case for prejudice if he had bad history with my dad. Uncle Sal would know. But if I tell him, I'm not sure he'll not blab to mom. She's not due back until Saturday, but I don't know how to phrase it so they won't both completely flip." He sighed. "You know, something else went through my mind. The night they came to question me, O'Shea instantly knew who I was, though we'd never met."

Carmine tilted his head. "Doesn't necessarily prove anything. Cops have access to DMV files."

"Fine, but still. Oh, and Nick called and gave me the number of a top lawyer if the old bastard persists in going after me. Not that I can afford him at seven fifty an hour. *Hundred,* in case that wasn't clear."

"Jesus," Terri said, eyes wide.

Carmine nodded. "Sounds about right, unless you go with a public defender."

Franco grimaced. "I'm fucked."

"Let it go, nothing good will come of this," Gino said ominously, refreshing his drink. "You'll only end up like our Uncle Guido. You don't want to screw around with the cops, they are relentless. Relentless, I tell you."

"Last week you said to let them handle everything."

"Yeah, well, that was last week, when it all looked like a big misunderstanding. Anyway, back in the 80s they harassed and tormented poor Uncle Guido for weeks, showing up at his work and home, accusing him of fencing stolen electronic equipment off the back of his delivery truck. They followed him everywhere, around the clock, and pretty soon his dry cleaning business suffered, Zia Carmen suffered, even the kids were getting shunned at school. I mean, we ate at their house every other Sunday...he's the sweetest, kindest man you can possibly imagine. And then one day, *boom,* the cops showed up and put him away for fifteen years."

Terri's eyes widened. "How can they do this to an innocent man?"

"Oh, well, no...he did it. They just added time for the illegal gambling he organized through his dry cleaning business."

With a *kill me now* face, Franco tossed up his hands. "How in the hell is that even remotely the same?"

"What? All I said was the cops are relentless. You wouldn't believe the stories Uncle Guido told us. Turns out, the cops knew about his more questionable dealings, and collected payoffs for years. Only after they increased their demands and he refused to pay more did they go after him, and threatened his family, so he'd comply and keep quiet."

Franco threw him a side glance. "This wouldn't by any chance be the same uncle you're buying this building from?"

"Yeah, why?"

Terri got off Carmine's lap, pulling up a chair next to Franco. "I'm sorry, babe, I wish you'd called." She kissed him on the lips and hugged him.

"Thanks, honey." He turned to the brothers. "See, *this* is what empathy looks like—watch and learn."

"*Merda,* what doesn't kill you makes you stronger," Gino said with a dismissive wave of his hand. "But I'd like to state for the record I think you should let it go. Lay low, don't draw attention to yourself."

Franco's expression turned grim. "Decades later, and all it takes is one piece of shit to keep rumors about my dad alive."

"Understandable, no one wants to hear that about the person they love," Gino said. "I can't begin to imagine what your mother must have gone through, raising two kids after losing her husband. Especially with *your* grandparents."

"Why, what happened?" Terri said.

"My dad thwarted their aspirations to expand the family business by marrying him off to a wealthy, competing store owner's daughter. Not sure what century they thought this was, but naturally he wanted nothing to do with it, and married my mom pretty much on the spot, though they'd only been dating four months. Huge drama ensued, families were disgraced, and the shunned father of the bride-not-to-be made it his life's work to destroy my grandparents' reputation and business. Mom never mentioned anything until they were both dead, and Sis and I were adults, but grandma and grandpa made her life hell. They only buried the hatchet for a while when I was born, the heir apparent."

"Turning in their graves, now, are they?" Carmine winked.

"I'm sorry, honey, I didn't know," Terri said, putting her arm around his shoulders. When Franco squinted, she vaguely resembled Angelina Jolie, after she'd been punched in the face a few times. Terri's nose had been broken more than once, and it veered slightly to the left. It didn't diminish her sex appeal in the slightest.

"I can't wait for all of this crap to be over," he said with a sigh. "Anyway, I think the whole fiasco concludes my foray into dating apps."

"And about time, too," Gino said between sips. "No one worth meeting spends time on there, anyway."

"Not true, I find guys worth meeting on Tinder all the time," Terri objected.

"Yeah, but you're a *ho* with a dick bigger than all of ours combined."

She let out a throaty chuckle. Never having made her active libido a secret, she saw no reason not to indulge in the same fun her male friends always bragged about, and would settle when she was good and ready.

"Excuse me, you there on the high horse," Franco said to Gino. "I'd like to think *I'm* worth meeting. There must be others who want more than a roll in the hay with enough attention span to get to know someone beyond the size of their dick."

"Of course you're worth meeting, *amore*, but I still believe the best connections are made in person, in everyday situations, like shopping for groceries, or at the gym."

"Listen to the expert," Carmine said sarcastically.

"Hey, I meet people wherever I go."

"I think you mean *alienate*."

Gino muttered something under his breath and Terri patted Franco's hand. "Someone somewhere will realize you're a great guy, don't worry."

"I simply want to meet a nice guy who is reasonably sane, shares my interests, and wants to have meaningful conversations over romantic dinners, before we grow old and wrinkly together."

"Says the guy whose balls have been fondled by more people than the *Charging Bull*'s," Carmine said, referring to Wall Street's bronze tourist attraction.

"Hey!" Franco said, laughing. He got up and stretched his back. "Thanks for letting me vent, guys, but it's a work night and I need my beauty sleep. I'm not twenty anymore."

Gino put his arm around his shoulder. "Hate to break it you, but you're not even forty anymore."

Chapter Seventeen

Friday, July 29

Thursday passed without a hitch, the damn cops, or any other difficulties, and Friday morning Franco woke relaxed and rested. Life appeared to return to normal. He rubbed sleep from his eyes and dragged his naked body out of bed.

Charles' funeral service was set for four, and Gino had already okayed him showing up late for his shift. Today would be a bear of a day, what with the funeral, Gino's, and bartending at Friction, but he welcomed the extra cash he was about to make.

He downed a small bowl of Greek yoghurt, changed into his workout gear, and headed downstairs where three workers in overalls installed a thick, new glass door. He grabbed his bike, put on his earphones, and pedaled past traffic and numerous construction sites on Canal Street, where jackhammers openly competed against the melee of traffic, and honking cars, drowning out the music in his ears.

Even Crunch'n'Punch seemed unusually busy, and he had to adjust his workout routine to coincide with available machines and free weights. He ran into a few acquaintances, but other than a quick *hello* or *how are you?* he refrained from long chitchats, focusing on his exercises. How he missed the days when he cleared entire dessert buffets without consequences, and just showing up at the gym burned enough calories to stay in shape.

He returned home two hours later, fixed himself grilled chicken salad for lunch, and finished editing his client's photos.

When the time came, he dressed in his Kiton suit, adding a new black dress-shirt, and a blue dotted '70s tie before heading to the Catholic church on Park and 84th.

A large crowd had already gathered, and black Town Cars lined up to drop off mourners. Huge clouds rolled in without cooling the sultry air, and Franco began to sweat in his suit. He scanned the nearby faces, didn't recognize anyone, and made his way inside the church, hoping to cool down.

Someone put a hand on his shoulder and he turned.

"I am glad you made it," Derek Brewster said quietly, taking Franco's hand. He hadn't seen him in person since the party at the foundation the previous year. He'd aged and looked like he hadn't slept all week.

"I am very sorry for your loss," Franco said. "Thank you for inviting me."

"I can't tell you how sorry I am you got involved in this tragedy. We have been scrambling to get this service together with some dignity. Charles was a great man, he deserved the best, though he would not want a fuss."

Franco nodded, uncertain what to say.

"He left a package addressed to you. It's been a crazy week and I haven't had the time, but I will send it as soon as I can."

Franco felt surprised, intrigued, and a tad worried. What if Torrance was right? "No rush, you have enough on your plate."

"Thank you. We loved the work you did for us and I am sure we'll be calling on your services again." Brewster cocked his head and his eyes glanced over Franco's shoulder. "Please, excuse me."

He went to meet new arrivals and Franco walked down the aisle of the church where the coffin lay amidst a sea of beautiful flowers, his portrait of Charles mounted on a stand beside it.

Not surprisingly, they'd forgone an open casket.

Franco stood there for a moment, suddenly unable to get Charles' deformed skull and massive injuries out of his mind. He grimaced and headed to the pews in the back to take a seat.

His mother had raised them Catholic, as their father would have wanted, but he'd broken with the church decades ago. Coming out made him reevaluate his life and question everything he'd been taught to believe. To each their own, but he knew his time was better spent striving to live life with an open mind, being kind to and accepting of others, and taking responsibility for his actions. To own his mistakes and pay it forward when he could. Didn't always work smoothly, but he tried.

He couldn't stand people conveniently hiding behind their religion, openly discriminating against anyone not of their faith, believing, come Sunday, some unseen deity would forgive all their sins over a few lousy prayers, before merrily returning to hypocrisy and bigotry by Monday.

He remembered attending Mass with grandma and grandpa DiMaso all too well, never realizing that the very people acting all pious and reverent on Sunday spent the rest of the week making his mother's life hell.

To her credit, she frequently let them spend time with their grandparents, accompanied by Uncle Sal and Aunt Angela, who did their best to mend the rift. Especially after their own daughter, Pamela, died when she was only ten.

Organ music filled the church, and he grew agitated. The service began with a thirty minute sermon by a priest, followed by Derek Brewster's eulogy of Charles. How he, after a dark period which included running from home, severe drug abuse, and living on the streets, completely turned his life around and went back to school, earning a degree in psychology. That he traveled extensively around the globe before inheriting a fortune after his mother's passing, creating the Charles Prescott Foundation in 1995. A philanthropist to educational organizations, he generously supported cancer research, the disease which had killed his mother. Two mourners in front of Franco whispered to each other that his fortune was estimated at thirty-million dollars, and Derek Brewster closed by calling Charles a modern day hero.

The more Franco heard, the worse he felt, having failed, again, to save someone's life. What if he hadn't been wasted, had been quicker?

The service ended an hour later with two modern songs, performed by the choir. Franco got up and nearly speed-walked out of the church, engulfed by an unexpected sadness. Someone touched his arm, startling him, but when he turned and saw Detective Torrance's face, his body relaxed.

He wondered what it felt like kissing him and blushed, hoping Torrance couldn't read his mind. And that his asshole partner wasn't anywhere near, or they'd have to turn this funeral into a double feature.

"Hello," Torrance said. Dressed in a light gray suit, he stood out in a crowd of black clad mourners.

"Hi." Franco felt drained, his emotions raw from the service, scattered all over the place.

"You came to pay your respects."

Franco nodded, spotting O'Shea twenty feet away, talking to Brewster inside the church. He felt his blood boiling. "I'm sorry, I have to go." He likely wouldn't see the detective anymore, and, oddly enough, couldn't decide whether to be happy or sorry about it. Maybe it was the funeral, but a profound sense of finality closed up his throat.

"Of course." Torrance held out his hand. "Goodbye."

Not trusting himself to speak, Franco simply nodded and walked away. He hurried across the street, taking in deep breaths, feeling better with each step. He reached the other side, stopped, and looked over his shoulder. O'Shea had caught up with Torrance, who was watching Franco across the street.

His heart beating a little faster, Franco sighed, turned, and took a step, ramming his right shoulder hard into the pole of the pedestrian light he could have sworn wasn't there a moment ago.

Thrown off balance, he gasped, the searing pain shooting down his arm making him see stars.

Keep walking—whatever you do, don't turn around.

Wanting to cry for completely different reasons now, he stared ahead, fighting the urge to rub his aching shoulder, and quickly made his way to the subway station.

* * *

Franco sat at a table in the back of the restaurant, eating a plate of leftover lasagna with one hand, an ice pack on his throbbing shoulder. The last customers left shortly after ten-forty, and the brothers decided to close early.

Carmine cleaned up behind the bar, and Gino returned from the kitchen in his apron, a fresh pack of ice in his hand. He handed it to Franco, then pulled up a chair and plumped down on it. "Oh, I meant to ask, how was the funeral?"

Franco lifted a brow in his direction. "An absolute riot. Clowns, ponies, the works. And when they cut the casket in half—"

Gino flicked his ear with a finger. "Be glad they didn't have strippers. *What*? They do in some parts of Taiwan and China," he said. "They hire professional mourners for a proper send-off, or as stand-ins when distant relatives can't make it. And, sometimes, pole dancers and strippers, to attract bigger crowds, which are considered a mark of prestige. The crowd, not the titties."

Franco chuckled. "Aren't you an effervescent fountain of useless information. *Anyway*, I thought the foundation did an amazing job pulling it all together on such short notice. The choir sang "Hallelujah" and "Bright Eyes"."

"Vince wants "MacArthur Park" when he kicks the bucket, the eighteen minute version," Gino said. "I'm not sure I want music at my funeral…well, maybe "The Wind" by Cat Stevens."

"How about "Ding-Dong! The Witch Is Dead"? Can I finish my damn story now? Anyhow, Derek Brewster said in his eulogy that Charles spent a year in Africa during his thirties, and helped build over forty clean water wells over the last two decades. He donated a boatload of money every year to help build schools and provide education to the poorest regions. Judging by the sounds going through the pews most people knew as little as I. He just did whatever he could to help others and never boasted about it."

Carmine pulled up a chair and joined them with a glass of whiskey. "Sounds like quite a guy."

Franco sighed. "He was. Probably sounds tactless, and I can't explain it, but ever since the service I feel a weight has lifted. I finally have this weird sense of closure, like this whole nightmare is over."

"No, man, I get it," Carmine said.

Franco noted the time and had to get cracking. He put down the icepack and raised his water glass in salute. "To Charles, wherever he is."

"And to the end of all your troubles," Gino added.

"Famous last words."

Chapter Eighteen

"Hey sexy, how are you?" someone shouted across the bar an hour later as Franco moved his hips to a bouncy edit of "Still Got the Magic." He recognized the cutie from last Saturday, the one who'd left the generous tip. Nate, if memory served.

Franco smiled, wiping sweat from his forehead. "Hey there, what can I get you?"

"Your number." Nate's grin exposed perfect white teeth, and Franco wondered how often he ever heard the word *no*. About to deflect again, Franco stopped himself. "And what would you like to drink with that?"

"Gin tonic, please."

Franco fixed the drink and served it with a napkin containing his scribbled number, old school style. He extended his hand. "I'm Franco."

"I know." Nate quickly put his behind Franco's neck and pulled him in for a kiss on the lips. They disengaged and Franco felt awkward about the public display of affection. Points for the kid's determination and execution, though. "Okay, gotta get back to work. See you later?"

"You bet, anything you want, daddy." Nate winked at him and disappeared into the crowd.

Franco's smile imploded. Ben set down a rack of glasses next to him. "What, someone tell you they gave you crabs?"

"Worse. Second time in a week someone called me *daddy*."

"Ha. Don't worry, you'll get used to it."

Franco scrunched up his lips and gave him a once-over. "Listen, because I like you, and it's impolite, I won't point out you're fifteen years my senior."

Ben barked a laugh. "But if I wanted to be called *daddy* I'd have had kids."

"You're overthinking this, it's just a fantasy. And besides, if you end up taking him home, there are easy ways to keep him from talking." Ben playfully tugged at his crotch before picking up a crate of empty bottles and heading for the storage room.

Franco grabbed a wet cloth and wiped down the counter, catching a glimpse of Terri and Carmine on the dance floor. They'd shown up twenty minutes ago, Gino in tow, and Franco wished he could join them. With everyone's lives moving in different directions, they shared few moments like this anymore, and he missed the old days.

Disco lights danced across the swaying crowd, and inside the DJ booth Vince smoothly blended "Cold Blooded" by Rick James into a contemporary club track called "Freesia."

Franco spotted Gino at the other end of the bar, talking to a slender, bearded guy with dark, curly shoulder length hair. Like an apostle, or a surfer, which, in his opinion, was pretty much the same thing once you got them naked.

"Bring me some ale, wench, and none of that swill you offload on your other customers," Carmine bellowed from across the bar with a good-natured grin.

Franco built himself up with the most sinister expression he could muster, planting his hands on the counter. "*Other customers* would indicate some form of payment, which you don't provide, so whaddayawant, and make it snappy, I ain't got all night."

Carmine chuckled. "Two Vodka tonics, if it please thee. How's your shoulder?"

"Pain pills kicked in. I'll live." He nodded his head toward the end of the bar as he poured the drinks. "Who's Gino talking to?"

"Beats me, he said he was going to the bathroom."

"Looks like someone made a new friend."

"Maybe he'll finally get laid and lighten the fuck up."

Franco handed him the drinks. "Here's your *ale,* now beat it, and don't let me catch you in this neck of the woods again."

Carmine laughed, grabbed the drinks, and dove into the crowd. Ten minutes later Ben told Franco he could take a break if he wanted to. Armed with a water bottle he raced out to the dance floor as Vince closed his set with an edit of "Club Lonely" before the next DJ took over.

Franco beamed from ear to ear. Minding his shoulder, he stripped off his T-shirt, and Terri draped her arm around his waist, mirroring his dance moves. They laughed and twirled under the big disco ball, completely lost in the music. The beat rocked, his friends were there, and he was being chased by a cutie. He had to admit, all else aside, life happened to be pretty damn grand at this very moment.

By the time he made it back to his building, the rising sun had already turned the sky blue. High on a great night and endorphins, he opened the dating app on his phone. Profiles of guys *looking* loaded on his screen, but something inside him shifted. Time for a break, maybe? Not forever, just for a while. He erased the app before he could change his mind.

He entered the main door and traipsed quietly up the stairs, re-reading his mom's text from the night before. One of her friends' husband would pick them all up in his new SUV and drive them home, relieving Franco of another airport run.

An oversized manila folder leaned against his door. He picked it up and read the attached note from Tony. *This came for you while you were out—thought I'd see you before leaving for the Hamptons again, but I guess my timing was off. Back Wednesday. Love, B&T*

The envelope's return address listed the Charles Prescott Foundation. He opened the door, put the parcel on the kitchen table, and headed for the shower. He returned ten minutes later, his skin damp and a towel around his waist, and tore open the package.

It contained a standard white envelope with his name, what appeared to be an old notebook, and a gold necklace wrapped in a plastic bag.

Charles' diary and jewelry? Shit, Torrance hit the nail on the head. This was worse than he thought.

Wary of reading Charles' love confessions, he took a deep breath and flipped through the small, battered notebook. Some of the dated entries were barely legible, the handwriting different from the envelope. No, not a diary. The first page on the left corner was marked *F.A.D.*, followed by a vaguely familiar number.

He frowned, studying the necklace with the small cross hanging from a broken chain. A chill crawled up his spine, a dark suspicion spreading in the back of his mind.

F.A.D.…Francesco Antonio DiMaso, the numerals his old badge number.

Franco held his breath and read the letter with numb fingers.

"Dearest Franco, if you are reading these words then I am no longer able to speak to you in person. Ever since our paths crossed, I have been trying to find the courage to confess my darkest secret to you. I can't imagine how devastating it must feel to find out this way, and I am so very sorry to do this to you, but you deserve the truth: In July of 1977 I killed your father."

Lower Manhattan, 1977

Wednesday, July 13, 9:22 pm

The man in the hoodie ran. Shaken to the core and scared to death, Charles bolted up the sidewalk and turned west on Spring Street. The hood slid off his greasy hair and he pulled it back up and down over his face, despite the sweltering heat. He tossed the gun in a pile of trash and sprinted across Lafayette Street without slowing down. His heart beat so furiously, he thought he'd pass out. Horns blared and cars came to a screeching halt. He barely avoided getting hit by an Oldsmobile Toronado, only to be knocked down by the driver of a Lincoln Town Coupe not quick enough to brake. He tumbled and hit the curb, scraping open his left arm, and losing one of his sneakers. Shaking, and with the wind knocked from his lungs, he scrambled to his feet, barely aware of pain in his intoxicated state.

People stared and pointed, and cold fear gripped him. Why did they stare at him like that? What did they want? Did they know…had they seen?

Charles pushed a man out of his way and bolted, wearing only one shoe. He stubbed his bare foot, but didn't slow down, his lungs protesting.

Leo…Jesus, how could he run when the cops threatened to kill him if Charles didn't do as instructed? But the boy…no one said anything about a kid. He'd panicked, and run as fast as he could, too terrified to return.

Charles desperately craved Quaaludes, or Secanol…anything to take the edge off. Perhaps he could score from Jack over on 6th. He'd return to the cops and Leo, then…when he'd calmed down, when the coast was clear.

They'd understand, right? They had to, and let Leo go, like they promised.

Oh God, he needed to turn around right now, pray they were still there, waiting for him. Before they hurt Leo any worse.

But he didn't slow down, seeing Leo's beaten body in his mind, lying on the ground, his face swollen and bloody. Why had he laughed at the cops and threatened to expose them? Too damn high, the stupid fool. If only he'd pretended to go along with their crazy plan, they could have found a way to escape together.

Charles couldn't stop the thoughts racing through his head. He needed a fix, now!

He didn't see the broken bottle in the growing darkness and stepped on it, crying out in pain. Bleeding, he limped on.

Only a bit farther, he recognized the buildings now. And then he'd find Leo, find his way back to the abandoned warehouse near the piers, where the cops had taken them. He'd explain. This wasn't his fault. He'd done what they said, and planted the key in the man's pockets, like they told him. They had to let them go, just *had to*...he'd done as they asked.

But...what if they didn't?

Tears streamed down his face, and he choked back sobs. He should never have run...

He remembered the face of the man he'd killed, saw the little kid in the car. Leaning against the wall of a building, crying openly now, he tried to rid himself of the images. But they wouldn't go.

He saw the woman cross to the other side of the street to avoid him, her eyes wary.

Did *she* know, could she see in his face he'd shot a man in cold blood?

He didn't have a choice, he wanted to shout, *no choice!*

She hurried away, her face a mask of disgust.

Oh God, he'd killed a complete stranger, someone's husband and father...a cop, they'd said. He couldn't stop shaking, smelling the sour stench exuding from his pores. He pushed himself off the wall and walked as fast as he could, limping more heavily now, and leaving bloody footprints in his wake.

He reached the rundown building Jack lived in and entered the dark hallway. A single light flickered above, and a figure lay motionless under a dirty blanket; dead or alive, he couldn't tell, and he didn't care. Only months ago he would have never set foot in a dangerous, scary place like this…but a lot changed since the day he'd fled from home.

Somewhere in the building a baby screamed and a man engaged in a shouting match with a woman. Charles entered the old elevator and impatiently pushed the button for the sixth level. His legs gave out under him and he sunk to the filthy floor, exhausted and shivering. How much time had passed…five minutes, fifty?

The doors closed and the elevator moved upwards, the walls of the cabin creaking ominously. He didn't have cash, but maybe if he was real nice to him, Jack would help him out. He just needed something to help him think straight again.

The single light above him flickered and went out, the elevator's engine died, and the cabin came to an abrupt stop. What was happening?

Charles crawled to the door in the darkness. He felt for the panel with the buttons and pushed and pounded against them, but nothing happened. He tried to shout, but he barely got a croak out of his parched throat. No one answered.

Delirious and scared, he waited in the dark. He felt weak, and so tired.

He shouldn't have run, should never have panicked. Oh God, what had he done?

Leo…whatever happened to Leo, it would be on him.

Chapter Nineteen

Manhattan, 2016

Saturday, July 30, 5:17 pm

Bodiless voices carry in the darkness, and the occasional beam of a flash cuts through the night. Between a sea of people rushing past him and his mother, he catches glimpses of his father's body lying on the pavement in a dark, wet pool. She is squeezing him tight, his head pressed against her chest as it shakes with each of her deep sobs. He holds on to her without making a single sound, terrified the man in the hood might return at any moment...

Now he's dressed in a dark suit, sitting on the sofa in his grandparents' apartment after his father's funeral, his feet barely sticking out over the edge. His grandmother's favorite perfume, something like sweet roses, lingers heavy in the air, and behind the closed bedroom door the harsh voices of his grandfather, uncle, and mother drown out his grandmother's wails. He doesn't understand what's going on, but everyone sounds angry, and he shrinks into the cushions, trembling...

Curled in a ball on his bed, staring at the wall, Franco asked himself for the millionth time what if? What if his dad had lived? What if he'd been around to raise him?

Would he have grown up a melancholic child who mostly kept to himself, even after his sister was born? He had no answers. Worst of all, he barely had any memories of his father and their time together, everything overshadowed by gruesome mental images of that horrible night.

Maybe he would have come to terms with everything sooner if he'd stayed with the therapist his mother had taken him to see, and dealt with his feelings, instead of nearly overdosing on sleeping pills, fourteen years later.

Making friends never came easy for him, growing up. Most kids felt as awkward around him as he did around them, and it wasn't until middle school that he discovered humor, and used it as a shield. His often witty, usually self-deprecating responses made them laugh, and, most of the time, leave him be. That suited him fine, then. He'd always been an introvert, a loner, and more so after realizing he was different, terrified someone would learn his secret, and expose him.

Before his suicide attempt, he'd not only been terrified to come out to his family, but nightmares and guilt over his father's death plagued him for months, weighing heavily on his conscience. Why hadn't he cried out and run for help? No one ever blamed him for it, but once the thoughts took hold, they festered in his brain, convincing him Dad would be alive if he hadn't been such a coward, and mustered an ounce of courage.

Unrequited love for a straight classmate only accelerated his desperate act at the time. He barely remembered Ken Porter now, or what had attracted him in the first place, only the humiliation when Ken outed him in front of his classmates, waving Franco's love letter in the air.

All of it, such a long time ago.

Franco sighed, his gaze fixed on nothing. He believed everything happened for a reason, even if the reason remained elusive, at times. One simply adapted and learned to live with it. *What ifs* were pointless wastes of time, of course, yet he couldn't stop himself.

His father's murder set wheels in motion he could have neither imagined nor comprehended back then. For years he'd been told so many things about that night, he couldn't even say for sure anymore which memories were truly his. Except for the man in the hoodie...his father, dead at his feet...and the moment he understood he wouldn't be coming home again.

He'd seen the man in the hoodie in his dreams a million times, but now, trying to picture a young Charles, he couldn't remember specific features, only feelings. And the terror they'd evoked.

Franco uncurled and rolled on his back. The setting sun's golden light flooded the loft, but he couldn't recall if he'd slept since coming home, or if he'd only drifted in and out of a semi-conscious state.

Everything he thought he knew had been torn to pieces, the truth, if he believed the letter, far from anything he could have ever imagined. Two days ago he'd attended the funeral of a man he barely knew, but respected, who just confessed to killing his father, thirty-nine years ago. His brain threatened to implode, trying to grasp the implications.

Waiting for the tears to come, Franco lay there, drained and catatonic. But they didn't, and a single word pushed to the front of his brain.

Enough.

He pushed himself up on his arms. Enough. He couldn't...no, *wouldn't* let grief and fear take control over his life and drag him down anymore. Too much of that, already.

Dragging himself out of bed, he showered and dressed, battling every urge to crawl back under the sheets, and pull the covers over his head, steadily performing one task after the other, as if remotely operated.

Then he folded the letter, put it in the back pocket of his jeans, and walked. First out of his apartment and down the stairs, then up the street. Without a plan or destination, he set one foot in front of the other as dusk invaded the city.

Chapter Twenty

Sunday, July 31

"I am not asking for your forgiveness because I do not deserve it," Franco read in a monotonous, detached voice, without looking at Carmine, Gino, Terry or Vince, who sat on the leather sofa in Vince's loft. After aimlessly wandering the streets, he'd ended up at the club around eight. Vince insisted on taking over Franco's shift while he, exhausted, finally got two hours of sleep on the couch upstairs, amidst the thumping bass downstairs. The rest of the gang arrived after midnight.

"I believe from the bottom of my heart that meeting you was fate," Franco continued, the letter in his hands. "My memory of those days is spotty. Too much time spent strung out in a haze of pills and powders. But I have been seeing a therapist, someone qualified to help me come to terms with my past, and the things I need to do now. I also procured the services of a private investigator because I do not trust the police. You will find their information attached to this letter, and if you wish to speak to them, they will assist you. I never knew the names of the police officers who grabbed us, or their reasons for wanting your father dead, but I am certain they knew him well. I will do everything in my power to bring them to justice, if they are still alive."

Muted sounds from the club filled the space for an instant, then he continued, "I dread the day I have to face you and confess, but I know it will come. Getting to know you has been one of my greatest privileges.

You grew into a wonderful and talented young man despite everything I did to you and your family. I am so very sorry for your loss, and for being the one who caused you all this pain. Sincerely, Charles Henry Prescott III, March 18, 2016."

For several beats no one spoke, their eyes wide and mouths open, until Carmine cleared his throat and said, "Who else knows about this?"

Franco shook his head and leaned against the wall, facing the foursome.

"He wrote the letter four months ago and never mentioned anything, all this time?"

Franco scrunched up his lips. "I guess he hadn't worked up the nerve, not that I blame him."

Terri got up and wrapped him in a tight embrace. "Jesus, honey, I am so sorry."

"What are you going to do?" Gino asked.

Franco shrugged again.

"Whatever you need, man, you know we're here for you," Carmine said.

"Thank you…I just can't wrap my head around it. My father was murdered by his…*buddies*?" He almost spat out the word. "Charles pulled the trigger, but cops were behind everything. No wonder the case remains unsolved. If Charles planted the key, my father was set up. But why?"

"Listen," Vince said gently, "don't mean to be Debby Downer, here, but you realize it will be near impossible to verify any of this information."

"Talking to the cops is out, too," Terri said. "Unless you have someone you trust."

"Yeah, no, hard pass." Franco rubbed his temples and grimaced.

"What?"

"Telling my family…is going to kill them." His mom had called earlier, probably to announce her return, but he hadn't picked up. No way he could talk to her just yet.

"I'll go with you," Terri said, but Franco shook his head.

"Thank you, but I need to do this on my own."

"Your mom is tougher than she looks," Gino said. "Why don't you stay with us for a few days?"

"I'm okay…thank you. I just need time to process this."

"I really don't think you should be alone, at least not tonight," Gino said softly. "I'll make some tea, or cook something."

"It's almost one," Franco said, forgetting who he was talking to.

Gino turned to Vince. "What's in your fridge?"

"Really, I don't need anything. I'll just go home."

"I'll stay with you tonight," Terri said. "And you can close your mouth again 'cause it's not up for discussion."

"Me too," Carmine added, and Vince said, "I'll get the blow up mattress." He got up and Carmine followed him to his office.

"Whatever it is, we're here for you," Terri said, and Franco nodded, his throat closing up.

They talked for another hour while Vince and Carmine brought out pillows and blankets for everyone, and Gino boiled pasta, complaining how he couldn't find a damn thing in Vince's understocked kitchen.

Franco hadn't eaten all day but pushed the plate away after three bites. The music from the club ceased at four, and Vince and Carmine headed downstairs to help close up.

Exhaustion finally hit, and though it took a while for everyone to settle down, Franco eventually found himself on the couch, fully dressed, under a light blanket, staring at the ceiling. He loved his friends more than ever for coming together as he waited for sleep to come, but his mind kept spinning, and refused to let him rest.

Chapter Twenty-One

Strangers levitate past him in enormous, sterile rooms, and Charles appears in a white, flowing gown, silent, his eyes tormented. Franco's blood boils, his fingers curl into fists. He struggles to find forgiveness within him, and before he knows it he jumps forward and grabs Charles and chokes him from behind with all his strength. Charles bucks wildly in his grasp, but an all-consuming hate tears through him, and he squeezes harder until he snaps Charles' neck, the sound like a cracking whip. Charles collapses and Franco jerks back, his hate replaced by panic. What has he done? Everything dims and Charles' features morph into a young face, obscured by long dark hair. Franco's insides cramp up. RUN. Then the man's eyelids pop open, the empty sockets bottomless black craters, and fingers like barbed wire shoot up and clamp around his throat...

Franco shot up with a sharp gasp. He winced at the painful dryness in his mouth, found no spit to swallow. His heart pounded and he took shaky breaths to calm himself. Dawn's weak light slowly spread out inside Vince's loft, outlining a sleeping Terri spooning Carmine on the mattress on the floor. Gino's and Vince's snoring had grown weaker over time, but he'd barely closed his eyes.

He checked his phone. 6:18 a.m.

Rising quietly, he slipped into his sneakers, and headed to the kitchen for a sip of water from the faucet. He wrote a short note for them, then tiptoed out of the loft, careful not to wake anyone. Sneaking out like that felt wrong, but he needed time to himself. They'd understand.

Out on the street he headed east on Little West 12th Street, then south on 9th Avenue, passing a handful of people stumbling home, and others on their way to work. Last night's conversations zapped through his mind, and part of him expected some kind of meltdown at any moment. Instead, he simply felt drained and untethered.

He found the loft as he'd left it the night before and headed for the kitchen where he collected the notebook and necklace from the table, returning them to the plastic bag. He hid them behind towels and amenities in his bathroom cabinet. He'd come up with a better place later. He collapsed on the bed and his limbs instantly slackened.

Five minutes, just five minutes...

Shouting voices from the street woke him at midday and Franco rubbed his eyes. He'd missed seven calls and received several messages, all from the gang. Torn between guilt and gratitude he decided to get back to everyone later, after he'd had a chance to gather his thoughts. He undressed and headed for the bathroom. Turning the water in the shower to cold midway through, he emerged with goosebumps, but finally awake.

He dressed in clean underwear and gathered the bag with its contents from the hiding place, then fixed himself an espresso. Sipping it, sitting at the kitchen table, he let the gang know via group text he was okay.

He eyed the bag on the table with a sigh. He had a few options, but dreaded all of them. Talking to Derek Brewster might shed light on Charles' story, but could he trust him? Would he help, or had he known all along, and would try to bury the story?

He had no idea what to expect from the therapist and the private investigator, and talking to the damn cops was out—if they were behind his dad's murder, chances were they'd killed Charles, too. Did they already know about the letter? Were they watching?

Franco's skin crawled with invisible caterpillars. He got up, dressed in gray shorts and a teal colored polo shirt, then stuffed the plastic bag and letter inside his backpack with a change of clothes, and headed out the door.

Rushing up the street, he repeatedly glanced over his shoulder, but it didn't appear he was being followed. Making his way to Canal Street, he boarded an R train to Prospect Avenue Station.

With each minute he grew more determined to find out the whole truth. But first he'd have to talk to his mother...though it meant breaking her heart all over again.

* * *

"Franco, honey, what are you doing here?" His mother's eyes lit up when he entered her home, using his key. She rushed to meet him with hugs and kisses. "You didn't have to come all the way out here, I could have come into the city."

"I have plenty of time, Mom, don't worry about it." He returned her affections, masking his anxiety as best as he could.

"You look exhausted, sweetheart, didn't you get any sleep—?"

"Hey, check you out, all tan and rested," he said cheerfully, trying to buy himself more time. "How was your trip?"

She beamed. "We had so much fun, although Betty got seasick and Audra got sunstroke halfway through. But the rest of us had a marvelous time. I even won four hundred dollars! St. Barts was absolutely beautiful and..." Her forehead furrowed. "Something's wrong. What's going on, honey?"

"Let's go sit," he said, wrapping his arm around her shoulder, no more ready than ten minutes ago.

"Is Andrea all right...the kids?"

"They are fine...I just have some news." He placed his backpack at his feet and sat next to her on the couch in her modest living room. She took his hand into hers in anticipation, her expression signaling a readiness to comfort him.

"It's about Dad."

Her brows drew together. "Dad? I...what do you mean?"

Franco opened his mouth, but he choked up. He swallowed hard, and her grip tensed. "I know what happened the night Dad...I know who killed him."

Her eyes widened and her face contorted, like he'd punched her. Franco reached into his backpack. "A man I knew died recently. His estate sent me this letter, his confession."

His mother let go of him and brought her hands up to her face, staring at him.

"He also sent these." He held out the plastic bag. She leaned slightly forward, reaching for it and stopping short, as if afraid of getting burned. On her second attempt, she delicately pulled out the golden necklace with the cross, her fingers gently curling around its shape.

She covered her mouth, and a heartbreaking wail escaped her lips. Franco put his arm around her, resting his head lightly against hers, as each of them struggled to hold it together to comfort the other.

Chapter Twenty-Two

Monday, August 1

Franco woke to sounds coming from the kitchen, and his eyes slowly adjusted to the shapes in his mother's study, where he'd spent the night on the blowup mattress. After her initial shock turned to numbness, the two of them talked for hours. He decided to omit witnessing Charles' death and the cops harassing him. The letter was bad enough.

He checked his phone and saw Nate from the club had sent him several messages, including several explicit bubble butt shots he'd have found most enticing under different circumstances. But he couldn't deal with any of this right now, much less get a rise out of it.

He shuffled to the bathroom and took a quick shower. Toweling off, he heard muffled voices through the door, recognizing one as Sal's. *Great.* He wished she'd waited to contact him, like they'd discussed. Of course Sal had a right to know, he'd just hoped later would be soon enough.

He dressed in yesterday's beige shorts and a fresh T-shirt and padded into the kitchen. His mother wore an oversized T-shirt over house pants, and cracked eggs on a skillet. Sal, in gray slacks and a striped, light green dress shirt, sat at the bistro table with the two chairs, his cane leaning against the wall, Charles' letter in his hand.

She turned her head at Franco with a confident expression, but he sensed a hint of an apology in her eyes.

"Franco, son." Sal pushed himself out of the chair, his face contorting in pain, and wrapped him in a tight hug. He held on for a small eternity, his body rocking and a choked sob escaping his throat.

Franco couldn't remember when they'd last hugged so freely, so sincerely. Their physical contact had been infrequent and awkward, overshadowed, he believed, by his coming out. His eyes welled up.

Sal disengaged and turned away, wiping his face with the back of his hand. He ran thick fingers through the thinning white hair on his scalp. He used to be nearly a head taller than Franco, but osteoporosis, and a hip replacement a few years earlier had taken a toll on his body and posture. He walked with a slight bend now, making it hard to imagine he'd been cycling and playing tennis only fifteen years ago, doing his best to reinvent his life after Aunt Angela's death. Their last time together was Christmas, and things had been uncomfortable, at best, post-Nick. He'd aged considerably since then.

"Can I get you coffee, honey?" his mother said, and Franco nodded.

"Here, sit." She motioned at the table's other chair, and Franco squeezed her lightly before sitting down.

"Did you sleep?" she asked.

"Not really. You?"

"No." She added a pinch of salt to the egg scramble in the pan. "A lot going through my head right now. I…called Sal early this morning."

Clearly.

"I can't believe it." Sal took his seat and Franco heard the tremor in his voice. "After all this time."

Franco pressed his lips into a thin line and nodded, but Sal stared at the table. What had been worse—the shocking news about who'd shot his brother, or that his own colleagues, men he'd possibly worked side by side with for years, were behind it?

His mother handed him a blue mug with coffee and he nodded a thanks, pouring a generous helping of sugar and milk into it.

"I've been thinking…" she said, putting a plate with eggs and toast before him.

"Thanks, Mom, but I'm not really hungry."

"I should be the one to tell your sister." She had nothing of her youthful appearance about her this morning. Either from lack of sleep, or she'd aged ten years in a single night. "I'll wait a couple of days, until we know more. No sense upsetting her now, she's got enough on her plate with the kids." She wiped her hands on her shirt absentmindedly. "I buried your father thirty-nine years ago and...there's not a day I don't think of him. I wondered so many nights about what really happened, why help didn't come sooner."

Franco grimaced, and she squeezed his shoulder. "Stop it right this minute. You know none of this was your fault! I just...wanted answers for so long. Now that I do, I almost wish I didn't."

"There's a chance we can get justice for Dad."

"Sweetheart, it's been such a long time, where would we even start? If that man told the truth, then the police...if they managed to keep this secret, all these years, then how can we...?" She shrugged and shook her head.

"There are ways, Julie," Sal said, raising his eyes as if waking from a dream.

She took a step back and crossed her arms. "I just don't know. I have been thinking about this...man, *Charles*. I'm so...angry, for what he did, for lacking the courage to come forward when it could have made a difference." She exhaled deeply. "But...I can't just ignore everything you told me about him, and all the good he's done, all these years."

"Doesn't matter," Sal said, his voice hard. "He was a thug, you owe those people nothing."

Franco sighed. He might never find it in his heart to forgive Charles, but someone out there was still getting away with murder. For now, he chose to direct his anger at them. He picked at his food without much enthusiasm, but since his mother had gone through the trouble of making it, he took a few bites. It tasted delicious.

"Who else knows about this?" Sal said.

"Just my friends. But I was going to talk to Charles' second in command, Derek Brewster, see what he knows."

Sal's jaw tensed and he nodded once. "All right, I'll go with you."

Franco shook his head. "I think I should talk to him alone."

"Bullshit, you need someone to ask the tough questions, make sure they answer for what this guy did."

"What this guy did was act on behalf of the fucking cops."

"Franco," his mom said sharply, and Sal's eyes narrowed.

"I can read," he said curtly, then his features softened. "I can't...I don't want to believe it...but..." His face showed the hurt and betrayal of a kid who's been told Santa isn't real. A seventy-three-year-old kid. "Part of me knows it all makes sense, why the investigation never went anywhere, why we hit a wall, everywhere we searched for answers. If this was an inside job..."

"I know you weren't part of the original investigation," Franco said, "but... did Charles' name ever come up before?"

Sal studied him, shook his head. "Carl Morrow and Ray Kane were decent dicks. We all started out around the same time, and I worked with them before I transferred to Midtown. But without witnesses or physical evidence they never got far." His fingers curled into fists. "I looked into Frank's death time and again, went back to hound Morrow and Kane every week for news." Julie touched his arm, nodding. "Checked everything from past arrests Frank had been part of to people who had a bone to pick with him, studied all his active cases. Even after I quit the force in '85 I stayed in touch with the guys in my precinct—nothing. And now this, gunned down by some goddamn fucking junkie?"

"What about the drug bust Dad was part of? That's how they linked—"

"He would have never taken any money," his mother said passionately.

"That's not what I'm saying." What was he saying? "I'm just...trying to connect the dots. Someone had to know *something*." He addressed his uncle. "Didn't you have copies of the case files? I remember you showed them to me, years ago."

Sal nodded. "Still do. I made copies of Kane and Morrows' notes, before I left, but I haven't looked at them since Angie died. Figured I'd spent enough years chasing ghosts."

Julie touched his shoulder. "You did everything you could."

He pressed his lips into a bloodless line. "I'm positive there was no mention of this Prescott guy, or anything like he claimed happened. I don't know what we could have missed. You can check yourself. But I'll call around, I might still know someone who knows someone."

Franco shook his head vigorously. "I don't want the cops to know."

Sal locked eyes with him, as if contemplating something, then nodded slowly. "No, you don't. And if what this Prescott says is true...you can't throw accusations like this around without evidence to back it up. Any half decent lawyer will get the case tossed before court's in session. If cops are behind this..." He shook his head. "Dangerous territory, son."

"Honey, listen to him," his mother said. "This is beginning to sound dangerous. Promise me you're not going to do anything rash. Let's...take a few days and think about everything. I don't want anyone else to get hurt."

He understood her concerns but felt frustrated, anyway. Hell, only days ago he'd been *this* close to getting his ass thrown, and potentially passed around, in jail.

He picked up a piece of toast. "What about trouble at work, did Dad ever mention anything or anyone connected to Charles?"

She shook her head again. "Your father never brought his work home to us. He loved protecting people and getting justice for those who no longer had a voice, but...it's a huge responsibility. I know you guys talked sometimes," she said, toughing Sal's shoulder. He nodded. "In many ways, you shared the same experiences, but he didn't want the ugliness to follow him home, to us, didn't want me worried." She sighed. "Sometimes he'd sit by himself in the bedroom, staring at the wall. He was a wonderful, kind, and generous man...but hardheaded. He had his secrets. Refused to talk about the stuff that got under his skin, and simply switched it off the moment he walked through the door. Or, at least, pretended to."

"He wasn't so different with me," Sal said. "We used to talk a lot, but in the year before your father died..." He glanced at Julie. "Things were difficult, lots of tensions in the family."

"Water under the bridge now," she said with a sad smile. "You had enough heartache to deal with, it wasn't your problem to fix."

Sal nodded, but seemed unconvinced. He turned to look at Franco. "With your cousin in and out of the hospital all the time...I didn't deal with it well, took it out on the people who loved me. Drank too much, too angry at the world, God." He sighed and shook his head. "Your dad was a good man, but…rigid. We talked about work, cases we were working on. But he never opened up about problems, never gossiped, or talked trash about anyone. I know some had issues with his approach to law enforcement, doing everything by the book, even if that meant letting a perp walk. He showed a compassion for some criminals many of us didn't understand or appreciate. But he believed every suspect deserved his day in court and didn't approve of some of our rougher approaches to get confessions. Some respected that about him, like his captain, but it could also drive you crazy."

Julie nodded. "One night, he came home black and blue, insisted things had gotten out of hand during a difficult arrest, but I didn't believe him. I knew his partner had a nasty temper and had hurt suspects during arrests. They didn't get along very well and Frank acted…different. I was truly worried and swore I wouldn't let it go this time, that'd he'd finally talk to me. We argued about it for two days, but he never changed his story."

"What was his partner's name?"

She thought for a moment, and Sal said, "O'Shea…Aengus O'Shea. I think he's still around."

Franco almost choked on his toast.

"Honey, are you all right?"

"Yeah, sorry," he coughed, "went down the wrong pipe." Mother. Fucker.

He caught Sal's eyes, and they were alert and full of questions. Shit.

"What is it, son?"

Franco waved a hand. "Nothing, really. So, what happened between them?"

His mom said, "They only partnered for a few months, but didn't see eye to eye on much. They had a falling out, but Frank never mentioned it, and I had to hear it from Sal much later. Sounded like the man had a drinking problem and almost got booted off the police force."

Franco suddenly couldn't wait to speak to a number of people, ideally far, far away from either of them. Sal still had a suspicious gleam in his eyes.

"Did they investigate him?" Franco asked, keeping his voice level.

"They interviewed him, because of an altercation between them at their precinct, before Frank died," Sal said. "But O'Shea was alibied by his wife. Look, I knew that precinct, started out there before I transferred. I know not everyone appreciated Frank's rigid approach to policing, but most of them were good, solid cops. Kane and Morrow cleared O'Shea, and once they found the drugs and the money..."

"I think I need to lie down," his mother said, exhausted. "All this talk...I'm tired."

Franco touched her arm and nodded. "Will you be all right if I head back to town?"

"Of course, honey, don't worry about me."

"I'll call you later." Franco got up and hugged her. He could barely focus, so many thoughts attacked his brain simultaneously, but he knew one thing for sure: shit was about to hit the fan.

Ten minutes later he was out the door, his backpack over his shoulder. He only made it half a flight down before he heard Sal call his name. His uncle closed the door quietly behind him, then stood against the banister, his fingers gripping the rail. He glanced over his shoulder, then back at Franco. "What aren't you telling us?"

Franco's cheeks stung. "What do you mean?"

"You forget who you're talking to." Sal's face showed no anger, only pain.

Franco sighed. "Let me talk to these people first, then we'll have another conversation."

"I should be there."

"Next time."

Sal's jaw moved silently. He stole another glance over his shoulder. "You don't understand." His head and shoulders drooped. "It's my fault he's dead."

Franco opened his mouth, but no words came out.

"You know things in the family hadn't been good in a long time, especially that year, with your cousin being in and out of the hospital all the time." He spoke quietly, his eyes avoiding Franco's, fixed on a spot on the steps before him. "Your granddad's business was failing because he kept making bad financial decisions, and forgetting stuff, then blamed everybody else around him for *his* mistakes. He was already curmudgeonly when we were kids, but it only got worse. He took it out on Julie, who wasn't to blame for anything. Dad was literally losing it, but because he never went to see a doctor, we didn't know until it was too late. Just thought he was even more of a piss-ant than usual." Sal looked up, his eyes finding Franco's. "The way Frank defied our parents and married Julie…there were better ways he could have done it, and wouldn't have caused the family so much pain. But your grandparents…they were just as bad, each blaming the other for making their lives miserable, yet incapable to stay away from each other, like moths to a flame. Angie and I tried our best to bring the family together, but after a while…I couldn't do it anymore. The week before he died, Frank went over the books with Dad, who started laying into him, blaming him for abandoning the business, and losing money, and then Dad said some truly vile things about Julie. Frank lost it and punched him in the face. Don't blame him, old bastard had it coming. The next day your grandmother pleaded with me to speak to Frank, and smooth things over, but I wasn't in a good place. We'd just brought Pamela home after another round of chemo."

He sighed, his eyes distant. "Doctors always gave us hope, but after all we'd gone through over the years…Angie didn't want to talk about it, but I knew I'd never get to walk my little girl down the aisle. It tore me apart." The hand on the banister trembled. "Between my girls, work, family, trying to save Dad's store, trying to restore the family peace…it broke me. I was fed up with always being expected to fix everyone else's shit because I was the oldest. So when Frank and I finally talked, it didn't go well."

Franco realized he'd been holding his breath and exhaled.

"After years of drama in the family, we'd reached a breaking point. He called me a coward, accused me of never standing up to our parents, of manipulating him, and I called him a selfish piece of shit who turned his back on his family, and walked away from his responsibilities…and worse. We almost traded blows ourselves. But we managed to walk away…and never spoke again. He tried to call a few days later, even told Angie it was urgent, but I couldn't let it go and refused to talk to him." He rubbed his eyes. "Every day I'm reminded my last words to my brother were *I fucking hate you.* He never told Julie about it or she'd have said…and I can't bear the thought of how she'd look at me if she knew. That I abandoned him when he needed me most, that I could have helped, and he'd be alive if I hadn't been…such a miserable piece of shit."

Franco swallowed. "You don't know that, Sal. All our lives, you guys were there for us. I know you did everything you could." Pam's death, two years after his dad's, devastated Sal and Angela. But instead of growing apart, the family began to draw closer again, like pieces of driftwood, crudely tied into a life-saving raft.

Franco felt a pull to let it all out and tell him everything. He climbed a few steps and placed his hand on Sal's arm. "I know Mom would understand. But I won't tell her, and neither should you. It won't change anything now. Just…be there for her, and I promise, we'll talk more about everything soon."

"Yes, we should talk more. About other things that need to be said…while there's still time." The sadness in Sal's eyes resuscitated his own guilt over failing to make an effort since Nick.

Sal's Adam's apple bobbed and his eyes locked on Franco's. "Let me help… make this right."

Franco squeezed his arm and nodded, then he turned and bolted down the stairs.

Chapter Twenty-Three

The lengthy ride back into town increased Franco's impatience with every minute. He called the foundation to set up an appointment with Derek Brewster, but his secretary said he was out for the day. It took a while to convince her Brewster would want to speak to Franco right away, but fifteen minutes later he had him on the line.

He managed to persuade the COO to meet without giving out details, suspecting Brewster already knew everything and simply didn't let on. He'd have to keep an eye on him to determine whether or not he could be trusted.

But first he hit Staples on Broadway and 57th and made copies of the original letter, then called Dr. Kruger's office, where the receptionist told him she could see him tomorrow at ten.

While there's still time, Sal had said.

They'd never really addressed the incident with Nick, both of them too stubborn to apologize, or make amends. Maybe Sal was too old to change, and Franco would have to be the bigger man. His Dad's and Sal's relationship had taken a terrible toll, he didn't want it to happen to them.

Shortly after one, Franco stood in Derek Brewster's elegantly decorated office, a nicely sized space featuring a small sitting area overlooking Central Park. Photos of him, some with Charles, others with celebrities and political figures, lined the walls.

Brewster rose from his chair behind the wooden desk, dressed in his usual conservative style of slacks and matching shirt and jacket, and shook Franco's hand. "Mr. DiMaso, it is good to see you again, but I'm afraid I only have a few moments."

"I'll be as brief as I can, but I thought you'd want to know about this before I take any further steps."

Brewster's brows lifted with curiosity. "You sounded cryptic on the phone. What may I help you with?"

Franco sat on a chair across from him. "I am afraid I have some bad news. The package you sent me from Charles contained...some shocking news." He watched Brewster closely for a tell, but his face remained confused.

"What do you mean?"

"Perhaps you should read it yourself." Franco handed him one of the copies and Brewster put on a pair of glasses. He read silently, and his face crumbled, his mouth opening and closing like a fish out of water. "Jesus," he stammered, "is this for real?"

"I'm afraid so."

"Good God!" Brewster picked up the phone, a tremor in his hand. "Janet, cancel my meetings for the rest of the day...no, all of them."

He hung up and read the letter again, his eyes giant disks. "I don't...I am beyond horrified. Please, don't misunderstand—I am so sorry for you and your family, but...this is absolutely disastrous for everything we've built here."

Brewster's shock seemed genuine and Franco relaxed. "I'm here searching for answers, not to create problems. My mother and I feel no one benefits from going public with this information right now." Brewster's face showed relief, and Franco said, "I can't put my emotions toward Charles in words, I'm still digesting it all, but we feel he was another victim in this...tragedy. We're really hoping for your cooperation to get answers."

"I am speechless." Brewster rose and walked around his desk, taking Franco's hand in his with a tormented expression on his face. "I am so sorry for you and your family. I knew Charles for twenty years and would have never dreamt to learn such...horrific news about him. I will do whatever I can to help, and thank you for your discretion. I know we have no right asking it of you, and I am grateful you feel the way you do. Have you contacted the police?"

"No, I wanted to speak to you first. Do you know the therapist and private investigator Charles mentioned?"

"No, the names don't sound familiar. He probably used personal contacts and funds to hire them. The foundation would not have records. He has an executor for his private affairs, and I will meet with her later today."

"Please, I need access to whatever you find that connects to my father's murder."

"I promise to contact you as soon as I know more. I just hope the police will be discreet."

"You realize they may be behind all this. Charles was convinced of it."

Brewster shook his head disbelievingly. "I can't imagine that to be true. You can't possibly hope to get to the bottom of this without them?"

"I think I should talk with the therapist and investigator before considering any next steps."

"I'd very much like to speak with them myself. I understand I'm in no position to ask this of you, but I would appreciate you letting me know if you find out anything that impacts the foundation. Before it ends up in the news."

Franco nodded and got up. "I won't let my current opinion of Charles affect everything you've built here together."

He shook Derek Brewster's hand, hoping he'd still feel that way tomorrow.

* * *

"I know you don't want to hear this, but you can't hold off talking to the cops forever," Vince said, leaning against the wall in Gino and Carmine's living room. The friends were gathered around the dinner table shortly before four. Everyone had something to say, all talking at once.

"He can't go to the cops, they're behind it," Gino said, turning to Franco, who sat across from him, next to Terri. "I told you they'd be nothing but trouble."

"*Ma vaffanculo*, everything is a conspiracy with you," Carmine snapped. "You're worse than Mama. There's gotta be someone trustworthy to reach out to, quietly. What about your uncle? Did you talk to the P.I.?"

Franco opened his mouth but Vince said, "You could always leak the story to the papers."

"Yes, take it to the *Times*, or *Newsweek*," Gino said. "Once it's all out in the open, the cops can't touch you. You don't owe that man and his foundation anything, screw his reputation."

Terri touched his arm. "Your poor mother, how is she taking it?"

"I can't imagine how she must feel after all this time," Gino added. "If everything in the letter is true, she should sue the department for compensation, or something."

"That requires concrete proof. You know, actual evidence?" Vince said. "And let's face it, all we have so far are a ton of maybes and a bunch of dead people." He shrugged apologetically at Franco. "Sorry."

Franco opened his mouth but Gino said, "This whole thing stinks. If you ask me—"

A piercing whistle cut through the air, and everyone flinched. Carmine pulled two fingers from his mouth and said, "Everyone, shut the fuck up, the man's been trying to speak for ten minutes."

With all eyes on him, he still waited a few beats to make sure. "I have no clue what to do, all right? Maybe the papers are an option. I left messages with the P.I., but he hasn't returned my calls, and I'll see the shrink tomorrow."

"Permission to speak," Vince said, raising his hand with a sheepish grin. "Whatever you decide, there's no rush, after all this time. Just consider all your options before making any hasty decisions."

Carmine nodded. "You want answers, but a few more days won't put a dent in it."

Franco lowered his head. "Years I've wondered *what if* Dad actually stole the money? Of course I didn't want to believe it, but you hear stories of desperate people doing stupid things every day. Now we know he was set up...but why, and by who?"

"You might never know," Vince said quietly.

"I can try." He reached into his backpack, handing out pieces of paper to everyone. "Copies, in case anything happens to the original. In the meantime, I'll go through Dad's notebook, see if I can decipher anything. Most of the entries seem to be in some kind of shorthand." Sal would be able to help.

"You're welcome to keep everything in our safe," Gino said, patting his arm. "We're here for you. There is a light at the end of the tunnel, you'll see."

"Yeah, it's called a truck."

Gino eyed his phone and shot up. "Shit, look at the time. Don't mean to be rude, honey, but if I don't get back to the kitchen, tonight's menu will be tepid water and stale crackers." An old friend of Carmine's had rented the space to celebrate someone's birthday. Franco rose, but Gino shook his head. "Go home and get some rest."

"We have twenty people coming," Franco protested.

Carmine mirrored his brother. "We got this. I'm here, and Mattia is already downstairs, prepping," he said. The distant cousin had immigrated from a small, remote town near Palermo a few months ago.

"Mattia speaks all of five words of English." Franco exaggerated, but not by much.

"He knows the words just fine, it's just no one can understand him," Gino said. The twenty-year-old had worked hard on improving his language skills. "He's young and hot, and he'll say it with his eyes. We'll manage, okay? Go, eat something, sleep, take a sick day for crying out loud."

Carmine said, "Contrary to what you may think you're *not* every woman, it's *not* all in you, and you need to listen to us, for once, and take a damn break."

Franco flashed a tired but grateful smile. "All right, fine, one night. I don't want special treatment."

Carmine winked. "Don't worry, the minute you're back to your old self we'll work you twice as hard for half the pay."

Chapter Twenty-Four

Tuesday, August 2

"My name is Charles Prescott the third and I am recording this confession on June 28th, in the presence of my therapist, Dr. Jacqueline Kruger. On the night of July 13th, 1977, I shot and killed Detective Francesco DiMaso."

Franco watched the screen in front of him, sitting on the expensive leather couch in Dr. Kruger's lavishly decorated 5th Avenue office, his cheeks flushed. She sat at an angle to his left, dressed in sleek, form-fitting black pants, and a light pink blouse, her dark hair tied in a loose, modern bun. He didn't have to look her way to know she was watching him intently through her Tom Fords.

"Leo and I used to hang out at the piers three, four days a week, back then," Charles continued in the video recording. "We were getting wasted that afternoon, cruising for sex and more drugs, when two detectives I had never seen before picked us up and took us to an abandoned warehouse nearby. I knew we were in trouble when they confiscated our whistles before they even took our drugs and money. We always knew the dangers, of attacks on gays, but nothing could keep us away." Franco knew many gay men carried whistles back then, to call for help if they were attacked.

Charles continued, explaining how the cops held them for hours. They ordered Leo to kill someone, another cop, but he, strung out of his mind, refused and threatened to expose them. The cops worked them over until

Leo lay bloodied and unconscious on the ground. Finally, Charles couldn't take it anymore, and agreed to do it himself to save his lover.

Franco watched Charles' lips move on the screen. He heard his words, saw the anguish in his face, knew how hard it must have been for him to say these things out loud, but only felt anger.

How could Charles not have told him? His fingers moistened and he dug them into his chinos.

On-screen Charles' eyes teared up, and his voice cracked. "They gave me drugs to take the edge off, and the younger cop drove me to an area in Little Italy. There we waited. He told me to make it look like a robbery and put a key in Mr. DiMaso's pocket. If I failed or tried anything, they would kill Leo, pin his murder on me, and make sure they were the ones making the arrest. After all, a jury would always believe decorated cops over a faggot junkie. I don't remember how many times I pulled the trigger, only that I did. Something inside me died that moment, but all I could think of was Leo. At least that's what I told myself. And yet I ran, did the one thing I knew could get him killed. Maybe I panicked, too high to think straight... and maybe I just never had the courage to admit I put myself first, grabbing the first chance to escape when it presented itself." He dropped his head, and his shoulders trembled. "I was unaware of Mr. DiMaso's identity at the time, and only learned it from the papers, weeks later. I do not recall taking his necklace and notebook, just seeing his son's terrified face, inside the car..." A deep sob shook Charles' body, and from somewhere off camera Dr. Kruger's voice gently said, "Would you like to take a break?"

Charles nodded, and the recording stopped.

Franco suppressed the urge to jump up and bolt from the office.

"I am afraid that is all. It took Charles nearly seven months of therapy to get to the point of being ready, but he insisted." Dr. Kruger's eyes seemed glued to Franco's, and he felt exposed. "Mr. DiMaso, I am very sorry we met under such tragic circumstances. How are you feeling?"

He exhaled sharply and shook his head. He didn't have words. His phone vibrated against his leg, but he ignored it.

"Charles was determined to face you in person, and I'm sad he didn't get the chance."

Franco struggled to push his anger aside. He'd come for answers and wasn't done. "Did he believe someone was after him?"

"No, but he believed the policemen who attacked him and Leo were still around. I know he hired a private investigator, but I am not sure of their progress." She waited a beat before she continued. "I spent a considerable amount of time with Charles over the past months, and I met a thoroughly changed person from the man he said he used to be. Please understand, I am not excusing his crime, and neither did he, but if you allow me, I'd like to share some things with you which might help you understand better."

Franco shrugged, his chest tight.

She talked about the abuse Charles suffered at his father's hands, his first trip to the emergency room at age eight, and the weak mother who failed to protect him, or herself. She talked about how Charles lived in fear when he discovered he was gay, and finding a soulmate in Leo in college, a troubled boy two years his senior. The love of his life, and the source of his decline into drugs and prostitution.

"He, too, came from a wealthy background, with absentee parents too busy to care, too quick to throw money at their son's quirks and rebellions. He was extroverted and cocky, the complete opposite of Charles, and yet the two became close. Leo introduced Charles to pot and Quaaludes, and, though reluctant at first, Charles eventually embraced how they made him feel, helped him forget. Charles said Leo was the first and only person who ever saw and loved him for who he was, and not surprisingly, he formed a deep dependency. When his father caught the boys kissing in Charles' room one day, he nearly beat his son unconscious. Leo interfered and the two of them escaped to a friend's home in the city. Fed up with his own parents, Leo promised they'd make a new start, create their own happiness. But Leo's friend was also his dealer and part-time lover, and though he took them in, living together caused a lot of tension. The two ran dry almost immediately and Charles came to find Leo wasn't above trading sexual favors for money and drugs, some of which he sold for profit. This wasn't the life Charles wanted for them, but he couldn't break free from Leo. Leo never hurt or beat him, but he manipulated Charles into using his body to help finance their new life, promising it would only be temporary. Charles would have done anything for Leo and believed it would only be a matter of time until they escaped to a better place. To cope, he delved deeper into drugs, failing to recognize the dangers of his and Leo's volatile relationship."

She stopped for a moment, studying Franco's face. "Charles didn't want to talk about any of this in his taped confession because he didn't want to make excuses for his actions. But I believe it is important you know what kind of person he was at the time, of the struggles he faced. He acted out of desperation, trying to save the life of the only person he ever loved."

He couldn't help feeling she tried to manipulate him. "The person he abandoned when he ran, you mean."

Dr. Kruger nodded. "Yes, and he died believing he killed two people that night. He fled to a friend's, hoping to score drugs to calm his nerves, but the blackout hit and the elevator got stuck, trapping him. Before someone in the building finally called for help, he'd been in there for nearly thirty hours without food and water. Paramedics found him unconscious and completely dehydrated. When he woke, days later, his mother was by his bedside. She'd been searching for him for months, and told him his father had died of a heart attack that June. Charles thought he ran away from home only three, four months ago, but had in reality been gone for nearly seven."

"No one ever followed up and asked him about his friend?"

"He lied about his whereabouts and injuries to the doctors and his family, and never mentioned Leo, out of fear. When he found out Leo's body had washed ashore two days after the blackout, he believed the cops had killed him. He kept his mouth shut, afraid for his life. But months passed without anyone coming for him, and he completed rehab, and, convinced he'd been given a second chance, turned his life around. He finished his education and involved himself with human welfare and social reforms, believing himself safe as long as he kept quiet. And he was, until the day he met you." She watched Franco for several beats before she continued. "Charles fought for months with the decision to seek counsel, and come clean about the murder, with all its consequences. Because so many lives depended on him, he needed time to get his affairs in order, well aware he'd go to prison once he confessed."

Franco felt anxious and eager to leave. Coming here had been necessary, but he still hated every minute of it. He regretted not taking Sal along, feeling utterly alone with the torrent of emotions plowing through him.

"Mr. DiMaso, may I ask how much you remember about the night Charles shot your father?"

"Not much. Snippets mostly, faces and sounds."

"How old were you?"

"Four."

"The experience must have been very traumatic for—"

"Sorry, Doctor, this is about Charles, not me."

She didn't seem to take offense at his abrupt tone. She handed him her business card. "Please know you don't have to deal with this alone. If you ever want to talk, don't hesitate to give me a call."

He considered returning the card and declining her offer, but got up, nodding instead. "Thanks for your time."

Chapter Twenty-Five

Franco rounded the corner to his street twenty minutes past noon. A vaguely familiar, unoccupied car stood parked in front of The Green Thumb. Inside the flower shop, the owner, Cody Granger, spoke to a few customers, but when she noticed him she waved excitedly. Franco returned the gesture without slowing down. Whatever she wanted could wait until he could think straight again.

He entered the building, collected several days' worth of mail from his overstuffed box, and headed upstairs. An official letter from a law firm stuck out between junk mail and bills, but before he could get a closer look, his phone vibrated again. He'd never checked, and now the screen showed a missed call from his mother, four from two different local numbers, and he had two voicemails, and a text from Derek Brewster, saying *Call me, urgent!*

Now what? He reached his floor, startled to find a tense Detective Torrance standing in front of his door.

Shit. "How'd you get in?"

"Hello to you too," Torrance said, his expression darkening. He looked sharp in a light gray suit, if you ignored the dark circles under his eyes. "The woman from the flower shop let me in, if that's all right with you. I called twice."

Why was he here? Given the tendency of his days going down the crapper every time Torrance showed up, Franco felt wary at best. "Sorry, I was just curious if our new security system was working," he said, squeezing past him. He set down his backpack and unlocked the door without opening it, planting his back against the hard surface. He wanted Torrance gone.

"I just spoke with the foundation," the detective said ominously. "I can't believe you'd withhold such crucial information from us."

So much for Brewster's discretion. "Look, I would have called, eventually. I just…needed time."

"We don't *have* time, and this news doesn't put you in the best of light."

Yeah, no shit, but now Franco's anger returned unfiltered. "*Hey*, since all of this started two weeks ago, you've gone out of your way to treat me like a criminal. Forgive me for feeling less than inclined to rush to you people for help. All I did was report a crime, and now I'm in the middle of my own father's murder." His blood boiled. "And no, I didn't get in touch with you because, frankly, after everything that happened I don't particularly trust any of you."

Torrance's forehead creased. "What are you talking about? You *can* trust me, but I—"

"Yeah, right, sure! In the end you just twist the truth until everyone looks guilty but the upstanding brothers in blue. Anything to avoid another scandal."

"You're not making sense."

Franco threw up his hands. "Stop playing games, I am so tired of this shit! You act all friendly, like you actually give a fuck, meanwhile you're the partner of the man behind all this."

That meltdown he'd been waiting for? Standing knee deep in it, front and center. He couldn't stop talking and trembled all over. "What are you gonna do, huh? Investigate O'Shea, or sweep everything under a rug again, so the NYPD's reputation isn't tarnished? Charles may have pulled the trigger, but you guys pulled every fucking string."

Torrance held up a warning hand, his face taut. "I get you're upset, but you better watch yourself, throwing around accusations like that."

Franco got in his face and pushed him roughly with both hands. "Don't tell me what to do."

Torrance grabbed his arms. "Stop it and calm down. You're hysterical."

Franco drove his body into him, provoking a confrontation, and his eyes welled up. "What's next, huh? Are you gonna come for *me*? Will I end up under a pile of garbage, just like Charles?"

He drove forward, but Torrance pushed back hard, and they slammed backwards into the door. A sharp sting pierced Franco's skull on impact, and he fully expected to get the shit beaten out of him at any moment.

Torrance's glowering face loomed only inches away, his green eyes gleaming dangerously. On the verge of a scream and unable to keep it inside any longer, Franco opened his lips. And kissed him, hard, a million alarm bells shrieking in his brain.

What the fuck are you doing? Are you insane?

Torrance's head reeled back, perplexed. Locked in a fighting stance, their heavy breathing filled the space between them.

That's it, you're dead.

Franco squinted, readying himself for a punch, but Torrance's grip on him tightened. Then he felt the cop's lips on his. He inhaled sharply, grabbing the back of Torrance's neck, his fingers lost in the thick hair. Their lips parted and their tongues explored each other's with an unexpected, frantic urgency. He thought he tasted blood and didn't care.

Franco inhaled Torrance's scent, a mix of a light soap and fresh sweat, and pulled at his white dress shirt. He was breathing hard and his heart beat furiously. Torrance's fingers dug into his back, his breath on his neck, and Franco reached behind him, fumbling the door open. The detective's full weight fell on him before he could balance his footing, and they crashed through it, landing hard on top of each other. The impact knocked the wind from Franco's lungs, and his head banged against the concrete floor.

He ignored the pain, didn't want the moment to end. Torrance's muscled chest pressed against his and Franco slid his fingers inside his pants, took hold of him. Torrance's body stiffened, and strong fingers gripped his.

"Stop…no, *stop*." He pushed himself off Franco. "We can't."

His head throbbing, and feeling exposed, Franco's first instinct was to apologize. But what the hell for? Wasn't like Torrance hadn't kissed him back.

Torrance grappled to his knees, then ran his fingers through his hair. "I'm sorry, Mr. Di—"

"*Mister*? You gotta be shitting me."

"All right, *Franco.* This is...not the right time or place." He didn't appear angry or embarrassed, and Franco relaxed a little.

"Is this what they call police misconduct?" He winked, but Aidan's face hardened.

"It isn't ethical, no."

"I'm kidding." Franco forced a smile, self-conscious again. "I am just... surprised. I thought you pretty much hated my guts."

"Ditto." Aidan rose and held his hand out to Franco, who pulled himself up. Catching Aidan discreetly arrange the tent in his pants gave him a satisfied tingle. His accomplishment, even if the fruits of his labor remained frustratingly elusive.

"I'm sorry I attacked you and said all those things." Franco rubbed the back of his head. "Some of them, anyway."

Aidan nodded. "I apologize for coming across aggressive. But...we have a problem. What just happened here...I don't have to tell you no one can know."

Franco pressed his lips together, but nodded.

"All the things you said about Prescott and your father...where does this come from?"

Franco squinted. "I thought that's..." But now he couldn't remember Aidan mentioning the letter. Damn. "Um, why are you here?"

"In a minute." Aidan watched him expectantly, and Franco chewed his lip. Could he trust him? Not like he had much of a choice at this point.

"Charles confessed to killing my dad in '77."

Aidan's eyes narrowed. "When?"

"A few days ago, his estate sent me a letter he wrote."

"May I see it?"

Conflicted, Franco retrieved his backpack, then closed the open door. He crossed the room and motioned at the kitchen table. "Can I get you anything to drink?"

"Water, if you have it."

Franco grabbed two bottles from the fridge and handed him one.

"Thank you." Aidan took off his jacket, revealing the holstered gun hanging from his belt, and sat down. Franco handed him the letter and watched him read it. His chest and nipples pressed lightly against the snug fabric of Aidan's damp shirt, and the short sleeves exposed smooth, nicely defined, tanned arms. Franco's eyes registered every pore on them, and the faint vein pulsating just at the base of his neck. He still held the pleasant, oddly comforting scent of Aidan's skin in his nose, and—

"There's nothing in here indicating O'Shea is involved in this, or even knew your father." Aidan's eyes lingered on his and Franco's cheeks warmed.

"My mother and uncle remember him. O'Shea physically assaulted him and almost got booted off the police force."

Aidan tilted his head. "Doesn't make him a killer."

"He hated my dad, and the man's a gigantic asshole."

"Not all assholes are killers."

Franco took a seat opposite him. "What? Asshole, killer…not a stretch."

Aidan sighed. "Look, Charles Prescott made some heavy accusations here, but is it possible he just tried to deflect from his own actions? He was a drug addict and admitted to pulling the trigger."

"*Reformed* drug addict, and why admit to murder just to claim 'someone made me do it'?"

"I'm just weighing all the options here."

"Sounds more like excuses to exonerate your partner."

"O'Shea's a tough nut and, yes, at times a royal dick. I've worked with the guy for a year now, and like to think I got him pegged pretty good. He's a lot of things, but not a killer."

"How can you defend him, now that we've firmly established your sexual proclivities? Clearly, he hates *fags*," Franco said sarcastically, making air quotes.

The lines around Aidan's eyes tightened. "One, he's not comfortable with *gay* people, and two, you don't know anything about the man, or me, for that matter. We all have baggage, all right? And despite his flaws, he's a decent cop. We don't discuss my private life, but I'm pretty sure he knows who I am. Maybe he only respects me because I'm good at my job and got his back, but bottom line is we get along, and he doesn't give me shit. He's got enough of his own to worry about."

Franco wondered who Aidan tried to convince. "He's an old drunk and a bigot."

"He's going through his third divorce, cut the guy some slack."

Franco snorted a laugh. "The real shocker is someone was dumb enough to marry the prick in the first place."

"Nice moments never last long with you, do they? You can be quite a pill."

"*Ditto*, not that it was a contest."

Aidan gave an apologetic nod. "I didn't mean to be arrogant, before...I just thought you were a slut."

"A *slut*? Wow, try saying that five times fast next time you have your tongue down my throat."

"All right, all right." Aidan held up a hand. "I am sorry I was quick to judge you. I shouldn't have. I know who I am, but it's no one's business. I don't need my work judged based on who I sleep with. And yes, I let my personal opinions reflect on your...choices because of my aversion to chatrooms and random hookups."

"No kidding," Franco said with a 'what-do-you-want-from-me' expression. He sighed, pointing at the letter. "O'Shea can't know about *any* of this."

"Forget it, I'm not going behind my partner's back."

"All I'm asking is we verify Charles' letter before you talk to him."

"When did this become a *we* thing? Don't get me wrong, you're cute, but *this*," Aidan waved his hand to where they were sucking face earlier, "doesn't change a thing. If there is anything you need to know, I will inform you accordingly."

Franco considered admitting O'Shea had been cleared back in '77, but annoyance took over. "Yeah, hell, no. I want answers and I'll do whatever it takes to get them."

Aidan exhaled sharply. "What about the therapist and the investigator, did you talk to them?"

"I met with Dr. Kruger earlier," he said, summarizing their encounter. "And I haven't been able to reach Ralph Sanders yet, but will keep trying. I promise not to go all *Murder She Wrote* on your ass, but if you think I'll just sit by the sidelines, you've got another thing coming." Aidan's face showed irritation, but Franco didn't care. "You can't tell O'Shea...*please*. He'll find a way to get in front of this. Two people are dead already."

Aidan studied his face for a few seconds, his jaw tense. Then he said, "O'Shea's taken a few sick days."

"In the middle of an investigation?"

"He had a temperature of a hundred and five yesterday. I can hold off telling him about this for a day or two, while he's out and I look into things. But I want to hear his side, eventually."

"Fine." Franco pressed his lips together, wishing he felt better about all this.

"Where are the necklace and the notebook?"

"I left the necklace with my mom, the notebook is here."

"They're evidence, I need them for forensics."

Franco stiffened. "You promised to keep this low profile."

"This is still a murder investigation."

Franco glowered at him, but he was right. He rose, reluctantly, and produced the plastic bag with the notebook from his backpack. Aidan pulled a latex glove from his jacket pocket and slipped it on.

"Isn't it a bit late for that?"

"No need to make it worse," Aidan said and carefully examined the notebook, flipping through the pages. "I'll have forensics go over it properly."

"I'm not letting you leave with it."

"This isn't how this works, Franco. Get it through your head. This is evidence and needs to be examined by professionals."

Franco growled, and Aidan returned the notebook to the bag. His eyes softened. "You're in over your head and I want to help you, but you have to let me." He rose and put his arms around him, and Franco didn't refuse the closeness, a tad unsettled by how much he craved it. "You're upset and confused, but I believe you want to trust me. I'm telling you that you can."

Aidan's position could open doors he'd never get through on his own. It just required a gigantic leap of faith. Franco unfurled himself from the hug.

"Okay."

"I'll give it twenty-four hours before I take it to my partner or my superiors."

Franco opened his mouth, but Aidan waved a hand. "Not up for debate. My job's on the line here. I may believe you're innocent but others likely won't, and this letter just provided the perfect motive."

"I didn't—"

"I know. Prescott's murder was planned, and you lack the calculation and organization it took to pull this off. Also, you're not really great at keeping your emotions in check, and not that good an actor."

Franco didn't know whether to feel relieved or insulted.

Aidan seemed to read his mind. "You want to argue my point, I'm willing to listen."

"No, that's okay."

"Whoever killed Prescott knew of his movements, and how to gain access, which means surveillance and planning. He most likely knew his killer or he wouldn't have opened the door, considering he kept the apartment secret from everyone."

Considering all of it fit him to a T, Franco kept his mouth shut.

"Can you tell me about your father's murder?" Aidan said, sitting again, and Franco gave him the five-minute version.

"A young couple stumbled upon us, some ten minutes later, but to me it felt like hours. We never found out what happened, or had any real leads... until now."

"Did your mother or uncle ever mention O'Shea before?"

"I've been racking my brain about that, but I don't recall hearing his name before last week. All my family ever talked about were the Romanos. My father refused to marry their daughter Anna, an arranged marriage sort of thing between our two families. I guess, their fathers' attempt to merge their respective businesses. Anyway, this all happened a few years before Dad died, but Romano never forgave my family, and ruined my grandparents' business, kind of an Italian delicatessen with lots of imported goods." A thought struck him, and he grew angry. "I can't believe Brewster told you about the letter after I specifically told him not to."

Aidan shook his head. "He didn't, I wanted to talk to you about the trust."

Franco uttered a humorless chuckle. "Yeah, well, considering how things went down between us, there really wasn't any—not that you can blame me." He took a healthy swig from the water bottle.

"No, I'm talking about the million dollar trust Charles Prescott left in your name." Aidan barely flinched before he wiped Franco's mouthful of water from his dripping face.

Lower Manhattan, 1977

Monday, July 11, 7:54 pm

Desk Sergeant Hank Porter stood behind the raised, twenty-foot wooden counter overlooking the waiting area inside the 8th precinct, barely able to hear himself think. The raucous laughter from a group of beat cops in the squad room competed with hollering from the drunk in the holding cell, drowning out the ringing phones.

It had been one of those days, and Hank hadn't caught a break in hours. He couldn't wait for his shift to end.

"Mac, keep an eye on things, will ya?" he said to the uniformed officer sitting behind him. "I gotta take a leak."

He stepped out from behind the old, weathered desk without awaiting a response. Crossing the squad room, he exited through the glass swinging doors into the narrow, bland hallway, which led past locker rooms to the precinct's back door. The building showed its age, though few places more clearly than in the shabby bathroom he entered through a recessed door. It creaked shut behind him, only marginally muting the noise from outside.

Relieved to find the space empty, he gladly traded its spicy odors for a moment of peace. He stepped up to the urinal and unzipped his fly. Days like this really made him wonder why he hadn't chosen another career. He hated carrying a gun and, as hard as he pretended otherwise, really wasn't much of a cop, at least not the way most people defined the word. As with most relevant things in his life, he'd let his family make the decision for him, continuing a tradition his great-grandfather started decades ago.

Hank didn't consider himself a brave man, still amazed at how he'd survived his years on the streets as a beat cop relatively unharmed. He avoided conflicts whenever possible, and frequently caught himself agreeing with opinions of a majority so he wouldn't have to form one of his own. He hated that about himself, wished he possessed more of a backbone, but then again, so far it had worked mostly in his favor. And from a bureaucratic standpoint he excelled at his job behind the counter, his domain, and was considered a loving father and family man by his peers.

Hank finished, zipped up, and washed his hands in the cracked, stained sink on the wall. He checked himself in the mirror and adjusted the tie on his blue uniform shirt, then straightened the black plastic name tag above the breast pocket.

The moment he stepped through the door, the noise level tripled. He stopped, exhaled, and leaned against the door after it closed behind him. Just one more peaceful moment before getting back into the lion's den.

From around the wall's corner harsh whispers reached his ears, spoken by two men no more than eight feet away.

"You know exactly what I mean! Where is it?"

"I don't know what you're talking about."

Hank almost started forward, wanting to avoid the brewing argument, but instead he held his breath and didn't move a muscle.

"Cut the shit, I know what I saw. Nothing's been logged, where is it?"

"Calm down, it's not what it looks like. This isn't the place to talk about it, let's go—"

Noise from the squad room drowned out the rest, making it difficult to recognize the voices. Hank didn't even want to know, worrying instead someone might think he was spying, if they happened to come upon him now.

"—At least fifty-thousand."

"No, listen—"

The laughter in the squad room increased and, against his instincts, Hank strained his ears.

"...you crazy? That's evidence."

"Calm down, I already said I'll take care of it and talk to him."

The voices retreated, as if the men were walking away.

"Make it right. I don't want any part of this, understand?"

"Cool your jets, I got—"

A wave of profanities filled the air, and through the glass doors Hank saw O'Malley and Turner drag another, strenuously resisting drunk toward the holding cell.

Footsteps approached and Hank opened the door behind him, backing into the restroom a few steps. Frank DiMaso rushed by without turning his way.

Hank wondered what could have upset the friendly young cop. Poor bastard definitely got the short end of the stick when they partnered him with that Irish hothead. And if their latest clash wasn't bad enough, O'Shea had shown up drunk a few nights ago, spouting death threats against DiMaso in a room full of cops. Barnes, Thomas and Kowalski had to physically drag him out and calm him down, before the idiot managed to get himself fired for good.

The backdoor squeaked and Hank peeked into the hallway. The man stepping into the alley had his back turned, but he recognized him immediately, and the hair on his arms bristled. Hank stole away before he could be discovered.

Chapter Twenty-Six

Manhattan, 2016

Tuesday, August 2, 12:45 pm

Aidan took the towel from Franco's hand and wiped his face. "How about from now on I give you news from another room, or over the phone?"

"I said I'm sorry," Franco said absentmindedly, sitting down. One million dollars. What the fuck? He fervently shook his head. "I had no idea. You gotta believe me."

"Yeah, I got that. But it will undoubtedly strengthen some people's argument for motive."

Franco clenched his teeth so hard, his jaw hurt. "What the fuck was Prescott thinking? Like money was gonna fix everything? Wasn't enough he destroyed our lives, now he reaches from beyond the grave to screw me?"

"I understand you're upset," Aidan said with empathy. "I would never tell you how to feel, but maybe, in time, this doesn't have to be as bad as you think it is now. Set it aside for a moment, and deal with it later, if you can. It's not going anywhere."

Franco huffed out air. "Now what?"

"There are a lot of people I need to talk to, the sooner the better—Dr. Kruger and Sanders, and if any are still around, people who knew and worked with your father. I need to pull your dad's file."

Franco opened his mouth, but caught himself in time. If it turned out Aidan could not be trusted, telling him about Sal's duplicates could backfire.

Aidan made a call and Franco began pacing around, no longer tired, but furious at Charles.

He dialed Sanders' number again, but only got his voicemail. Aidan wrapped up his call and Franco said, "What the hell is with this Sanders guy? I've left five messages. Why can't he just call me back?"

"Maybe it's time I pay him a visit."

Franco nodded. "Ready in two."

"You're not going."

"Like hell I'm not. I got a right to know, and I was going there myself, anyway."

"Franco, I'm serious."

Franco shot him a look, then tapped the screen on his phone. "You don't want me in your car, *fine*."

"What are you doing?"

"Getting an Uber."

Aidan sighed and shook his head. "Anyone ever tell you you're a piece of work?"

Franco threw him a quick glance. "Yeah…but I like to think of myself as a masterpiece of work."

* * *

They arrived at a remodeled warehouse on East 37th at twenty past one. The sun had disappeared behind a wall of thick, streaked clouds, the air was thick and humid. Big signs listed all the different businesses and shops housed in the giant structure.

Franco's shirt stuck to his damp skin. The whole way over, his mind circled around the trust fund Charles set up in his name. Why did it infuriate him so much? Others would be ecstatic, already making lists of ways to spend it, but he was offended. He'd trade every cent for Charles to have had the guts to face him.

Aidan was quiet, clearly less than thrilled to have him tag along, but Franco didn't care.

They walked wordlessly through abandoned corridors, and it took them ten minutes to locate Sanders' office on the third floor, nestled between a row of storage units. They didn't encounter anyone anywhere, but amidst a muted baseline from another floor, Justin Timberlake went to great lengths to explain just why he couldn't stop the feeling.

Aidan knocked on the door. "NYPD, Mr. Sanders. Please open up."

Nothing moved, and he knocked again, getting the same result.

Franco pulled out his phone and redialed Ralph Sanders' number. "Maybe he's on vaca—"

Aidan shushed him. "Is that you?" He pointed at the door through which came the faint sound of a ringing phone. Aidan banged on the door. "Mr. Sanders, police. Open up!"

The call transferred to voicemail, and the ringing ceased.

"Mr. Sanders, open up, or we're coming in."

He grabbed Franco's arm and pulled him behind, then reached for the gun in his holster. "Stay, don't move."

Franco backed away, eyes wide.

Aidan grabbed the doorknob, found the door was unlocked, and pushed it open, his gun raised before him.

"Mr. Sander's, NYPD, I'm coming in." He swung around, gun held out in front of him with both hands, and stepped into the room.

Franco inched closer to the door and peeked in. Someone had taken the small office apart, leaving drawers hanging and papers strewn about. Aidan cleared the room and its adjacent bathroom, then tried the handle of a connecting door to another unit. Locked. He backtracked to the hallway, passing Franco, then tried the handle of the adjoining unit. Locked as well.

"No one's here," Aidan said, holstering his gun. He reentered Sanders' office and Franco followed.

"Stay," Aidan said, holding up a hand.

Franco shrugged, annoyed. "What? You just said no one's here."

"I doubt he decorated it this way. This is a crime scene, stand back."

Franco raised his hands in mock surrender, fingers around his phone. He watched Aidan scan the room, gingerly stepping over the mess on the floor to a desk by the window. "His phone," Aidan said, pointing at a black device. "No wonder he didn't get back to you."

"So, where the hell is he?"

Aidan shrugged. "Looks like someone paid him a visit." He pointed at the ceiling corner, where a small camera dangled on cable. "With a little luck we'll find where these connect to. They might have recorded the break-in."

"All right, gentlemen, easy now—no stupid moves," the smoky voice of a man behind him said, too close for comfort. "I got a license to carry, and no qualms about blowing either of your heads off."

Franco didn't dare turn, but ahead, Aidan looked furious. "Are you insane? You're holding a gun on an NYPD officer. Stand down!"

"Sorry, pal, that doesn't count for much around here."

Franco instinctively raised his hands, still clutching the phone. The man he still hadn't laid eyes on, but presumed to be Ralph Sanders, roughly pushed him against the wall, and his cheek smacked against the plaster. His body stiffened as big hands patted him down roughly, his heart pounding in his throat.

Franco's eyes searched Aidan's, but he looked past him. "Mr. Sanders, I'm Detective Aidan Torrance. You're interfering with an NYPD investigation. Lower your weapon and put your hands behind your head."

"Here's what's gonna happen," Sanders said. "You'll both smile for the camera over there and hold up identification—real slow. Don't even think about going for your gun. Everything happening in here is uploaded to an off-site computer, and will go public in fifteen minutes if anything happens to me."

"We're not here to hurt you," Aidan said. "We're here about Charles Prescott."

"Identification."

Franco said, "No, listen to him. My name is Franco DiMaso, you must know who I am."

Sanders snatched the phone from his hand and pushed him forward until he stood next to Aidan. The husky, bald man, likely in his late fifties, pointed a big, silver handgun at them. In boots, blue jeans, a dark flannel shirt and gray windbreaker, he'd clearly dressed for a colder climate, maybe Vermont in October, not the tinder box outside.

"Yeah, I recognize you." Sanders handed Franco his phone, his tone less aggressive. He put his gun on the floor, spread his fingers, and put his hands behind his head. "All right, take it easy now."

Aidan rushed forward, kicked the gun out of reach, and spun the investigator around. He patted him down and picked up the gun.

"Sorry about that," Sanders said, utterly unapologetic. "I have no intention of ending up like Prescott."

Aidan ejected the gun's magazine, emptied the chamber, and laid everything out on the desk.

"What the fuck were you thinking? I should arrest you right now," he said, his face crimson.

Sanders' expression matched Aidan's. "I was thinking the same NYPD pieces of shit who'd ransacked my office last week were back to finish the job."

"What the hell are you talking about? We didn't do this."

"You don't know shit, do you? Wake up, buddy, the call's coming from inside your house."

"All right, prove it. Show me the footage of the break-in."

Sanders sneered. "They didn't hold up their badges for the camera, they wore masks. But they knew they were being filmed and didn't care. They wanted me to see them trash my place."

"So really, this could have been anyone."

"Let me tell you something," Sanders said in a menacing tone, pointing a finger at Aidan. "Prescott hired me three months ago to find something, *anything* on an unsolved, forty-year-old murder no one's been giving a fuck about in decades." He shrugged at Franco. "Sorry. Anyway, the minute I start digging someone puts a tail on me, Charles gets bumped off, and DiMaso's case files disappear."

Aidan took half a step forward. "I just put in a request for them."

"Well, don't hold your breath. Betamax will make a comeback before they do."

"How do you know all this?" Aidan sounded doubtful.

"I'm good at what I do."

"Oh for fuck's sake, are you two done measuring?" Franco snapped, glaring at Sanders. "You're in a less than ideal situation yourself, from what I can see, so how about we skip to the part where we stop wasting time, pull resources, and help each other out?"

Sanders studied him and sighed. "What do you want to know?"

Aidan said, "When did the break-in occur?"

"Monday, a week ago."

"And your last contact with Prescott?"

"Wednesday, the week before."

"How often did you report to him?"

Sanders shrugged. "Whenever I had news. I wasn't on a schedule, and we didn't talk daily." He pushed the gun and magazine out of the way, then parked his generous butt on the desk. "When Charles hired me, he gave me a name and a date, and told me to get as much info as I could without alerting anyone to my investigation, especially the NYPD. That was it. After I exhausted all the usual channels and came up mostly empty, I persuaded Charles to let me use a trusted source in the department. It took some convincing, but they finally agreed to locate the murder book. I never saw the original, but they provided me with copies of crime scene photos, names of witnesses, and interviews from the initial investigation, what little there was of one. But when my source went back for another look, it was gone."

"Do you still have the copies?" Aidan asked, and Sanders nodded.

"They took the paper files, but I backed them up to my cloud." He eyed Franco. "How much do you know about your dad's case?"

"What my mom and uncle told me."

"That crime scene, pardon my French, was a giant cluster fuck, from what I can tell. A residential neighborhood at dusk, but no one saw or heard anything? Then again, Little Italy was a different place back then. The Mob had a strong presence there, not uncommon people looked the other way to avoid trouble. When the blackout hit, all hell broke loose. By the time the cops showed up, any kind of physical evidence had been destroyed between those trying to reanimate your dad, and gawkers crowding the crime scene. The autopsy eventually concluded he was shot with a .44, like Son of Sam used, but after Charles coughed up the truth, a few weeks ago, I suspect that may have been an orchestrated effort to muddy the waters. Because his wallet and some personal items were missing, it seemed plausible he'd been the victim of a robbery." He sighed and ran a big hand over his jaw.

"Nevertheless, the cops investigated a number of people who'd made threats against your father, including his old partner, and a few criminals he'd arrested a few weeks earlier, out on bail again. Everyone alibied out. Same for Romano, a suspected low-level mobster who owned a series of stores in Little Italy, and apparently engaged in a bitter feud with your folks, after your dad dumped his little girl at the altar."

"My father and Anna Romano were only friends, they never even dated."

"Her old man clearly didn't see it that way. Anyway, after the cops discovered drugs and money in a lockbox your dad supposedly kept at Penn Station, the whole investigation came to a screeching halt, and never really gained steam after that. And here we are." Sanders sighed, his eyelids at half-mast. "Gotta say, I'm not confident you'll ever know what really happened. It's just been too long, without much to go on to begin with. Most people are dead or moved on, and the rest aren't very talkative."

"Like who?" Aidan asked.

"Hank Porter, the precinct's old desk sergeant. Sourly old chap, and none too pleased to see me. Owns a small diner on JFK Boulevard over in Jersey. Knows more than he let on, you ask me."

"When did you talk to him?"

"Two weeks ago. I meant to go back and work my charms, but then Charles got killed, and my office got raided, and I decided to lay low for a while."

Aidan said, "Could Porter be involved?"

Sanders shrugged. "He might have tipped someone off. He wasn't happy to see me, I can tell you that."

"Anyone else?"

"Gian-Carlo Romano." He turned to Franco. "Your grandparents were convinced his grudge against them escalated to murder, but they had no proof. The cops suspected he had ties to the Mob, but they only questioned and never arrested him. He's over ninety now. Located him in a hospital a few weeks ago, but he was in a medically induced coma. He did wake up, but I never got to talk to him, and his daughter Anna hung up on me."

"So you didn't follow up with any of these leads," Aidan concluded.

"Listen, I liked Prescott, and he was a generous fella, but I ain't risking my health just to end up at the bottom of the Hudson." He eyed Franco. "That's why I didn't return your calls."

"All right," Aidan said, fishing a card from his wallet. "I need your footage and whatever information you dug up. I don't know who vandalized your place, but you got my word I'll follow this to wherever it leads."

"That's noble, Detective, but forgive me for not holding my breath." He glanced at the card. "I'll send you what I have within the hour."

They said their goodbyes, and five minutes later Franco and Aidan walked back to the car. "I'll need to talk to your mother and uncle."

"They don't know I saw Charles get killed. I don't want them freaking out."

"I understand, but it's important I speak with them, and sooner or later you'll have to tell them."

Franco flashed a pained smile. "Later sounds great. How about later?"

Chapter Twenty-Seven

Franco sat inside a small coffee shop a few blocks from Sanders' office, watching through the window as Aidan paced up and down on the sidewalk, talking on the phone. Was he calling O'Shea? Was Franco an idiot for trusting him?

What a mess. No, he didn't fully trust Aidan, but saw him differently now. It worried him. He'd been fooled by a nice face before, and duped by guys with seemingly good intentions—except this one could land him in the slammer, charged with murder.

State Department's "Slow Love" played in the background, but failed to cheer him up. He'd learned so much the past few days, yet still knew next to nothing. He plopped his head in his hands and massaged his temples.

"Are you okay?"

He hadn't heard Aidan return and flinched. "My mom just finished lunch with my uncle, and they're on their way to her place now. We can see them in half an hour. Just...don't screw up. I'll say you're an acquaintance who can help."

"I have done this once or twice before," Aidan said, but his tone lacked malice. "Just let me do the talking."

A waitress approached and brought them both lattes and apple turnovers.

"I didn't know what to get you," Franco said.

"Just black coffee would have been okay, but thanks." Aidan pushed the pastry toward Franco, who took one and bit into it while generously pouring sugar from a dispenser into his coffee.

"I hadn't figured you for a sugar junkie."

"Fast metabolism," Franco said through a mouth full of pastry. He tasted his coffee and added more sugar.

Aidan grimaced. "I'm amazed you still have your own teeth." His eyes softened. "How are you doing?"

Franco shrugged. "I am just so angry. Hell, I don't even know *who* to be angry at. We have absolutely nothing to go on. After all these years we're digging up the whole sordid past again without any guarantee we'll get any further."

"We know a lot more than forty years ago. But this must be very hard on your mother."

"Probably, though she seems remarkably collected. We all learned to move on, somehow, but it was quite literally the darkest night of her life."

Aidan sipped his coffee. "I heard that blackout was quite severe?"

"You never heard of the '77 blackout before now? It was all over the news for days...hell, The Trammps even had a hit record about it."

"Sorry, before my time, and I thought disco was dead."

Franco grabbed his chest in feigned shock. "No one says that to my face and lives. Just...exactly how old are you?"

"Thirty-eight."

Franco chewed his lip. "Well, around here people generally remember where they were that night. Admittedly, my own memories are fuzzy, but I read a lot about it later. New York was going through a massive heatwave and lightning bolts blew out transmission lines, and shut down Edison's power system. *Snap, crackle, and pop*, and nine million people without juice. Most made a night of it, sitting in the streets, talking, and listening to music on battery-powered radios. Some restaurants in Manhattan moved tables out to the sidewalks and served people by candlelight, and several Broadway shows continued while stagehands held flashlights, and actors did their own soundtracks. But eventually everything from elevators to subways and water pumps stopped working, and it became pretty clear the city was screwed. Things remained relatively calm here in most parts of Manhattan, but in the Bronx, Harlem, and Brooklyn, shit hit the fan." He shook his head and wiped his mouth with a napkin. "I mean, people were losing it. Looters smashed in windows and ransacked stores for food, clothes, jewelry, TVs, whole fucking washing machines. And we're not just talking poor people... everybody joined in. Some store owners trying to protect their businesses came face to face with longtime friends and neighbors stealing from them. Hell, a group of guys hot-wired fifty Pontiacs and drove them right off a lot. Whatever people couldn't take, they destroyed or set on fire. The cops arrested thousands of people while neighborhoods burned half the night... just utter frigging chaos."

"I'm afraid your blackout didn't leave as lasting an impression in California," Aidan said, finishing his coffee. "We've got earthquakes to worry about."

"That where you're from?"

"Los Feliz, yes. I only moved here a little over a year ago."

"How'd you end up here?"

Aidan sipped his coffee, avoiding his eyes. "I feel we're getting off topic here."

Franco cocked a brow at him. After several silent beats Aidan said, "My now *ex* got an offer in New York he felt was going to be his big break. Actor. We did the long distance thing for a little over a year, but it wasn't working. I put in for a transfer, left the LAPD, and ended up at my precinct late spring, last year."

"Moving across the continent for love, how hopelessly romantic."

"More like hopelessly stupid." Aidan stared at the coffee cup, his features hardening. "Five months after the move, I found out he'd been having an affair for a year. Another actor, someone he met after moving to Manhattan. And then he got one of the leads in a new drama series back in L.A. They left, I stayed." He sighed. "Manhattan is nothing like home, but...maybe I needed a change."

"I'm sorry."

"Don't be, that's life." Aidan's tone indicated unresolved feelings, something Franco knew about all too well. "We rarely speak, but today of all days he calls out of the blue and we got into an argument..." He shrugged with an unreadable expression.

Franco guessed it hadn't gone well. "So...he's the reason you kissed me."

Aidan opened his mouth, stopped himself, and lowered his head. "Sorry... that happened for all the wrong reasons."

Oh good, an apology *and* genuine regret.

An uncomfortable silence spread, and Franco said, "So, what made you join the co...police?"

"My best friend was shot and killed on our way home from school, a few weeks before graduation," Aidan said, his tone neutral. "Random drive-by. He was not even the intended target. Died in my arms, choking on his own blood. Until then, I'd always dreamt of a career in architecture, like my mother, but that day changed my life. The police never found the killers, and I always felt if I were a cop I'd do better." His mouth twitched. "Suffice it to say fifteen years on the force, seven in homicide, thoroughly schooled my teenage naivete. On patrol you frequently get to help people before something terrible happens, you can make a difference. But I always knew I wanted to be in homicide someday, and let's face it—we only ever enter the picture after the worst has already occurred. All we can do is try and bring closure to the ones left behind, find answers, and catch the responsible ones. And often not even that. But...it's what I believe I was born to do."

Franco nodded. "Were you out in the LAPD?"

"I've always kept my personal life private, but my partner there, his wife, and a handful of others met Josh. I came out late."

"I figured. I busted out of the closet at eighteen, with a bang, so to speak," Franco said. "It was a difficult time, nothing made sense in my life. I was terrified to disappoint my mom. Needlessly, as it turned out, because her reaction was, "Honey, I knew the day my eight-year-old son instructed me to only buy soda water henceforth, so he could rinse his hair like Farrah Fawcett. What?"

"The light makes your eyes look intense, almost black."

"Like my soul, you mean?" Why couldn't he just take the damn compliment?

Aidan shook his head and Franco stared out the window. "This is all just so...bizarre. Like watching a movie where everything is happening to someone else." He exhaled sharply. "Did you get any further with Charles' investigation?"

Aidan seemed reluctant, but offered, "We talked to a number of employees and friends, many who noticed a change in him several months back, said he seemed to withdraw a bit, and appeared preoccupied. Security cameras from his building show his driver dropping him off at his primary residence after work that day, but minutes later he leaves on foot. He did this several evenings, the week before he died, sometimes hailing a cab or an Uber. Took a while, but we found most of those trips ended a block from your home. Do you remember when the first new tenants moved in across the street?"

Franco shook his head. "Few weeks back, maybe?" His phone lit up. "Okay, they're home. Let's go…and not a word."

* * *

Franco listened quietly as Aidan, Sal and Julie spoke, all of them sitting around the glass coffee table in her living room. Aidan's phone sat between them, recording their conversation.

When they got to the family feud with the Romanos, Julie said, "I know her father never forgave him, but Frank and Anna remained friendly. They never intended to get married to one another, that was all the families' meddling."

"The whole idea was ridiculous and my parents had no right," Sal said. "But they were conservative and old fashioned, and where they were from back in Italy, arranged marriages were common. Kids had little say in it."

Julie nodded. "Anna left the country around the time Frank died and didn't speak to her family for years. In fact, I didn't hear from her until she wrote last year, out of the blue."

"What? Why didn't you say anything?" Franco said, the first words he'd spoken in half an hour.

Julie shrugged. "It wasn't important, and you don't know her. She apologized for leaving and not staying in touch for so many years. Said she thought about us often, and if I ever wanted to talk, I should look her up. I mean, we were friendly back then, but I never really knew her. I appreciated her gesture, but didn't see the need to walk down memory lane with a stranger, and forgot about it."

"Do you still have the letter, Mrs. DiMaso?"

She nodded. "I'll get it for you."

"And...I'm sorry to do this, but I understand you have a necklace that was taken from your husband the night of the murder?"

"Yes, a Confirmation gift from his parents. He always wore it."

"If you could get it so I can tag it as evidence, at least for the time being. I promise to return it to you as soon as I can."

Her face fell, but she nodded and left.Franco put a hand on Aidan's arm. "Why do you think Anna bolted right after my father died?"

"Could be any number of reasons," Aidan said, removing his arm.

Franco let go, but the corners of Sal's watchful eyes already twitched. "So, what are your next steps, Detective?"

"There are still a few more people to talk to."

"And you're not afraid to go down the rabbit hole? The letter made some pretty heavy allegations."

"Allegations being the key word," Aidan said, a slight edge to his formal tone.

"It's been a while, but I'm happy to help in any capacity I can."

"Thank you," Aidan said, "but if you think of anyone who might have information, let me know, and *I'll* contact them. This situation is highly sensitive and I don't want us to get ahead of ourselves."

"In other words, butt out," Sal said, matching Aidan's tone.

"I'm sorry."

Sal flashed a bitter smile, about to say something, but Julie returned and handed Aidan an envelope. "Here it is. Anna's last name is Alvarez now." Her eyes lingered on the necklace, and it broke Franco's heart.

"Can't you let her keep it, she has nothing else left of him."

Aidan glanced at him sternly, and Franco pressed his lips together until they practically disappeared.

"It's okay, I...understand," his mom said. "If you could please just..."

"I'll get it back to you as soon as possible."

She nodded. "I don't know what good this will do after all this time. My husband was a good, *honest* man. He deserves his name to be cleared."

Aidan nodded, and Franco excused himself to go to the bathroom.

When he returned, his mother and Aidan talked by the door. Sal stepped in his path, suspicion in his eyes.

"You trust him?" he said in a low voice. Franco hesitated a second before he said "yes," certain Sal hadn't missed it.

His uncle shook his head, something like frustration or disappointment flitting across his face. "I hope you know what you're doing," he said, his tone insinuating Franco was thinking with his dick again.

Franco squinted. "What are you saying?"

"Two days ago you hated every cop in town and told me to lay low, now you show up with this one, all buddy-buddy?"

"Franco, I'm sorry but we need to get going," Aidan said and Franco nodded.

Sal's expression remained wary.

"We'll talk soon," Franco said. Clearly, they were all overly sensitive, the situation tense, and he patted his uncle on the back.

"So, what about these?" Sal pointed at a box by the door.

Aidan looked at the box, then at him. What to do: prove his uncle's suspicions right, or risk potentially sensitive information falling into the wrong hands?

"My uncle's copies of my dad's murder book," he said, trying to sound less deflated than he felt.

Aidan's features tightened and he addressed Sal, "How long have you had these?"

"Since day one. Over the years, the original investigators let me check on their progress, usually leaving me alone with the files for a moment. Interdepartmental courtesy between old friends. I've gone over them so many times I can recite them by heart. Never got any closer, though."

Aidan picked up the box. "Thank you, I'll keep them safe."

An uncomfortable silence spread, so Franco hugged his mother, and they all said their goodbyes.

Outside, Aidan walked ahead of him, descending the stairs. When they reached the bottom floor, he turned around, his eyes hard. "When exactly where you gonna tell me about this?"

Franco blushed.

"You make my job that much harder when you keep things from me."

"My uncle's not supposed to have these, okay? I didn't want to get him in trouble," he said, but Aidan's expression said he saw right through him.

"Look, I'm sorry I didn't tell you, I thought you'd have access to the originals. You're right, this is all a bit much, and I hate feeling like I've got no control over any of it, like everyone's pushing me around."

Aidan studied him a moment before he said, "I understand, and I get you're upset. You're doing that lip thing again. But the sooner you accept I actually know what I'm doing, the sooner you'll feel better." His eyes and voice softened. "I *am* trying to help you, but you have to trust me, or this is only going to get harder. For both of us." He turned and walked out to the car.

Chapter Twenty-Eight

Aidan sat at his desk, staring at the computer screen. The squad room had quieted over the past hour, and only a handful of day shift dicks remained working at their stations. He rubbed his forehead and eyed his empty coffee mug. The clock on the wall said 6:22 p.m., and he was getting hungry.

He'd spent the last two hours going over the documents Sanders had provided to his private email account, accessing them through his phone. Sal's box he'd stored at his condo before returning to the precinct. Withholding them from evidence could bring serious repercussions, but what if logging them exposed him to whoever was working against them? Frank DiMaso's murder book had to have been tagged somehow. How else explain its disappearance the moment people came looking for it?

Actually, the record department clerk's exact words were "files can't be located," not unheard of with paperwork this old. She said the file hadn't been pulled in the past two decades, except for one entry on the day of Prescott's murder: Detective Aengus O'Shea.

Aidan's mood tanked. There had to be a logical, non-incriminating explanation, short of asking O'Shea point blank.

He pulled up his notes on Prescott: only child, never married, his homosexuality not a secret, but kept his personal life fiercely guarded. Brewster provided names of men Prescott had dated, the last relationship having ended five years ago, but everyone Aidan spoke to alibied out. Everyone only said nice things about him, but none had been in touch for months.

He went over the murder timeline again, then let his mind wander. He'd been at home that night, completing his DD5s on the Banks case. O'Shea didn't answer his calls when he tried him to verify some info in the files. He didn't think much of it then, but now he wondered where he'd been.

Was O'Shea one of the men Franco claimed he saw, *sort of*, through his drug induced fog? He didn't want to believe it, but it explained why O'Shea went out of his way to implicate Franco.

Aidan raised his head and caught Burt Tanner's eye a few desks over, one of the few people here who got along well enough with O'Shea. The detective got up from his chair, turned off his computer, and nodded in his direction before heading out for the day.

Aidan rubbed his temples. Someone out there had gotten rid of the DiMaso files, and if not O'Shea then who?

He checked his emails. Forensics hadn't made progress in cracking Prescott's password protected personal computer, and still no okay to access his private cloud accounts. Frustrating.

He'd texted O'Shea two hours ago to check in, but still hadn't received a reply.

Though he promised to call Franco if he had news, he didn't want to fuel his conspiracy theories any further. It could wait, not least because part of him really didn't want to deal with this unexpected, highly unprofessional situation.

What the hell was he thinking? He didn't know what to make of the man, nor could he deny the intense connection he felt when they'd gotten intimate. Still, the dumbest thing he'd done all year. This could expose him to the department, and he had enough shit to deal—

"Torrance."

Aidan raised his head. "Captain."

How long had Kaplan been standing there? Facial lines like ravines dated his boss well beyond his fifty-nine years, his piercing brown eyes locked on him. Aidan discreetly scanned his desk for incriminating files, found none, and got up.

"Where's your partner?"

"On sick leave, Captain."

"I know that, I sent him there. The DA has questions about the Faulkner case and can't get him on the damn phone."

"I haven't spoken to him since yesterday. He was running a high fever, and is probably just sleeping, trying to get back to his old self."

Kaplan's sardonic expression said he wasn't impressed with O'Shea's old self. "Yes, I've been meaning to talk to you about that, and your progress on Prescott. My office, five minutes." He turned and walked off without waiting for a confirmation.

O'Shea's and Kaplan's relationship qualified as frosty at best, and Aidan didn't like where this was headed.

* * *

Franco stacked the last of the dirty plates on the kitchen counter, where Carmine rinsed them off in the sink before putting them into the industrial dishwasher. Behind him, Gino wiped down the stove and glanced at the clock on the wall. "Eleven?" he muttered, "Shit, my bones say 3 a.m."

Franco nodded. He'd been largely silent all night, regretting parting with Aidan on a sour note.

The guys had inquired about his visit to the shrink, but there hadn't been enough time to get into it. Work somewhat took his mind off the day's developments, but now it required every ounce of self-restraint not to contact Aidan for news.

Gino wiped his hands on his stained apron and sighed dramatically. "I'm beat."

Carmine said, "Maybe if you'd gone to bed at a decent hour instead of three in the morning…"

Franco glanced at Gino. "Ah, that explains those Birkins under your eyes." He opened the fridge and grabbed the box of Spicy Basil Chicken he brought to work, but didn't have time to eat and re-heated it in the microwave.

Terri entered with a full tray of dirty glasses. She'd stopped by after a work dinner, looking sharp in slim black pants, a white blouse, and high heels. "Okay, tables are cleared. Now let's hear it, how was your hot date?"

Franco's heart stuttered and his cheeks stung, but she wasn't talking to him.

"*Che cazzo*, stop making such a fuss, there's nothing to tell," Gino said. "He came over last night and we had a few beers after work."

"Not what I heard," Terri said, giving him a once-over with a mischievous grin.

Franco said, "Who are we talking about, exactly?"

"The guy from Friday night, Goldilocks," Carmine said.

Gino sighed dramatically. "Anyway, you can all relax, it's not gonna work out."

"Why?" Terri asked.

"He dated Carl Myers, and before him, Patrick, from that travel agency over on Bleeker." Gino grimaced.

Franco knew those guys fleetingly, and they seemed nice enough. He shrugged at Carmine. "Did I miss something?"

"He only dates fat people." Gino grimaced like he'd just licked a bunch of turnstiles at Grand Central.

"Kate Moss over there feels offended," Carmine barked with an apathetic wave of his hand.

"Excuse me, but Carl Myers is my height and weighs close to three hundred pounds. I look nothing like those two *and* I just lost a ton of weight."

"Eighteen pounds," Franco corrected between bites.

"Twenty-four, as of yesterday, thanks very much."

"So you're gonna pass on this hot number because he likes some meat on his men? You know, twenty-four pounds don't qualify you as anorexic yet."

Gino folded his arms across his chest. "He likes a certain type of man and I'm not that man."

"So, what, you had a lousy time?" Terri asked.

Gino tilted his head. "No, he's actually rather nice. Intelligent, funny…a carpenter, of all things, and good with his hands."

"Geez, have some fun," she said. "Your last serious relationship was, what, four years ago?"

"So I gotta jump on the first man who shows an interest?" Gino, sounding incredulous, shook his hand with his fingertips pinched together.

Franco put down his food. "No, this is about you judging and eliminating someone before they can do it to you." Gino opened his mouth to protest, but Franco held up a hand. *"Ah-pa-pap,* let me finish. It's your trademark, you know it, we know it, half of New York State knows it. Not everyone's out to get you, okay?"

Terri looped her arm through Carmine's and said, "Franco's right, what's the harm? Hell, you might even get laid."

"Like I care about such things?"

"You should, you're forty-six, not dead. How long has it been, anyway?"

Gino opened and closed his mouth, then scrunched up his lips.

"Shit, *gurl,*" Terri laughed, "if you can't remember, it's been too long. You're going on another date with this guy if I have to drag you there by the balls myself."

Gino raised his hands in surrender. "All right, fine. Maybe I'll call him next week."

Franco shook his head at Carmine. "Slap him, you're closer."

Gino took a step back with a warning finger. *"Non ti permettere! Attento che ti faccio ricordare natale."*

He and Carmine broke out laughing, and Franco asked, "What about Christmas?"

"One Christmas morning, I was maybe eight or nine, Gino and I were fighting over presents until Dad gave us such an ass-whupping, we couldn't sit for two days. After that, whenever anyone got rowdy, he'd just stare at us, raise a hand, and say 'watch it, or I'll make you remember Christmas.'"

"Wow, rough crowd," Terri laughed, and Franco checked his phone. No messages.

Gino sighed. "Are you on that damn cruising app again?"

"No, just seeing if Aidan called."

"Who's Aidan?" Terri said, picking at Franco's food.

"The, um, detective working my case."

Gino's eyes narrowed with suspicion. "The stud? Since when are we on a first name basis?"

Everyone stared at Franco.

"You fucked him...didn't you?" Gino said flatly.

Terri laughed. "You didn't."

"We didn't get that far."

She said, "I thought you guys hated each other's guts?"

"Well..."

"You are something else." Gino didn't elaborate *what,* but his tart expression suggested nothing good. "After everything you've just been through, and we've talked about, you go and do something stupid like that."

"Hey, I didn't plan this, okay? We were at each other's throats one moment and...down them the next. Bottom line, Aidan wants to help."

"Oh, sure," Gino said, his tone facetious, "a little tonsil hockey and suddenly you're besties."

Franco grew defensive. "It just happened, okay? Maybe he can make a difference. I'm not saying everything's changed, I hardly know the man, but I need professional help."

"Yeah, start with your head. You're a fool to trust him."

Carmine slapped Gino's arm. "Lay off, why are you making such a big deal? This may be for the best." He turned to Franco. "Didn't his partner want to lock you up?"

"We sort of reached an agreement not to tell him anything for now." Aidan was adamant Franco not share information on the investigation, especially with his friends. But he just couldn't hold out on his family, feeling at least mildly guilty as he relayed what happened earlier. All except Charles' money, he had enough to deal with for now.

"Held at gunpoint?" Gino threw up his hands. "What is wrong with you, are you trying to get yourself killed?"

"Jesus, relax, it was an honest mistake. At least now we finally have some answers. I made it clear I won't sit by the sidelines, though he's not happy about it, that's for damn sure." He reached for the wrapped fortune cookie.

"This is getting out of hand," Gino muttered, and Carmine sighed. "I hate to say it, but I agree it's all getting a bit...intense."

Terri touched Franco's arm. "How is your family?"

He shrugged. "My sister still doesn't know, but I think this is all much harder on Mom than she lets on."

"Like someone else we know," Gino said, his tone mellow again. "Look, I'm sorry I snapped at you. But this is getting dangerous, and it worries me. I don't want to see you get hurt. You're not always the most perceptive when it comes to trusting people, is all I'm saying."

No argument there. "Aw, you care about me," Franco said, the corner of his mouth lifting.

"Don't put words in mouth." But Gino gave him a hug.

Franco said, "Not sure if Vince mentioned something, but any chance I can leave early Thursday to help out at the club?"

Carmine nodded. "Yeah, I'm here, you can head out by ten."

Terri said, "Just a thought, but you've been through a lot...have you considered talking to someone about it?"

"No...but the shrink gave me her card."

"Really, talking to the therapist of the man who killed your father?"

Franco shrugged with a tilt of his head. "Hey, on the bright side, I'd save a shitload of money trying to get to the root of things."

He cracked open the fortune cookie and popped one half into his mouth. "Ha, listen to this...*You are as intelligent as you are good-looking.*"

Carmine patted him on the shoulder with feigned sympathy. "Man, that's just mean. If I were you, I'd sue."

Chapter Twenty-Nine

Wednesday, August 3

Aidan woke after a rough night of little sleep, Tuesday's events leaving a stale taste in his mouth. He pushed away thoughts of Josh and Franco and took a shower. The talk with the captain in his office had gone better than he feared, and though Kaplan wanted an update, none too pleased with the lack of progress, he seemed more interested in O'Shea's state of mind and their working relationship. He gave Aidan the impression he was angling for ways to get rid of the old cop before his official retirement at the end of the year.

But he backed O'Shea and didn't change his story for Kaplan. His partner's aggressive behavior in recent weeks hadn't gone unnoticed. The unexplained absences were likely bar-related, considering Aidan occasionally caught the whiff of booze around him despite his best attempts to mask it with mints. Now Aidan wasn't so sure anymore.

He dressed, popped a capsule into the Nespresso machine, then carried his coffee over to the laptop and Sal's files he'd left on the walnut dinner table in the living room last night. By far the one-bedroom apartment's best feature was wide floor to ceiling windows in the bedroom and living room, flooding the space with ample natural daylight. It wasn't much, but it was his, at least until it made sense to sell without losing more money than he already had.

After a quick glance at the Jersey shoreline in the distance, he repeated last night's exercise by going over everything again, and familiarizing himself with DiMaso's case, checking names and statements on his rather short witness list: a former neighbor of the DiMasos, who'd moved to Florida, and the people Ralph Sanders already located, Hank Porter, and Gian-Carlo Romano.

He received a text from O'Shea: *fever breaking, back tomorrow.*

Aidan texted back he should contact Kaplan, or the DA, as soon as possible and wished him a quick recovery.

He called Dr. Kruger's office and made an appointment to see her at noon, then focused on Francesco DiMaso's notebook. His last entry was dated Tuesday, June 12, 1977, the day before his murder. According to Detective Morrow's notes, DiMaso ended his last shift early Wednesday morning and wasn't due back until Friday morning.

Circled in black, the entry read *MC/W/$$-??.* Aidan backtracked from there, trying to decipher what or who the initials stood for, but the preceding entries only featured more initials and few explanations. Occasionally, DiMaso made full entries, but seemingly every time he referred to people or things he knew, he switched to initials.

An entry on July 10 described a drug bust DiMaso had been part of. *MC/W* appeared again, and a name in full, Guido Simoni, whom they'd arrested with drugs and cash. Another circle around *$80k?.* DiMaso's estimate of the confiscated drugs and money? Aidan made a note to talk to Sal DiMaso again, hoping he could shed light on his brother's handwriting.

He flipped forward and found another entry, a potential homicide DiMaso investigated on June 30th. He referenced OS a few times, potentially referring to O'Shea, which would indicate *MC/W* also referred to a person or persons. DiMaso's old station house had closed down in the late 90s, and the personnel reassigned. Clearly, he needed the old list of names from records sooner than later. He checked his email again, but no luck.

A witness statement in the detectives' notes detailed O'Shea's assault on DiMaso during an arrest gone horribly wrong, and another the death threats he'd uttered at the precinct, two nights before the murder, drunk off his ass in a room full of cops. He couldn't find an official incident report, but there was mention of O'Shea's suspension in DiMaso's murder files. His first wife alibied him back then, though she was divorcing him at the time. Any chance she could have been lying?

One way to find out.

* * *

"What's wrong, Papi?" The woman's thick, red lipstick had smeared all over Jesús' throbbing dick, the enormous shaft with the inked scorpion rapidly deflated in her tiny hands. She blinked her eyes at him, her surgically enhanced breasts like medicine balls sewn on a rag doll. "I can suck it more, make you feel real good."

No, she couldn't, as sufficiently demonstrated over the last five minutes. He shoved her away. "Get me a beer."

She pouted, and he gave her a cold stare. She knew better than to argue, or point out it was only 10 a.m., and had the bruises to prove it. She rolled off him and trotted into the kitchen.

His mother's choice to christen him Jesús was an irony not lost on most of those unfortunate enough to cross him. Some considered him the devil, but he quite liked that. Kept people in line.

Sweat glistened on his sculpted abs and he leaned back against the pillow, reaching for the joint on the busted nightstand with one hand, and running the other through his newly short hair. Still felt odd to him, but necessary.

"Maricón," he spat under his breath. Things could have gone smoothly, had the old cop not rushed him, turning a simple hit into a complete fucking mess. Though not a professional, killing never bothered him. Did his first at fourteen and beat some little punk to death because he'd given him the stink eye. There were others, but he was always careful...and lucky. The cops never got him, not on those, anyway.

Mac was the problem. He'd bailed Jesús out of a few sticky situations as a teen, and used him to collect money, or provide muscle. Worked well enough at the time, and he preferred it to the slammer. But Jesús always knew a bigger payback would be expected someday. Except lately the old-timer treated him like he owned him or some shit, and he wouldn't put up with that. No one disrespected him, cop or not.

His orders had been simple: follow the old cocksucker, learn his routine—nothing more. No idea why a rich fart like Prescott felt the need to sit in an empty apartment, three, four times a week, in a neighborhood far away from his actual dope crib, so he could stare across the street at another homo. You asked him, his kinda dough could have bought him better and younger.

So he cozied up to the man one night, pretending to be one of the new tenants on the wrong floor, looking for the rooftop. He knew how to act non-threatening, clean up nice, and make a good impression. He deliberately wore a tight top over white sweatpants, his fat dick perfectly outlined against the fabric. Old guy practically salivated. So, Prescott let his guard down, two nights later, not expecting trouble, when Jesús knocked on his door, claiming he'd lost electricity in his unit.

Everything would have gone smoothly if Mac hadn't rushed him, and that *cabrón* across the street hadn't seen them.

That and the fucking security cameras in Prescott's, they'd not expected those. No way to get rid of the footage on the cloud, either, because the guy's fingerprints hadn't unlocked his phone. Too fucking late to ask for the password, now.

So they changed plans, dropped the body out the hallway window, and discarded him in the garbage container, a few houses over.

He hadn't planned on returning, but his ass was on the line, not Mac's. He thought he knew where the photo dude lived, then, but made a mistake. No doubts, now.

No way in fucking hell he'd go back in the hole, and only one way to make sure. Once and for all.

Chapter Thirty

Thursday, August 4

Franco held on to the orange railing of the Staten Island Ferry and inhaled the salty air, listening to a beautifully dreamy, somewhat wistful version of Nina Simone's "Here Comes the Sun." As always, the song evoked images of deserted sandy beaches and lost loves. He closed his eyes, letting the morning sun warm his skin while the wind brushed against his face.

He had forgotten how much he used to love the occasional ferry ride as a kid. Now he felt anxious, unsure he was doing the right thing...or remotely prepared for what lay ahead.

A murmur went through the crowd, and several camera-wielding tourists speaking a mix of French, German, and Italian all raced to the ferry's other side. Franco remained in his spot, along with other locals who no longer got overly excited by the Statue of Liberty passing on their right.

He probably should have called Aidan, given him the courtesy of an advance notice. He hadn't heard from him since Tuesday, but chances were he'd only tell him to butt out. Franco pulled his phone from his jeans and googled Gian-Carlo Romano, finding a few old entries about his small chain of Italian goods stores, which went belly up in the early 2000s. Two news stories alluded to his Mob ties, and allegations his businesses were part in a money laundering scheme in the 70s and 80s, before gangster Mick Lombardi was assassinated.

His phone vibrated and Aidan's name popped up on the screen. Shit. Accept, or ignore and deal with the consequences later?

He pulled the buds from his ears and answered the phone. "Hi, what's up?" he said, but the words came out sounding defensive.

"Guess who I just got off the phone with?" Interestingly, Aidan's tone left no doubt he wasn't anywhere near a mood for guessing games. "Ralph Sanders. Asked if we learned anything from Romano, you know, given you called him and asked for the old man's address."

Franco remained silent, but his cheeks tingled.

"What the hell do you think you're doing?"

"Turns out he was released from the hospital," Franco said, trying to sound upbeat. "I figured if I just show up at his home, it'll be harder to get rid of me. Besides, Anna contacted my mother."

"Where are you?"

"St. George, in fifteen minutes."

"You reach the station and sit your ass tight until I get there."

"Listen, I—"

"That, or I'll have local police pick you up and detain you the moment you reach Romano's home. Your choice." Aidan sounded mad enough to actually do it.

"All right." Franco ended the call, his mood thoroughly soured. He'd barely put his phone away when it vibrated again.

Sal.

Franco hadn't spoken to him since Tuesday either, and felt a pang of guilt. "Morning, what's up? I was just about to call Mom."

"Yes...sort of the reason for my call," Sal said, his tone serious. "She's quite worried. We talked a lot, the last few days and...I made some calls."

Exactly what Aidan told Sal *not* to do, not that Franco had room to point fingers, there. The sun hit his eyes and he blinked, waiting for Sal to go on.

"When you asked about Frank's old partner, Monday...that's what you didn't tell us, isn't it?" he said. "That he's investigating this Prescott guy's murder, the one listing you as a primary witness."

Franco closed his eyes. "You didn't tell her."

"Not yet, though your mother has every right to know. What the fuck did you get yourself mixed up in?"

"Look, I was gonna tell you both…when the time was right." *AKA never.* "How the hell did you find out, anyway?"

"That's *so* not the issue, right now," he said in the taut tone Franco remembered well from childhood, the few times Sal stepped in for a fatherly heart to heart, usually preceding a stern lecture. "This is much worse than you led us to believe. If the letter is right and O'Shea's involved in your father's murder, then this Torrance—"

"I know that, okay, but Aid…*Detective Torrance* is making real progress, and promised to help. Behind his partner's back, by the way. I trust him and know what I'm doing." To a degree, and not really, but no turning back now.

"I don't scare easy, Franco, but if the people who killed your dad bumped off this Prescott guy…"

They had almost reached the Staten Island Terminal and were getting ready to dock.

"You can't tell Mom, not yet. I don't want her freaking out. Promise."

"If you promise to step away from this. You're dealing with things way over your head."

"I can't—"

"God damn it, Franco, stop being so fucking stubborn. There's not just one way to approach this, all right? But that's gonna be as much your mother's decision as yours. I don't know how you and this Torrance know each other," he said, his tone suggesting he had a pretty clear idea, and didn't like it, "but you can't trust him blindly."

"All right, *fine*," Franco said, his go-to phrase since his teens, whenever he wanted to end a tedious argument without any intentions of following through.

"All right fine, *what*?" his mom would say, making him spell it out to hold him accountable later, but, apparently, Sal didn't seem to know or remember that trick.

Franco promised to call later, and they hung up. His screen lit up with a message from Nate, who sounded positively pissed he hadn't gotten back to him. He *had* forgotten all about him, and texted an apology, adding that this was a really bad time.

Nate's reply came promptly. *Flake.*

Great, not even ten o'clock, and he'd already alienated every person he'd come in contact with since getting out of bed. Why weren't they handing out medals for that?

He pushed the buds back into his ears and Curtis Mayfield assured him if there was a hell below, they were all gonna go. Much as he loved the brilliant track, its gloomy lyrics didn't instill confidence. He took a deep breath and made his way downstairs to exit the ferry.

Thirty minutes later, Aidan arrived in his unmarked department car, and Franco opened the door. Before he could speak, Aidan silenced him with a hard stare, holding up his hand.

"I'm back at the station, where are you?" O'Shea's barked over the car's speaker, and Franco tensed.

Aidan said, "I have something to take care of, but I'll be there in about ninety minutes, two hours tops."

"Lead in the Prescott case?"

"No." Aidan pressed his lips together. "Hey, listen, did you ever get back to the DA? He needs your notes on the Faulkner case. He isn't happy."

"Fuck him," O'Shea growled. "I'm out two days and suddenly everyone's in a fucking panic about everything."

"Just do it. We'll go over Prescott's file when I get back, I know the DA really wants to talk to you."

"Whatever. Later." O'Shea disengaged.

"The man's one gigantic ray of sunshine," Franco said, sliding into the passenger seat.

"Fuck!" Aidan slammed his fist on the steering wheel and Franco flinched. "I just lied to my partner about an ongoing investigation. How long do you think it'll take him to find that list of beneficiaries from the Prescott estate and know something's up?" Franco crossed his arms and clamped his lips shut. "You have no business being out here, messing with my investigation.

It was stupid of me to agree to this. We'll see Romano together, but after this all cards go on the table."

Aidan pulled out of the parking lot. During the thirty-minute ride, which they spent in a tense silence, Franco's lips did not reappear.

* * *

Franco practically jumped out of the car the moment Aidan parked in front of a gray, two-story family home near Blueberry Park. The white trim and picket fence gave it a quaint appearance, but someone had spent considerable time planting flowers in the front yard, setting the home apart from others. He smelled salty air from the waterfront a few blocks down the street.

Aidan led the way to the front porch. "Let me do the talking, okay?" he said, sounding calm again. Franco relaxed a bit. He knocked, and after a moment a stout woman in her sixties opened the door. Dressed in cream-colored jeans and a blue blouse, she wore no makeup, her curly hair short.

"Mrs. Alvarez? My name is Aidan Torrance, NYPD." He held up his badge. "We'd like to speak to your father. May we come in?"

Her inquisitive eyes turned suspicious, and her hands grabbed the door frame tighter. "What is this about? I am a bit busy." She eyed Franco. "You're not a cop, who are you?"

"You don't know me, Mrs. Alvarez, but you knew my family. My name is Franco DiMa—"

"Yes." Her posture relaxed, and she opened the door a smidge. "I have been expecting you."

If Aidan felt as surprised as Franco, he didn't show it, and they both entered.

The conservatively decorated home was meticulous, making the sour odor hanging in the air seem completely out of place. Franco scrunched up his nose before he could stop himself.

"Cancer," she said in a monotonous voice.

He glanced at her apologetically. "Sorry."

"I will only let you see him under the condition you ask your questions in a civilized manner." She spoke in a way that he half expected her to instruct him to put shoes on the belt, and remove liquids from his hand luggage next. "He's weak, his system is failing, and I don't want you to upset him unnecessarily. I thought we'd reached the end of the road at the hospital, three weeks ago, but somehow he bounced back. It was his wish to die at home, so I brought him home." She studied Aidan's expression. "I *am* a professionally trained nurse, and I assure you my father has the best care he could possibly hope for."

Yet her tone suggested part of her couldn't wait for the old man to cease being a burden.

She turned and led the way down the hall where the sharp scent intensified. They entered a small room fully equipped with a modern, state-of-the-art hospital bed, IV drip, and medical supplies. Anna Alvarez hadn't been kidding.

An old, bald man with dark eyes and sunken in cheeks lay in the bed, his delicate skin an unhealthy shade of yellow. He kept caressing the blanket across his chest with a noticeable tremor in his gnarled hands, and his head bobbed gently, clearly no longer under his control.

Franco studied Romano's face but didn't remember ever having met him before.

"*Papà*, these are Detective Torrance from the NYPD, and Franco DiMaso… Santo's grandson." The old man turned his head toward the window with a view of a broken fence, and the crumbling stucco of the neighboring house. Anna circled around the bed until she stood in front of him, but he turned his head away from her again, staring straight ahead.

"*Papà*, we had a deal! *L'avevi promesso*." You promised.

Aidan pulled out his phone and put it on a table near the bed.

"Mr. Romano, I am Detective Torrance, and I am going to record this interview. I want to ask you about Francesco DiMaso's murder."

"I have nothing to say, find another stool pigeon," Romano said, his hollow voice indignant.

"Enough!" Anna said, her voice like the crack of a gun. Even the old man flinched. "You promised Mama when she died, and you promised me before

I agreed to come back here. This all ends now, or I swear I'll leave you here to rot by yourself."

But he remained quiet and Aidan said, "Mr. Romano, were you involved in the murder of Francesco DiMaso?"

The old man closed his eyes. After a long silence he finally said, "Turn off your recorder."

"Mr. Romano, I need—"

"Turn it off or leave."

Aidan looked pissed, but he stopped the recording.

Romano reached for the handle hanging above his bed and struggled to pull himself up. Anna propped a pillow behind his back.

"No," he said, staring straight ahead, "I had nothing to do with DiMaso's death, though I wished I had..."

"*Papà!*" Anna balled her fists and Franco followed suit.

"You want the truth, you get the truth...my way." Romano slowly turned his head, his eyes resting on Franco. "You are Santo's grandson?"

"Yes," he said through clenched teeth.

"Your father dishonored my family and your grandfather betrayed me. Where I come from honor is sacred. Actions have consequences." He coughed. "No, I never denied the rumors, it bought me respect and fear. Some believed I had reclaimed my family's honor. But, alas...I had nothing to do with the death of your father." Romano coughed again Anna handed him a cup with a straw. After he drank she attempted to wipe his mouth but he batted her hand away. "I vowed to ruin your family, and your grandparents died believing I took their son. But...I had an alibi, witnesses. The cops had nothing on me."

"You were an affiliate of Mick Lombardo's."

"That man knew about honor and respect. Mick and his crew looked out for me...and I for him."

Anna walked away from the bed, shaking her head in frustration. Franco could see why she'd sounded so detached earlier. He'd only just met the old fart and already wished him dead. Not a shred of remorse or compassion in his voice.

As if reading his mind, Anna Alvarez said harshly, "You talk of respect and honor? What respect have you shown this man, talking about his family and your stupid feud the way you do?" She pointed at Franco. "He was an innocent child who lost his father. He deserves the truth."

Romano's tremors increased noticeably. He turned his head toward the window and didn't speak for several seconds.

"I chiromanti."

Aidan turned to Anna with a shrug.

"Fortune tellers," she translated.

Romano turned his head. "It's what Mick called them…the cops who killed for him."

Franco felt a jolt and held his breath. Aidan's eyes narrowed. "What are you talking about?"

"Detective, don't tell me your mind can't grasp the concept of corruption inside your precious blue walls," Romano said with contempt. "Your institution practically invented it."

"You have proof?"

"Your job." Romano sounded exhausted, but Franco felt no sympathy. "What I am telling you I am doing for my daughter and my beautiful wife, may she rest in peace. And because I *am* a man of honor. I won't testify, ever…but I made a promise, and intend to keep it."

Another coughing fit shook his body. Anna reached for a portable oxygen tank, but he waved her off. When he recovered he said, "I only met them once, when they came to pick up money I owed Mick for…services rendered. They did not introduce themselves, but the way they carried themselves, talked, it was obvious. They were…very unpleasant men, and I considered talking to Mick about them. But then I heard he was friends with one of their fathers…and I thought better than to push my luck. I did not see them again for years, until Mick's *capo* pointed them out to me one night at a restaurant, told me they were on Lombardi's payroll. Providing tips on drug deals so Lombardi's crew could rip off the competition, warning him before cops raided his own properties. Fortune tellers. They handled drop offs and provided muscle when Mick went on one of his infamous personal visits.

Few people got to walk away from those alive."

He stopped to catch his breath, studying Franco's face. "Your father was part of a drug raid led by Mick's cops...but drugs and money went missing. Mick's drugs and money. A few days later your father was dead, and the stolen goods were discovered in his lockbox."

"He was set up." Franco didn't bother hiding his anger.

A borderline grotesque smile touched Gian-Carlo Romano's thin lips. "You think your family is so pure? You are a fool...as was I. In the end, Lombardi got everything your family lost." He barked a chuckle, spittle flying from his mouth. "You make a deal with the devil, you better not mind the fire."

What the fuck was that supposed to mean? Franco stepped forward, his face taut, but Aidan stopped him.

Romano coughed. "Your father did something he shouldn't have, so Lombardi's cops took care of it."

Franco opened his mouth, but Aidan beat him to it. "How many, and who were they?"

"Two that I know of for sure, no names. Few people knew, apart from Mick, and he took it to his grave. Gunned down with two of his sons and five of his closest associates, in '85. At their local hangout, of all places..." He looked mournful, sighed. "Wasn't right...the end of an era. The rest of his crew scattered in the wind, though his youngest should still be around. So...good luck with your investigation." He coughed so hard his face turned beet red. Anna managed to put the oxygen mask over his nose and mouth, and he didn't resist.

"Detective, enough, please let him rest," she said.

"We'll wait," Aidan said, but she shook her head.

"He told you all he knows." She tried to usher them out of the room, but Aidan didn't budge.

"Did he ever mention the name Charles Prescott?"

"No, but I'll ask him later."

"Why did you leave the country right after the murder?"

"Please, outside," she said, and this time Aidan followed her.

Franco watched the old man whose eyes were now closed, his breathing labored. How many years and chances had been wasted because of this cruel old fuck? He turned and walked out of the room.

In the hallway, Aidan asked Anna again why she'd left the country.

"My father never accepted my husband and believed I married Joaquim only because Frank married Julie. It didn't matter that I loved him, and he came from a respectable, wealthy family in Brazil—his dark skin was reason enough for my father to disapprove. He wasn't good enough for our family, for him. My opinion never mattered, or my mother's, only his." She lowered her head. "I never understood why my father wanted to be a made man, keeping company with thugs. My mother said he wasn't always this way, and his obsession broke her heart. I wanted nothing to do with that life. I told him again and again I made my own choices, that Frank had nothing to do with any of them. But he was a stubborn man, hurt in his pride, and he needed someone to blame. So, he did everything to ruin the DiMasos, because he could."

But Romano had claimed Lombardi ended up with everything. Franco said as much.

"He did, somehow, and I remember my father was very disappointed. It may have been the first time he realized Mick Lombardi would always put Mick Lombardi first."

Anna's eyes welled up. "I loved my father…suppose a part of me still does. I'm here, aren't I? But he turned into a cruel man, hungry for power, and for what he perceived as respect. When Frank was killed I was beside myself, and when he acted like he had something to do with it, I confronted him. 'It's done, he got what he deserved,' he said, and it stopped my heart cold. I honestly believed he had Frank killed and, terrified for my husband's safety, I persuaded Joaquim to leave with me. So we did, and started fresh with his family in Brazil."

She turned to Franco. "I couldn't bring myself to tell Julie. I had no proof and couldn't stand to hurt my mother. I didn't speak to my father for years. When she died, I returned home and found out the truth, but he refused to go to the police. Then Joaquin died, and the following year the doctors diagnosed my father with cancer. They gave him one year to live. He begged me to come home, begged my forgiveness. It's been two years, but we're at the end of the road now. I agreed to take care of him if he promised to make things right. He refused to go to the police, but we reached a compromise, and he agreed to tell the truth if someone came asking. That's when I wrote to your mother, hoping she would contact me. She never did."

"She didn't mean to offend you, I think she simply forgot over time," Franco said. "She's doing really well, and she's happy."

"I'm glad." Anna turned to Aidan. "I hope you find these men. The day they came to our store, the younger of the two tried to get fresh with me. He acted arrogant and rude, like he owned me, and my father got very upset. He gave them a package and told them to leave, but the young cop got in his face and said something I couldn't hear. Papa never told me what he said, but I'd never seen him look that...terrified."

"Could you identify the men if you saw them again?" Franco asked.

"It's been forty years," she said, shaking her head. "But the younger one suffered from *nevus flammeus,* port wine stains on his elbows."

Chapter Thirty-One

Aidan walked back to the car while Franco said goodbye to Anna Alvarez. He got in, checked his mail for the attachment he'd been waiting for, and sighed with relief. Finally, a lead. And a confirmation, providing some good news. For a moment he considered sharing them with Franco, when he joined him in the car. Instead, he put his phone away, and they took off.

After ten minutes of riding in silence and trying to figure out his next step, Aidan decided to grab the bull by the horns. At a red light just before entering the Verrazzano-Narrows Bridge, he sent out a text he still wasn't convinced was the right thing to do.

Franco had been gazing out the window, seemingly lost in his own thoughts, but now he said, "Everything, the whole fucking mess, because of a lie. *Now* do you believe what I've been saying all along?"

Aidan glanced at him. "So far, all we have is stories. We need witnesses backing up their claims. Even if Romano agreed to testify, you've seen him. I doubt he'll make it past Tuesday."

"Miserable piece of shit. My grandparents were assholes, no loss there, but not even I felt that kind of hatred toward them. And the way he spoke about my dad, like he brought it all on himself. We *know* what happened to him, Romano said he was set up, and murdered by corrupt cops."

Aidan cleared his throat. "Not exactly what he said. I know you don't want to hear it, but there's a possibility whatever we find on your father may still not be what you want to hear."

Franco exhaled deeply. "That maybe he *was* just another crooked cop?

Well, then you might as well stab my mother in the chest now and get it over with, because that news will definitely kill her." He held out his phone. "Here...not sure it's legal, but it's Romano's confession. What? He told *you* to stop recording, he never said a damn thing to me."

Aidan nodded. "We have one-party consent laws for taped conversations in New York."

"Well, I consent, and he can rot in Hell."

"Forward the recording to my number."

Franco nodded and exhaled sharply. "Bunch of corrupt cops, guess I shouldn't be surprised."

Aidan's fingers gripped the wheel harder and his cheeks tingled. "I get you're upset, but stop. It's insulting."

Franco's eyes twitched.

"Most of us are damn hardworking, honest cops who take the law seriously with every fiber of our being. We protect and serve, and risk our lives every damn day so you and the rest of the city can sleep better. To judge the many because of the faults of a few is a slap in the face of every decent law enforcement officer out there, busting their ass."

Franco's jaw tightened, but when he spoke several seconds later, his tone was contrite. "So, what about these mystery men? Anything in my dad's file about them?"

Aidan swallowed his frustration and took a deep breath. "Lombardo's organization was smaller than any of the other Mob family's, but ambitious. Getting cops on his payroll for inside information was...smart, and he wasn't alone, unfortunately. Crime was running rampant in the 70s and 80s, the Mob had a hand in nearly everything. When the FBI cracked down in '85 and arrested the heads of every crime family, people panicked. Loyalties were tested, and some saw opportunities and began scheming. Not impossible Lombardi became a casualty of internal politics."

"What about Dad's notes?"

"Slow going. I found several entries I'm not sure what to make of. I talked to Dr. Kruger and got Prescott's video confession. It's compelling, but without him around to testify..." He glanced at Franco. "For what it's worth, he sounded sincere, and I think he would have gone through with the whole thing, made it right...well, as much as possible." His phone rang, and he answered using his earpiece.

Franco leaned his head against the window and blocked out Aidan's voice as he watched the asphalt streak past. He hated the tension between them, knew he was to blame for much of it. He clearly wasn't himself lately, and as little as he wanted to admit everyone was right, things were outpacing him.

The Belt Parkway took them close to his mother's condo, and his conscience chided for not calling her sooner. He would do it...but later.

Aidan ended his call just as they reentered Manhattan, but they remained silent. Heading north on Church, he took a turn, then maneuvered the car into a subterranean garage of a high-rise.

Franco turned his way. "Where are we going?"

"My place. I want to show you something."

He perked up. Maybe there was a chance they could pick up where they left off? Aidan parked, and they rode the elevator up to the eighteenth floor. Franco's anticipation increased, and by the time Aidan unlocked the door to his apartment, he felt positively giddy.

The brightly lit living room connected to a small, open kitchen, and floor to ceiling windows provided a partial view of Hudson River and New Jersey, peaking out between other high-rises.

"Nice," he said. "The NYPD pays better than I thought."

"Not exactly." Aidan closed the door behind them. "Josh and I got this place together...a bit hasty, in hindsight. I wasn't ready to move again, so I'm stuck paying off him *and* the mortgage."

"Ouch."

"Yeah." The corners of Aidan's mouth lifted, but he seemed tense. "Can I get you anything to drink?"

"Water's fine." The sleek Nordic decor, consisting of a brown mid-century sectional and glass coffee table, walnut bookcase, and dining room table with four chairs fit Franco's tastes to a T. "Cool place. How many bed—?"

A sharp rap at the door made them turn their heads. Aidan's expression darkened, and he opened it.

O'Shea stood outside, and Franco's jaw dropped. O'Shea seemed equally surprised to see him and instantly adopted his trademarked *expired milk* expression. "What the hell's he doing here?" He sounded congested.

Only Aidan didn't seem the least bit shocked, and Franco's blood pressure spiked. "Aidan, what the fuck?"

"Yeah, *Aidan,*" O'Shea said, entering, and mimicking Franco's familiar tone. "What the fuck, indeed?"

Aidan shut the door and positioned himself in front of them. "Time we all sat down and talked face to face."

"Are you crazy?" Franco snapped. "Why the hell don't you hand him a gun, too?"

O'Shea, his skin pastier than usual, scowled at him as he casually lifted the side of his jacket to reveal his holstered weapon.

Aidan raised a hand. "You said you'd do whatever it takes to get answers, and I'm telling you this *is* what it takes. Trust me." Aidan turned to O'Shea. "Take off your jacket."

"What?"

"Please, do it, and roll up your sleeves."

O'Shea placed his hands on his hips and squared his shoulders. "Not until you tell me what the fuck is going on here."

"Show him your elbows."

"My what? Are you nuts?"

"Just do it. He thinks you killed his father."

Franco threw up his hands, his eyes to the ceiling. "Oh, you gotta be fucking kidding me."

"Are you out of your mind?" O'Shea pinched his eyes. "Is that why you called my ex?"

Annoyed, Aidan said, "Guess the good news is, she doesn't dislike you as much as she claimed, or she'd have kept the call confidential, like I asked."

"Screw you." O'Shea took off his jacket, revealing a rumpled and sweat-stained white dress shirt. He rolled up his sleeves and held out his pudgy white arms. "Happy?"

No marks or scars anywhere. Franco crossed his arms. "He could have had the spots surgically removed."

O'Shea threw him a tired look. "Have you met me?"

Fine, he had him there. Franco glared at Aidan. "I can't believe this. You promised."

"Franco, *he didn't do it.* I had to prove it to you in person or I'd be talking until the cows turn blue."

O'Shea rolled down his sleeves. "You better start talking and making sense."

"First, I want to show you something." He walked to the table and opened his laptop. A moment later he pulled up a screen. "Early this morning we finally got access to Prescott's cloud, and footage from the condo's security cameras." He hit a button.

The recording showed the inside of Prescott's unit in near darkness. The night glow from the clouds illuminated the space enough to outline Charles sitting in a chair, looking out his window. There was no audio, but he suddenly turned his head at the door and got up, then hesitated. After a few seconds he moved closer and switched on a light, and opened the door a few inches. His head moved for a moment, as if speaking to someone, then the door blew open, and an arm struck forward, hitting him in the throat. Charles stumbled back, raising his hand, and a man with long hair shot forward.

Franco's insides turned cold and he inhaled sharply.

Charles slammed backwards into the window as the attacker grabbed him and swung him around. He appeared young and strong, but the long hair got in the way of a clear face shot. Another man with a New York Rangers cap rushed in and instantly headed for the camera. The shot only showed glimpses of his face. The screen went dark mid-fight.

"Carter sent me this an hour ago. He and his team are working on enhancing their faces," Aidan said to O'Shea, tilting his head toward Franco. "Clearly, he wasn't there, and DNA results came through, too. He's no match for the samples from Prescott's nails, either."

Franco perked up, relief washing over him. O'Shea grumbled but didn't speak.

Aidan said, "I have to ask you questions and you're not gonna like them... but your name keeps coming up in connection with his father's murder. Why?"

O'Shea's expression darkened. "Careful, Torrance, you're walking on thin ice here."

Franco clenched his fists, debating which one of them to murder first. How could Aidan betray him like this?

"Answer me," Aidan said.

His eyes like slits, O'Shea said, "I have no fucking idea because I had nothing to do with his father's murder."

"Bullshit," Franco spat, but Aidan silenced him with a raised hand.

"We know you guys had bad history. What happened?"

"*We*? What the fuck is this?"

"Prescott confessed to shooting Frank DiMaso in '77 in a letter sent to Franco by his estate, and his therapist supplied a taped confession. He claims two cops forced him to commit the murder while they held a friend hostage."

"Is this a joke?"

"No, and I also want to know why you pulled the DiMaso file two weeks ago, and where it is now."

O'Shea glared. "I never pulled DiMaso's file. Why the hell would I?"

"You tell me. Your name is on record the day Prescott was killed."

He stabbed a finger at him. "I'm telling you, I never saw that file. And what's this bullshit about cops killing cops? Everyone knows DiMaso was dirty and got knocked off by the people he screwed over."

"DiMaso was set up. Prescott confessed he was instructed to plant the key to the lockbox on his body, and Gian-Carlo Romano pretty much confirmed it."

O'Shea shook his head with contempt. "The wanna be wise-guy? Who'd believe anything he says?"

"His story adds up. He's been carrying it around for decades, ready to take it to his grave. He claims he met the cops, and they worked for Mick Lombardi."

O'Shea stared at him, his mouth agape.

"You were DiMaso's partner, you have to know the cops he was talking about."

O'Shea walked over to the window and stared outside. "This is crazy," he said, seeming genuinely flustered. He turned around, his face tired. "Show me the letter."

Franco tensed, but Aidan reached for a file on his table and handed it to O'Shea. He read it, put it back on the table, and continued staring out the window, his back to them.

"Everything was different back then," he said after a while, his voice almost melancholy. "People in the department used to call me a hothead. But they appreciated my approach to get criminals to...cooperate. A lot less restrictions in those days. Frank and I were a terrible match, but Reynolds, our captain, believed he'd be a good influence on me, could rein me in if necessary. Muscle and brains." Hands behind his back, he barely made eye contact with Aidan, and none at all with Franco. "Frank followed protocol to a T, and had a way of talking to people, getting them to open up, but we disagreed on almost everything. I thought he was too soft on perps and didn't have what it took to be a real cop, but Reynolds refused to reassign us." He sighed and looked at Aidan. "I know I was a loose cannon in those days, drinking too much. I sometimes took it out on the perps we arrested, figured they had it coming." He turned his head and locked eyes with Franco. "And once, when he got in the way, your father. Nearly put him in the ER. Reynolds suspended me without pay for two weeks and threatened to can me for good if I didn't clean up my act, get my anger issues under control. I said some stuff and when Frank was killed a few days later, they came for me. But I was nowhere near him and had an alibi. The rest is history. I was lucky to still have a job after that, and kept my head down until everything blew over."

Franco let out a humorless chuckle. "What a stand-up guy."

"I didn't trust the guy, and finding all that shit in his locker only convinced me he was another lying crook behind his righteous act. Wasn't the first, either, and I'm still not convinced I'm wrong."

Franco stiffened, and Aidan said, "I'm pretty sure DiMaso was set up, and I'm thinking so were you, because if you didn't pull DiMaso's file someone sure made it look like you did. And now they're gone."

"For the last time, I never saw the file."

Aidan gestured at the table. "Sit...both of you."

"He has no business being here," O'Shea said, nodding toward Franco.

"He deserves to know the truth."

Franco sat at a safe distance from O'Shea.

"Both Prescott and Romano spoke of two cops," Aidan continued. "A younger one with a skin condition on the elbows, and an older one who seemed in charge. Who were they talking about?"

O'Shea's eyes twitched, and his muscles tensed. He seemed to mull it over in his mind, then said, "We were assigned to a new task force against organized crime, two months before Frank's murder. The division consisted of six people: DiMaso, me, Pat Monaghan, Pete Stanton, and Sean MacCaffrey."

"That's five."

O'Shea nodded slowly. "He was a detective back then, but you'd know him as Raymond Lee Walker, candidate for the next mayor of New York City."

Lower East Side, 1977

Saturday, July 09, 4:23pm

The tan colored Coupe de Ville Caddy cut the corner into Alphabet City with squealing tires, speeding down 4th street toward the East River. Frank DiMaso held on to the door handle and pressed his knees against the passenger seat to keep from being tossed around in the backseat.

"We get there, you stay by the car, keep an eye out." MacCaffrey's tone left no room for debate as he navigated the unmarked car down the block as if trying to impress people at NASCAR. "We can handle the rest."

Frank caught a glimpse of the young cop's disgruntled face in the rearview mirror. Walker, sitting next to him in the passenger seat, kept quiet, but they clearly didn't want him here. Reynolds had given the orders, and here he was, bruises and all—fresh out of a partner, there to assist other teams on arrests.

MacCaffrey acted unusually hostile, territorial. Frank didn't think he and O'Shea were close enough for MacCaffrey to care or take sides in his recent suspension, but the captain's decision had created tension in the unit.

Frank wanted to put it behind him and focus on work. O'Shea had crossed a line. His problems were his, and if he didn't get a grip on his life, his downfall was pre-programmed. Frank was done being understanding.

The Ford came to a rough halt in front of a row of rundown buildings, and MacCaffrey and Walker got out. Frank followed suit and MacCaffrey swirled around. "*Stay*...and keep your eyes open."

Down the street, a bunch of kids stopped playing ball and stood watching them with suspicion.

"What about the fire escape?" Frank said.

"We got it covered, there's only one way in or out," Walker said, his tone smooth. "Just make sure no one gets by you."

They unholstered their guns and trotted across the street into a five-story building showing old fire damage on the upper west corner.

The tip about a drug deal going down came in minutes earlier, but chances were anyone who had been there had already hightailed it by now. Frank walked toward an overgrown lot, parts of a demolished building's original foundation still visible. A sagging mesh fence was cut open in places where people had disposed of garbage and broken furniture among a sea of old bricks.

The city kept rotting away. Poverty and crime were increasing, entire neighborhoods falling apart, everyone waiting for someone else to clean up the mess.

Frank studied the building's eastern facade with its single row of narrow windows. No one would try and go out this way, risking a free fall over several floors.

A muted gunshot bellowed through the air. Frank turned and bolted to the car, radioed for backup, and sprinted across the street. He shouted at the kids to get lost, but they just moved to one side of the street, watching.

He drew his revolver and ran into the building, weapon raised. Slowly advancing up the stairs, he strained his ears for sounds. A faint thumping noise from somewhere above preceded someone yelling instructions, and something heavy being pushed or dragged across the floor. The door to an apartment on the second floor stood open, abandoned, save for a few pieces of furniture, a layer of dust covering the filthy ground.

He reached the third floor landing and carefully peeked around the corner through the open door. He heard a scraping noise. "Walker, MacCaffrey, everything all right?"

"What the fuck are you doing here?" MacCaffrey appeared in the doorway of a bedroom farther down, his hand outstretched. "Lower your damn piece,

I told you we got it covered."

"I heard shots and called for backup." MacCaffrey muttered something under his breath and Frank stepped into the small apartment, lowering his arm. A window to the back stood open, and a pair of unmoving legs lay on the ground, Walker kneeling beside them.

"It's okay, Frank, we got this," Walker said, rising. "One guy took off through the window, the other one shot at us, but I managed to knock him out."

Frank advanced into the tiny living room where the man lay face down on the floor, out cold, arms handcuffed behind his back. To the side, Frank glimpsed a table with white bags and pills, and an old gym bag on its side, cash piling out of it. MacCaffrey stepped in front of him, blocking his view, and stabbed a finger at him. "Get downstairs."

Frank batted away his hand away and Walker moved between them.

"Go canvass the neighborhood." He spoke calmly.

Frank glanced at the man on the ground and the table with the drugs, nodded, and headed out. Walker and MacCaffrey had been at this longer than he had, and were a well-oiled team, but the whole thing still seemed off.

On his way down, he quietly entered the abandoned unit. He noticed footprints on the floor and determined they were fresh. He raised his gun and checked both rooms, found them empty, then advanced the window. No one on the fire escape. Had the other guy been waiting in here when he passed the apartment the first time?

He made his way downstairs and around the back of the building, where the lower part of the fire escape was heavily damaged. Unlikely someone jumped from the second floor, nearly twenty feet above ground, but also not unheard of. He made a mental note to call hospitals in the area, check if anyone came in with injuries.

Backup arrived and they searched the area, but an hour later they called it a day. No one in the neighborhood copped to seeing anyone or anything, unwilling to help the pigs, as one of them eloquently put it.

Frank spent the rest of the day behind his desk filing his report, then headed home to his pregnant wife and four-year-old son. But a nagging feeling wouldn't let him rest, resulting in a trip to the evidence locker the next day.

He left only three minutes later, the nagging feeling in his head turning into a dark suspicion.

Chapter Thirty-Two

Manhattan, 2016

Thursday, August 4, 4:51 pm

"Walker and MacCaffrey led a number of successful drug busts in the mid-70s, which didn't go unnoticed by the brass," O'Shea said with a grim expression, leaning back in his chair. "Some of us were assigned to a temporary special division to track and target organized crime, getting drugs, guns, and wise-guys off the street. The experiment started in June, but after my...suspension...I never rejoined the team and eventually got assigned a new partner. Reynolds retired in '78, and Walker and MacCaffrey transferred to another precinct two years later, where Walker headed a new anti-drug unit. He's been rising in the ranks ever since."

"And these are the guys Romano spoke of?" Aidan sat between him and Franco, taking notes, his back to the kitchen. "Was MacCaffrey one of the men in the video?"

"Hard to say, haven't seen him in years. But you said one of them had purple elbows, and that's Sean MacCaffrey Junior. His dad was Walker's partner before he dropped dead of a heart attack chasing a perp in December of '76. Sean Junior is a couple of years younger than Walker, but he joined Walker's plain clothes OC unit that year at his request. He'd barely survived the layoffs in '75, lost his mother to cancer the same year, and his dad ten months later. Frankly, many believed he only caught a break because of his dad's legacy and connections. Most cleared cases in the precinct's history, medals of honor, personal friend of the mayor, you name it. Everyone figured Walker was more a son to him than his own flesh and blood, but Sean Junior and Ray got along like brothers. Couldn't have been more different, though. Walker's cool, collected, sharp as a tack, charismatic, when he wants or needs to be, but behind closed doors the guy shows little empathy for anything. I've never seen anyone able to switch it on and off like he does. MacCaffrey and I were more alike, with the quick temper and the fists...but he was a pompous loudmouth."

Franco cocked a brow his way, but clenched his mouth shut.

"What about the other two, Monaghan and Stanton?"

"Walker brought them into the unit. Both were already in their forties, then, and died years ago."

Aidan sighed. "What about rumors of ties to the mob?"

O'Shea slowly shook his head. "No, but Walker's a slick son of a bitch. His connections reach far beyond the department, and nothing ever sticks to him. There were a number of complaints of misconduct, allegations of bribery, back in the day. Intimidating witnesses, coerced confessions, that sort of stuff, but all were shut down, and witnesses recanted. Simply powered through everything, coming out the other end smelling of roses. He's an intimidating son of a bitch for sure, but his operations were largely successful, and he put away a lot of bad guys. Many believed the accusations were fabrications by the opposition, to bring him down." O'Shea raised a hand. "Don't get me wrong, Walker isn't my kinda guy, but he got the job done, and cracked down on crime. If you're telling me he's tied to Lombardi, working for the guys he was supposed to put away? Hard pill to swallow, to say the least. Less so about MacCaffrey."

"Could they have worked with others?" Aidan said, making notes on a pad.

O'Shea shrugged. "Those two were attached at the hip, hard to say who else they worked with, off the clock. They got along well enough with DiMaso, but I never got the impression they were close. Either way, good luck proving it. Walker's got a lot of friends in very high places. Guy's been playing politics for decades, and he's damn good at it. Easier to go after MacCaffrey, he's always been a blow-hard, and a washout. I think he quit the force a while back and runs some sort of private security company."

Aidan said, "Anything ever suggest Walker and MacCaffrey were on the take? Large, unexplained sums of money?"

"Not that I recall. MacCaffrey could be a showoff, but we figured he got it after his folks croaked. Fact is, a lot of guys found ways to fatten their wallets, back then, and few thought twice about it. Perks of the job. I'm talking about harmless stuff, like eating and drinking at restaurants without paying a dime, filling up at the gas station…but some got greedy. Whorehouses, bars, and clubs, they all paid someone to operate and get protection, usually on both ends of the law."

Aidan tapped his pencil against the table's surface. "Romano said Lombardi was friends with the young cop's father, which would be MacCaffrey Senior."

"Don't know, but if he did, he didn't parade it around. You could check school and military records."

"What about Hank Porter?" Aidan picked up his phone and swiped across the screen.

"Porter's a coward, but he had no love for Walker…or me."

"Shocker," Franco finally said, ignoring O'Shea's scowl. "So, what, we talk to Porter next?"

"*We* aren't doing shit," O'Shea said. "You're not a cop."

Aidan cut Franco off before his lips finished forming a sharp *F*. "I'm sorry, but O'Shea's right. Let us do our job."

Franco folded his arms across the chest, his forehead deeply creased. He wanted to believe they were all on the same page, except he still hated O'Shea's guts, and didn't trust him. But the prick *did* have a problem: someone went out of their way to make him the fall guy, something Franco hoped would motivate him enough to get off his fat ass, and do some actual police work.

"*Fine*." Franco pushed back his chair and got up. His shift started in less than an hour.

Aidan held his phone's screen up for him to see. "Is this one of the men you saw attacking Prescott?" The portrait showed a mature man in a sharp suit, with silver hair and piercing blue eyes, smiling at the camera.

"No, that's the guy that was at your precinct when you almost arrested me, last week." He shot O'Shea a dirty look, but he didn't acknowledge Franco.

"Walker," O'Shea said. "I remember seeing him there. He and the captain go way back. If you wanna take any of this to Kaplan, you better have an ironclad case. And he'll likely still run straight to Walker."

Aidan showed Franco a black-and-white photo of a group of uniformed cops. "What about him, the one in the middle?"

"No, doesn't look familiar. Um, can I talk to you for a moment?"

Aidan nodded and walked him to the door. Neither O'Shea nor Franco said goodbyes.

They stepped into the hallway and Aidan closed the door behind him. "I *am* sorry I blindsided you, but if I had to, I'd do it again."

"Hell of an apology."

Aidan's eyes hardened. "Oh, stop acting like a five-year-old. We cleared the air, made progress, and have a lead because we shared important information. *You're welcome.*"

Franco clenched his fists, mirroring Aidan's expression. "I'm aware I have trust issues, and if you knew me better you'd understand why. What you did didn't help matters, but…I get why you did it. You better be damned sure you can trust him."

"I am." Aidan sighed. "I want to get the people responsible for your dad's murder."

Whether or not he liked how they'd arrived there, Franco couldn't deny progress. "I gotta go, and you have work to do." He waved a halfhearted farewell and walked away. He pressed the button for the elevator and looked back at Aidan. "Hey, listen, I'm sorry…about earlier. My experience with the police has been less than…anyway, I know you're doing your best, and I shouldn't have implied you're all crooks." He nodded his head toward Aidan's apartment. "Still not sure about that one, though."

The elevator dinged, the doors opened, and he left.

Aidan closed the door behind him. O'Shea, standing in front of the table, threw him a harsh glance. "Are you two…?"

"Are we what?"

"Oh for fuck's sake, don't make me say it."

Aidan crossed the space and picked up the files from his table. "No, and I don't know what this has to do with anything, or how that's any of your business."

O'Shea grimaced. "Well, I guess there's my answer, right there. I don't have to tell you how unprofessional that is."

"No, you truly are the last person to speak to me about police conduct."

O'Shea sighed. "Fine, but if this gets back to the department or the DA, it's my ass on the line, too."

Aidan locked eyes with him. "Then let's make sure it won't get to that."

Chapter Thirty-Three

Aidan played O'Shea Romano's confession, then filled him in on the rest, including the news about Franco's trust fund, on their ride out to New Jersey. O'Shea reacted as expected. "A million bucks sounds like a lot of motive to me. Even buys you a hitman or two. Just because he wasn't in the room doesn't mean he's not connected. And given your...involvement with DiMaso, your judgement is hardly the soundest."

"Let it go. He had nothing to do with Prescott's murder. Guy's barely hanging on as it is."

O'Shea growled, and Aidan pulled into the parking lot of Hank Porter's Blue River Diner. A few tattered and neglected stores next to a row of older, three-story homes lined the road on either side.

They exited the car and entered the small diner, a hollow sounding bell above the door announcing their arrival. The fifties interior, like the neighborhood, lacked proper care, having lost its luster over the years.

A group of teenagers occupied two of the booths, cackling and talking over one another, as Frank Sinatra sang from the speakers about flying to the moon. A woman in her sixties waited on two old-timers sitting at the counter. She glanced at Aidan, grabbed a menu, and headed their way.

"Anywhere you like, honey," she said warmly. She wore her red hair in a ponytail, and her considerable curves tested the limits of her uniform's elasticity in several places.

"We're not eating," O'Shea said, flashing his badge. "We're here to see Hank Porter."

She nodded. "My brother's in the kitchen. I'll get him for you. Coffee while you wait?"

"No," Aidan said, smiling. "Thank you."

O'Shea observed the diner with his nose scrunched up. "Place is a dump."

"How about you keep that to yourself. We're here to get answers, not alienate more people."

A man Aidan's height approached, wiping his hands on a stained apron. He sized them up and his eyes turned suspicious faster than he managed to produce a saccharine smile. "What can I do for my brothers in blue?"

Judging by the white hair and lines around his mouth and eyes, Aidan guessed him in his seventies, but the T-shirt under his apron exposed a hard frame and muscular arms. Porter's good-natured expression cracked when he recognized O'Shea. He nodded at him, then shook Aidan's hand. "What brings you out here, Detectives? Aren't you out of your jurisdiction?"

"Aidan Torrance, Mr. Porter. We're hoping you can help shed some light on an old case."

"Really, which case is that?" Porter's eye twitched, belying his rendition of a poker face.

Aidan kept his tone level, watching him closely. "We're taking another crack at the DiMaso case."

Porter's eyes darted between them, his voice calm when he spoke. "Such a long time ago, not sure how much help I'll be. Follow me, best to talk outside," he said quietly, nodding towards the kitchen door. They followed him behind the counter and through the kitchen before exiting into a small backyard.

"I've been off the job for nearly two decades, I don't really keep in the loop anymore." Porter's chuckle sounded forced. Ever the diplomat, O'Shea said, "Hard to believe, considering you had your nose in everyone's business back in the day."

Porter's expression tightened. "I wouldn't go that far, but yes, people talked to me. I was approachable," he said curtly, the *unlike you* implied.

"Frank DiMaso," O'Shea said. "What do you know about his relationship with Walker and MacCaffrey?"

"You're asking me? You were his *partner*," he said, pronouncing the word facetiously.

"You know we didn't hang out and exchange cooking recipes. Did he talk to you about them?"

"No, even you should know better than that." Hank Porter's face twitched with anger. But Aidan got the impression he was also afraid of O'Shea. "Frank was a stand-up guy, he never talked about anyone behind their backs, including you."

"Yes, a real saint."

Porter's jammed his lips together, and O'Shea took a step forward. "You were the desk sergeant and knew everybody's business. If you have such respect for the guy, how about you grow some balls and show it?"

Porter raised his shoulders and drew his neck in like a turtle. "I may not have been your idea of a great cop, but I did my job well. I don't need your approval." Despite his meek posture, he seemed ready for battle. "You wanna know what happened to Frank? Start by looking at yourself, why don't you? Where were you forty years ago, when you could have made a difference?" He pointed at O'Shea. "I'm not the one who beat the crap out of the person who had my back, too pissed at my mess of a life, and drowning every problem in an ocean of booze. You talk a big game, but if it weren't for Frank, you wouldn't be standing here today, carrying a badge."

"Fuck you, I don't owe that man a damn thing!"

Porter took an instinctive step back, and Aidan positioned himself between the two men.

Porter said, "You think you'd still have a job if he hadn't spoken up for you after you nearly beat him to a pulp? And that bogus alibi of yours, think you'd still be around, had the truth come out?"

O'Shea's angry mask cracked, and Porter smirked. His shoulders relaxed, and he grew several inches, but Aidan's stomach lurched. "Lucky for you I didn't speak up then, either, or Reynolds would have kicked your ass to the curb right then and there."

O'Shea stepped back. He caught Aidan's inquisitive look and said, "I spent the night at the drunk tank, over at the 10th. Reynolds put me on suspension after my incident with Frank…after I showed up drunk and made those threats against him, a few nights before he died. Reynolds gave me an ultimatum: never touch booze again, and work through my anger issues, or he'd personally kick me off the force and make sure I'd not land so much as a shopping mall gig."

"And yet, only days later, you got wasted again," Porter said with contempt. "Your pals at the 10th kept their mouths shut, and let you sleep it off, and so did I. Lucky for you, the blackout kept everyone's attention on more pressing matters. But your career could have ended right there, and should have."

For once O'Shea kept quiet, leaning with his back against the building's wall.

"What else?" Aidan said, and Porter's triumphant expression evaporated.

"I didn't know this until a few years later," he said, lowering his head, sounding defensive. "Reynolds and I still talked from time to time, after he retired. He was always wary of old MacCaffrey and his protégé, Walker. Their collars always *appeared* sound, and they worked well as a team, but Reynolds suspected something was off. Before she died, he visited MacCaffrey's wife at their home, said their house resembled a top-notch hospital, one few of us could afford. The equipment, the round-the-clock nurses, the nice home, all on a cop's salary? MacCaffrey explained they'd come into some money on his wife's side, but Burt wasn't convinced."

Porter stopped talking and Aidan prodded, "Did he look into it?"

"No. Within a year MacCaffrey and his wife were dead, and Burt decided to let sleeping dogs lie. Walker took MacCaffrey Junior under his wing, and when they formed the organized crime division, Reynolds assigned Frank and O'Shea to the team. He knew Frank would never stand for police misconduct or mistreatment of suspects and hoped to plant a spy of sorts. Frank didn't know Reynolds was using him to keep an eye on Walker, or bring him down, if necessary."

"Why didn't you come forward then?" Aidan said.

"I had my own problems, and it wasn't my fight. Besides, I was not going to repeat hearsay against a someone like Walker." Aidan opened his mouth, but Porter shook his head. "There's no such thing as a confidential informant.

Rats don't do well in the department, and my career would have been ruined, or worse."

He had a point. Whistleblowers were often openly shunned and The Blue Wall of Silence prevented many honest cops from ratting on crooked colleagues, afraid of repercussions within their own ranks.

"Did you ever suspect Walker and MacCaffrey were involved in DiMaso's murder?"

Porter shrugged. "Walker is a cold blooded son of a bitch, hard to think he'd go that far. Still…"

"What?" O'Shea said impatiently.

Porter glowered at him, then addressed Aidan. "I overheard them argue, Frank and Walker, two nights before the murder. At first, I couldn't see who spoke. One of them demanded to know what had happened to some evidence, and the other claimed not to know what he was talking about. I later believed hearing Walker finally admit *someone* took it, without naming the person, and promising he'd make it right, that DiMaso should cool his jets. It was a crazy busy night and the squad room noise drowned out everything else. But I remember one of them giving the other an ultimatum."

Porter lowered his head again, remorseful. "Frank stormed right past without noticing me, and Walker left out the back door with his head turned. I forgot about it, but when news broke Frank had been killed I thought about talking to Reynolds. But truth is, I didn't want to get involved. Frank was a standup guy and would have given you the shirt off his back. I never saw him do or say anything questionable, and yet, when they found money and drugs allegedly belonging to him, I began to wonder. That maybe I misheard, and Walker confronted Frank, not the other way around. And the more I thought about it, the less I wanted to know."

"We'll need your official statement," Aidan said, but Porter shook his head.

"I've seen witnesses against Walker recant, and in one case, disappear. I quit the force, Detective, I'm out. My wife is already in Florida and I will follow in a week, and my sister's family will continue running the diner. I told you what you came to hear, and that's as far as I'll go."

"Coward." O'Shea stared at Hank Porter, who shrank back, his face crimson.

"You're the last person to point fingers. You think you get a free pass because you were a drunk at the time? You don't get to judge, least of all me."

Keeping his frustration in check, Aidan said, "Mr. Porter, I understand you're worried, but Frank's family deserves justice."

"I am sorry, Detective. Frank was a good guy, and I knew his brother Sal from his time at our station house. But I have my own life to live, my own family to worry about."

"We can protect—"

"No." Porter shook his head. "I'll take my chances on my own terms, thank you very much."

Aidan pulled out a business card. "Please, at least think about it. I promise to keep your information confidential as far as I can."

"What's the use?" O'Shea spat on the ground. "Once a coward always a coward." He turned and stomped back into the diner, the door slamming behind him.

Aidan shook Hank Porter's hand and followed after O'Shea. He caught up with him in the parking lot, the sun dipping toward the horizon.

"This prick is a disgrace. He should have never been a cop." O'Shea got into the car and slammed the door. Considering his lousy treatment of his former partner, Aidan felt O'Shea was in no position to judge. But he only said, "Let him sleep on it, I'll try talking to him again. What's our next move?"

O'Shea turned in his seat and studied him for a moment. "You sure you wanna do this? I'm out in a few, but you have your entire career ahead of you."

"And when I look back, I want to be able to say I didn't take the easy road. I want to get to the truth."

"All I'm saying is, he better be worth it."

Aidan narrowed his eyes. "Let me make this clear, I'm not doing this as a *favor* to anyone. I'm going where the evidence takes me. If Walker and MacCaffrey are guilty, they need to be stopped." He remembered something.

"How well did you know Kane and Morrow, the detectives who investigated DiMaso's murder?"

O'Shea shrugged. "They were all right. Old school, but thorough, and why Reynolds assigned them. Not that it made much of a difference. Why?"

"I checked the copies I got from Sal DiMaso against the files Sanders provided, and they don't match up. DiMaso's are missing two witness statements, one by a Kathy Simmons, a forty-one-year-old school teacher who was walking her dog, two blocks over. She didn't hear the shooting but reported a car without lights nearly running her over, describing it as something the police would drive undercover, like on the TV shows, and remembered half a New York license plate. The other was a Ron Salerno, a sixty-year-old banker who gave a description of a running homeless man who almost caused a traffic accident. Think Morrow and Kane could've been holding out on DiMaso?"

O'Shea shook his head. "Don't see it. Why would they? They all went way back."

"How close were Morrow and Kane with Walker and MacCaffrey?"

O'Shea pursed his lips. "I see what you're saying." He sighed and shook his head. "Don't know. Then again, I didn't think any of what you told me could be true, so...all right, let's go back, pull all available files on everyone, see what shakes loose. They've been careful, clearly, but I guarantee you no one passes through life without making a single mistake. Let's find theirs."

Chapter Thirty-Four

After leaving Aidan's place, Franco barely had enough time to rush home and change into fresh clothes before racing over to the restaurant. His failure to trust him unquestioningly frustrated him, and his fixation on O'Shea as a killer had made him develop tunnel vision.

Yes, Franco had made some spectacularly bad decisions when he was younger. Wanting to belong, longing to be liked, he'd put his trust in some people who used him, and hurt him deeply. But Aidan had shown he was on his side, even if Franco didn't like his approach.

At least they knew names now. He couldn't find much on MacCaffrey, but Walker made the news a few times in recent years, especially since becoming an official contender as the next mayor. Silver-haired and blue-eyed, the gaunt man rarely smiled in any of the photos, and Franco couldn't believe how close he'd stood to the person responsible for his father's murder.

He finally called his mother, and they spoke for a few minutes. He didn't tell her about his trip, but promised to go see her and talk more on the weekend. He'd fill her in then.

Gino and Carmine knew something was up the minute he walked through the door, but Franco stalled, promising to talk more later. He finished his shift and reached Friction a little after ten. The club filled quickly, and the guys had their hands full all night. Thursdays featured guest DJs playing a more contemporary, electronic club vibe, largely stripped of vocals, and generally attracting a younger crowd.

Around three in the morning, only a handful of people remained, finishing their drinks at the bar.

Ben winced as he put a rack with dirty glasses on the counter next to Franco. "I'm getting too old for this shit, my back is killing me."

Franco nodded. "Tell me about it. Some nights I feel like I aged a decade in four hours."

Cheryl Lynn's "You Saved My Day" announced Vince's arrival behind the turntable for the last couple of songs for the night.

Jerry returned to the bar with a crate of empty beer bottles. "We're gonna grab brunch over at Tartine on West 11th, later, wanna join?"

"Hells, yeah," Franco said, his face brightening, "I've been craving their apple pancakes for weeks."

Ben winked. "It's a date, then."

Franco's bladder pushed uncomfortably, and he excused himself. He made his way through the swinging doors and down to the end of hallway into the empty, dimly lit men's room. Bottles, plastic cups, and tumblers lay wherever guests had left, and in some cases dropped them, and lingering wafts of urine and stale beer stifled his enthusiasm to return and collect the mess in a bit. The joys of club life.

He stepped up to the urinal, unbuttoned his jeans, and got to it. The door to his left opened and a tall guy entered, setting up shop next to him. Franco turned his head, giving the dark-haired, thirty-ish hunk with the smooth, light brown skin, and white T-shirt stretched tight across an impressive chest a quick once-over. A toothpick dangled from the left corner of his mouth, and Franco wondered if he'd walked into the wrong club by mistake.

"'Sup?" he said, looking vaguely familiar.

"Hey," Franco replied, trying to concentrate on the task at hand. Company tended to jam him up. He casually lowered his gaze down the man's sculpted arms, covered with exquisite Japanese tattoos, to the guy's hand, holding the biggest dong he'd ever seen. A tattooed scorpion graced the brown shaft all the way up to below the navel. Franco nearly dropped his jaw and averted his eyes, wincing inwardly at the pain he must have endured getting the ink, not to mention any poor bastard on the receiving end of that monster.

He finished and with a quick nod, made his way to the sink. He took two steps.

Japanese sleeves, not shirt sleeves! The short hair was wrong, but that face...

Heart in his throat, Franco spun around, wide eyed. But the stranger had already zipped up and traded his dick for a switchblade. He advanced so fast Franco could barely stumble backwards. Frantically grabbing at anything near him, he snatched an empty beer bottle and threw it at his attacker. And missed. The guy veered toward a stall to avoid the projectile. Franco slipped on the wet floor and fell, just as the man came at him again. The blade slashed Franco's shoulder, and he yelled out in pain. But his fall threw his attacker off balance, too. Franco kicked the guy's groin and he doubled over with a sharp grunt, steadying himself against the wall.

He scrambled away, seeing smears of his own blood on the floor, and his mouth filled with the bitter taste of bile.

Don't look, *get out!* His hands slipped as he crawled away while frantically kicking his attacker's wrist. The guy yelled in pain and dropped the blade, sending it skittering across the floor.

Franco pulled himself up at the sink, ripped open the door, and stumbled into the empty hallway. Cheryl still carried on at full volume. Hands grabbed him roughly from behind before he'd taken two steps, slamming him against the wall. His head smacked against the hard surface, the pain temporarily drowning out all sound, but featuring a spectacular light show.

From behind, one muscular arm clamped around his throat like a vise, and a fist punched him in the kidneys. His eyes watered, and his cut-off air supply was all that kept him from throwing up. Franco twisted and bucked, clawing at the arm crushing his throat, but he couldn't break free.

He felt himself dragged backward through the emergency exit, and hot jolts shot through him. If they made it into the back alley, he'd be dead.

Letting go of the arm around his throat, he grabbed the door frame, his fingers slipping. Tears ran down his face, and everything dimmed.

In a final effort he braced his shoes against the door frame, let go, and pushed off as hard as he could. His stomach lurched and the world toppled over. Hurtling down the stairs, pain assaulted him from every angle, but the pressure around his throat ceased. Suddenly free, Franco slammed against the metal railing and landed face first in a pile of trash bags at the bottom of the stairs. He gasped for air and retched, his throat on fire.

Pushing himself up, he coughed, managing three steps before collapsing to his knees again. He saw the guy's fist a split second before it plowed into his jaw. Numb and faint, a deafening ringing in his ears, Franco hit the pavement. He rolled onto his back and tasted blood, the guy looming over him like a demon.

Everything around him tuned out, and he squeezed his eyes shut amidst thoughts of his mother and sister, and the faint realization he'd never even had a chance to wash his hands.

Chapter Thirty-Five

Friday, August 5

Numbing pain registered a good deal before Franco succeeded in blinking at dark, backlit shapes hovering over him. He flinched reflexively and yelped, fighting the urge to vomit.

"He's coming to," Ben said. Franco's eyes slowly focused on three concerned faces gazing down at him. His effort to sit up ceased halfway through, his teeth gritted.

"Easy, lie still." Ben was kneeling beside him and gingerly touched his shoulder. "Something may be broken."

Franco lifted a hand to his stinging throat, the simple gesture nearly wiping him out.

"What the hell happened, who was that guy?" Jerry said.

A chill gripped Franco's insides. He'd almost died. His stomach churned and his eyes brimmed with hot tears.

"Are you all right?"

Franco raised his head with a weak nod. Vince had a bloody gash above his eye, and his clothes were disheveled.

"What...happened...to you?"

"He hit a brick wall," Jerry said, sounding impressed. "I couldn't believe my eyes."

"The emergency door triggered the silent alarm," Vince said. "I came to check, and saw the guy beating the crap out of you."

Franco tensed, wishing he hadn't. "Where...is he?"

"We chased him off. Lie still. I'll take you to the emergency room. Be right back." Vince groaned as he got up and headed up the stairs.

"Who was that guy?" Jerry said again.

Franco coughed. "Killed Charles."

"Holy shit, are you serious?"

"Am...I bleeding?"

"Yeah, we should get you to a hospital. Good thing Vince jumped in when he did, literally," Jerry said. "I never thought I'd see the day that man excelled at *anything* physical."

Franco blinked. "What?"

"When I got to the door, Vince leapt off the staircase like frigging Wonder Woman," he said with an admiring chuckle. "Granted, motherfucker batted him away like a gnat, but he hightailed it as soon as he saw us coming."

Franco fidgeted, but his arm weighed a ton. "Gotta call...Aidan. My phone..."

"Let me do it." Ben awkwardly stuck his hand into Franco's jeans pocket, fingers fumbling for the device.

Franco clenched his jaw. "Last time...you showed more finesse."

"Last time your pants were around your ankles."

Clanging steps on the metal stairs announced Vince's return. "Okay, let's get you to the emergency room."

"Do you need help?" Jerry asked.

"I'll manage, I'd rather you stay and close up here."

Ben nodded. "Call if you need us."

Franco looked at Vince and choked up, his words trapped in his throat. Vince nodded with a smile and squeezed his hand. "Can you stand, or should we call the paramedics?"

"No...I can manage."

With Jerry and Ben's help, he rose to a sitting position, ignoring the pain.

Ben eyed him with concern. "You don't look so good."

"Don't worry, I'm fine," Franco said, and tossed his cookies.

* * *

"You are very lucky, young man. No broken bones." Dr. Sims eyed Franco over her glasses as she read from a file on the clipboard in her hands. Her short cropped gray hair stood in stark contrast to her smooth, nearly wrinkle free dark skin.

"Young man?" Vince said, cocking a brow. Franco discreetly extended half a middle finger in his direction. Sitting topless on a hospital bed in the bright, modern examination room at Lenox Health, he'd patiently waited his turn before spending two hours being poked, prodded, and bandaged.

"You have a couple of bruised ribs," she continued, "and your jaw will hurt the next few days, but from everything you described things could have gone far worse. How are you feeling?"

"Peachy…the painkillers kicked in."

"Good, but you should still get as much rest as you can, you bumped your head pretty good."

A nurse had applied medical strips across the cuts on his right temple and left brow, and he'd received six stitches for the nasty gash across his deltoid and triceps. Bandages covered the patches of torn skin on his ribcage he got from skidding across the pavement.

"Please contact your primary physician immediately if nausea and dizziness increase. Minor head traumas can take two, three weeks before you feel back to your old self again, so try limiting your time in front of computers, or the TV. And you should avoid strenuous labor, including the gym, for at least two weeks."

Franco groaned and the hint of a smile dashed across her subtly painted red lips. She gave him the number of a physiatrist and told him to keep his wounds clean to avoid an infection. "And try to breathe normally, even if it's uncomfortable."

Franco spotted Aidan speaking to a nurse, who pointed him in their direction. As angry as he'd been earlier, he couldn't recall a moment he'd been happier to see him. In tan jeans and a white polo, he'd dressed more casual than Franco had ever seen him.

"Are you all right?"

"I'll live."

Aidan gently put a hand on his good shoulder, and his skin tingled. "Did you recognize the man who attacked you?"

"He's the guy from the video, the one who killed Charles."

Dr. Sims' eyes widened, but she remained quiet.

"Did he say anything to you?"

"No, he was too busy dismantling me. He walked up to me at the urinal, and I thought he was checking me out. His attack caught me completely off guard…but Vince jumped him, literally."

"Call me Tarzan," Vince introduced himself with a wink, shaking Aidan's hand. "Nice to finally meet you."

"You, too. Have you ever seen the man at your club before?"

"I only saw him from behind," Vince said, shaking his head. "And by the time my barmen caught up, he'd run off. But we have six cameras recording the premises, he's got to be on one of them."

Aidan fished a business card out of his pocket and handed it to Vince. "Please get me the footage as soon as possible."

"Of course, I'll do it as soon as I get home."

Franco addressed Dr. Sims. "Am I free to go, or do you need to run more tests?"

Dr. Sims shook her head, handing him a release form. "No, sign here at the bottom and you are good to go."

He did as instructed, thanked her, then she said goodbye and departed.

With Aidan's help, Franco slowly pushed himself off the bed. Vince handed him the remnants of his torn T-shirt and helped him put it back on over his head.

Franco winced.

"I'm taking you to my place," Aidan said. Standing behind him, Vince suggestively wiggled his eyebrows at Franco. With the guys supporting him on either side, he limped down the corridor, thrilled to leave the hospital.

Outside, Vince said, "Call me if you need anything, okay?"

Franco hugged him as hard as he could manage. "Thank you, Vince. For everything…"

"Of course," he said, smiling. "And that's Mr. Weissmuller to you."

"Weissmuller?" Franco blinked, flashing an innocent smile. "Wasn't Cheetah played by an ape?"

Chapter Thirty-Six

Saturday, August 6

Aidan took one last sip of his coffee and set the mug on the dining room table. Stifling a yawn, he leaned back in his chair, his eyes gazing out the living room window, the caffeine only barely keeping him awake at one in the afternoon. He watched the sunlight dance across the Hudson River in the distance and pushed away a half-eaten sandwich.

He gently massaged his temples and closed his tired eyes. No time to slow down, even after spending half the night combing through old databases and newspaper stories, picking Franco up at the hospital, and spending the rest of the morning watching footage from Prescott's apartment. At least, the new information finally formed a clearer picture.

Prescott's cloud stored a week of recordings up to the night of his death, showing him at the apartment on four other nights. Every time he would arrive, maybe eat something he brought along, then spend the rest of the time sitting on a chair, gazing out the window, all of it in total darkness. Sometimes he slept on the mattress, sometimes he left again. Prescott never behaved sexually inappropriately, and though still a bit creepy, Aidan got the impression he really was only there to make sure Franco was all right.

He'd only scratched the surface on the extensive files on Lombardi. Too soon to tell how much connected to his case, but they confirmed he and MacCaffrey Senior indeed grew up in the same neighborhood in Queens in the thirties, and attended the same schools. Though both made the news several times later in life for entirely different reasons, no report mentioned them as friends, and it would require deeper digging to find people or documents confirming their connection. He felt confident he would, in time, except, of course, he had none.

He'd finally accessed the NYPD's Domain Awareness System, and NCIC, the FBI's National Crime Information Center for more information, although he worried about exposure, in case anyone had flagged files or names connected to their case. Nothing he could do about it now.

MacCaffrey Junior and Walker made the news a few times throughout the 80s and 90s. Usually with arrests of various lower and middle status members from every one of New York City's most prominent Mob families...except the Lombardis. Granted, Mick Lombardi ran a much smaller operation, but it raised Aidan's suspicions.

Cops doing the Mob's dirty work was tough to swallow. But it had happened before, and he couldn't deny the possibility any longer. Every few years a new scandal rocked one of the nation's major police units, exposing crooks ranging from patrol cops to the highest ranking officers abusing their positions and powers. He was tired of it, hated that actions of a few undermined the efforts of tens of thousands of honest and hardworking women and men, tarnishing an increasingly strained relationship between law enforcement and the public.

He got up and stood by the window, basking in the warmth penetrating the glass.

Documents and news reports all showed MacCaffrey retired from the force in 2001 at the rank of detective second grade, and Walker made it all the way to captain. He left in 2009 steadily climbing the ranks outside of the department, both politically and as a security expert for huge corporations, before throwing his hat into the mayoral race. And though he wasn't the most popular contender, he had strong political allies, as well as support from the police department. No wonder he'd been ahead of the investigation every step of the way.

Aidan stretched his limbs and returned to the table, revisiting everything he thought he knew so far: Frank DiMaso got wind Walker and MacCaffrey were working for Lombardi, confronted them. They picked up junkie snitch Leo Bauer and his lover, Prescott. But Bauer refused, despite heavy duress, and Prescott agreed to do it instead. Things didn't go well, and he promptly fled the scene after the murder.

With DiMaso dead and Prescott in rehab, keeping his mouth shut, he posed no imminent threat to Walker, MacCaffrey or Lombardi. Then Lombardi was killed in '85 and everyone sort of disbanded. The media reported Lombardi's business meetings had always been top secret, yet the killers knew exactly where to strike, and when, suggesting the Mob's commission had been cleaning house. Witnesses couldn't agree whether two, three, or four masked men were spotted leaving the closed restaurant, and no further descriptions were given, no arrests made.

Fast forward thirty years, Franco and Prescott meet, and Prescott grows a conscience. Within months he's dead and DiMaso's murder book disappears. The attack on Franco left no doubt he was next in line.

Aidan yawned again. He was supposed to drive up to New Rochelle and relieve O'Shea, who had been surveilling MacCaffrey's house all night, but the attempt on Franco's life changed everything. Aidan had underestimated the situation, and the attack rattled him more than he thought possible, surprised by his feelings for Franco.

It bothered him. He couldn't afford to be distracted, and besides, he wasn't ready for anything new after Josh. Something still prevented him from moving on. Himself, probably.

The ringing phone ripped him from his wandering thoughts, and he answered.

"Not much happening out here, what's the word on your end?" O'Shea said.

"Why are you still up? We agreed you'd go home and get some sleep."

"I did plenty of thirty hour stakeouts in my day, this isn't going to kill me. Besides, after everything that went down last night we can't afford to lose sight of MacCaffrey. He didn't leave the house until this morning. Swung by a hardware store, and a diner. Now we're back at his house."

"If I leave now, I can relieve you in about an hour."

"Anything on DiMaso's attacker?"

"The perp blocked out the club's security camera in the hallway, so there's no footage of the attack inside. But the outdoor cameras got everything. Carter is working on pulling a clear face shot. Hold on a sec."

Aidan opened his computer and checked his inbox. Bingo. The tech's message contained a digital rap sheet featuring the photo of a handsome man with light brown skin and black, shoulder length hair, facing the camera in utter boredom.

"Got him. Name's Jesús Armando Martinez, age thirty-three. Arrest record dates back to '98."

"Early start."

"Various charges of assault, armed robbery...and possession of drugs with intent to sell. Charged with rape on two occasions, but both victims recanted. Suspected in two homicides in 2005 and 2012, but not enough evidence to make it stick." Aidan sighed, scrolled down. "Did three years in Rikers for the drugs and has been staying all over the place since he got out, two years ago, usually with a girlfriend. There's an address for his mother's place in Brownsville, but it says here she's recently deceased. Outstanding features are Japanese sleeves on both arms, a skull on his left calf, and...a scorpion on his dick."

"That ought to narrow it down."

Aidan's fingers flew across the computer's keyboard. Armed with Martinez' name, his search in the DAS and NCIC produced fast results. He felt a rush of adrenaline. "We got two sealed arrests from when he was still a juvenile. Not sure a judge will grant us access, but guess the name of the arresting officer on the others."

"Walker."

"MacCaffrey, and Martinez walked on both with nary a dent."

O'Shea grunted. "Must have been more valuable to MacCaffrey to keep the kid on the streets."

"I can't find a paper trail of Martinez as an informant, but it doesn't mean he wasn't."

"He might be hiding out at his mom's place. Let's check."

"Give me five minutes, I'll call you back and text you the address."

Of course Franco had secretly wished to find himself in Aidan's bed, someday, barely able to move. He'd just imagined it would be from hours of mind-blowing, acrobatic sex, not recuperating from a thrashing by a psycho.

Dressed in a blue sports brief, his eyes traveled down his bruised, bandaged, aching body. Clearly, swimsuit season had wrapped early for him. Memories of his attacker's arm squeezing the air from his throat flooded back, and he choked up. Someone almost succeeded in killing him, and if not for Vince...

Behind him the door creaked, and Franco slowly raised himself to a sitting position, teeth gritted. Aidan entered, holding his laptop. "How are you feeling?"

Franco tilted his head and sighed. "Sore, the good stuff's wearing off. I should call my mom, but part of me really doesn't want to. Telling her what happened is only gonna make everything *so* much worse. She'll insist on coming into town, and I don't want her to become another target."

Aidan sat next to him on the bed. "Then wait a day. You're pretty banged up, and maybe tomorrow you'll look less gruesome."

"Thanks."

"You know what I mean. Imagine how she'd feel seeing you like this." He touched Franco's arm. "I think we identified the man who attacked you." He turned the computer's screen towards him. The photo was a few years old, but Franco tensed anyway.

"He cut his hair. Did they get him?"

"No, we found him in the system from the security footage. We're trying to locate him. Clearly, he's aware you saw him the night he killed Prescott, and considers you a loose end. Chances are he'll try again."

Franco's heart thumped against his chest. "Great pep talk." Would he be looking over his shoulders for the rest of his potentially brief life?

"Sorry, I didn't mean to scare you. He may have already fled the city, but

I'm not willing to take that chance. O'Shea and I are going after him."

Franco pushed himself off the bed with a low groan.

"What are you doing?"

"Coming with you."

"You can't come." Aidan shook his head, lifting his hand in a calming, broad arc. "You have to heal. You'll be safe here."

Franco mimicked his gesture. "Is that supposed to be some kind of Jedi mind trick? Forget it. You're taking off on a wild goose chase without a clue where that asshole may or may not be, *and* you just said he might come after me again. For all I know he's creeping about in your hallway, waiting for you to leave."

"Listen—"

"There's no safer place than with you. Bind me, gag me, lock me in the fucking trunk of your car for all I care—I'm coming, end of discussion."

Aidan's phone rang, and he answered, his face doing a near perfect impression of O'Shea. "Yes."

"Get moving, something's up!" O'Shea said over his car's revving engine. "MacCaffrey bolted out of his home and took off like a bat out of hell, talking to someone on his phone."

"Did you lose him?"

"I'll pretend I didn't hear that. I'm four cars behind and I think he's headed for the I-678. He seemed furious. How much you want to bet he's meeting up with Martinez or Walker?"

Aidan chewed his lip, but Franco couldn't read his expression.

"Okay, we're on our way," Aidan said, "Call you when I'm in the car."

"*We? What—?*"

Aidan ended the call and threw Franco a stern look. "All right, you got one minute to get dressed."

"Like you had a choice."

Aidan's stare silenced him, and he hurried as fast as his injuries permitted. He put on his jeans and borrowed one of Aidan's polos, then limped after him out the door. He didn't want to be left behind, but the prospect of what lay ahead didn't excite him in the least.

It terrified him.

Chapter Thirty-Seven

The Ford barreled down the streets with howling sirens and blazing lights. Aidan expertly navigated them out of Manhattan, and across the Williamsburg Bridge. Franco slid down in his seat and held on to door and dashboard to keep from being tossed around, the seatbelt cutting painfully into his injuries.

Aidan stared out the window, his expression grim. No question, he didn't want him along, but Franco couldn't tell whether he was pissed or concerned. To top things off, he'd forgotten his pain pills.

"I don't want you to get hurt," Aidan finally said.

"Thanks, but I'd say that ship has sailed. For all we know, no one's there," he added, more for his benefit than Aidan's.

They hit the parkway, then turned left. A car ahead of them slowed down. Aidan's sirens seemed to confuse the driver and, seemingly unsure which way to turn, and the car came to a complete halt in the middle of the street.

Aidan's phone rang, and he put it on speaker.

"Where the hell are you?" O'Shea sounded tense. "MacCaffrey entered Martinez's home two minutes ago."

"Howard Avenue, a car is blocking us." The vehicle ahead of them lurched to one side, and they zoomed past it. "You saw Martinez?"

"No, the door opened just wide enough for MacCaffrey to enter. I snapped a few shots with my phone."

"Okay, we're about four minutes out, where are you?"

"I'm one block down the street and approaching the house on foot. I'm sure he didn't make me, but something feels off." O'Shea's voice turned to a harsh whisper. "I can hear them argue."

"Hear them? How close to the damn house are you? Did you call for backup?"

"And risk tipping someone off? If this gets to Walker, we lose any chance of surprise. I want evidence before we make a move."

"I don't like it, it's too—"

"Just get here. If Martinez is there, we'll arrest him, but I wanna see how this plays out with MacCaffrey first. And kill the fucking sirens." O'Shea hung up.

"God damn it!" Aidan hit the wheel and shut off the sirens. "Fucking traffic, *move.*" He bypassed another car by using half of the empty sidewalk and turned a corner with squealing tires. Franco's eyes doubled in size, but he clamped his mouth shut as they raced past rows of homes, more than a few suffering from age and neglect, their doors and windows covered by thick iron bars.

"You'll stay in the car."

"Not a problem." Franco wouldn't go near Martinez until he was in shackles.

Three blocks later Aidan slowed down, then brought the car to a halt next to a graffiti covered, abandoned two story building. Franco craned his neck and studied his surroundings. Heavy gray clouds darkened the sky. He couldn't spot a single person on the street. Aidan got out of the car, popped the trunk, and reappeared a moment later on Franco's side, wearing a dark bulletproof vest over his polo. He opened the door and handed a spare to Franco. "Put this on and keep your ass glued to the seat."

Fastening a portable radio to his belt, Aidan trotted down the street, swearing under his breath. He couldn't see O'Shea anywhere. The old coot had better have waited and not gone off and done something stupid. He unholstered his Glock and carefully advanced the single-story house across the street. The teal paint on the roof and walls was chipped, the untended lawn covered in yellow grass. Dying shrubs covered two front facing windows protected by corroding iron bars, and curtains prevented him from seeing into the home.

He heard shouting, but couldn't make out any words.

Two shots rang through the air in quick succession, and Aidan's adrenaline spiked. He ducked and sprinted toward the house, then pushed himself against the wall on the door's left side, straining his ears for sounds. Nothing.

He reached for the knob and opened the door as quietly as possible. A wall of baked stale odor hit his nose.

Inside the gloomy place furniture lay upturned, with beer cans and old pizza boxes strewn about the floor. But no movement. He entered the small living room quietly and let his eyes adjust, the Glock raised waist-high.

Blood pounded in his ears as he tried to control his breathing. Where was O'Shea? Who'd fired the shots?

He knew failure to announce his presence could backfire, but giving away his position could end things real fast if Martinez or MacCaffrey were hiding and waiting.

Why the hell was it so quiet?

Ahead, a narrow corridor with two doors on the right led from the living room. He moved forward cautiously, then saw a pair of feet sticking out from behind an old recliner. His eyes darted back toward the hallway to verify it was empty, then he rushed over to the unmoving, half naked man lying on the floor.

Aidan touched the guy's neck, not really expecting to find a pulse, considering he'd been shot in the face point blank. Twice.

The gaping wounds were fresh, but Aidan could have sworn the shots had come from the other end of the house. The head of a tattooed scorpion peeked out from the dead man's jeans. Martinez. Damn it, he'd wanted him alive.

Aidan clenched his teeth and scanned the floor for a weapon, but couldn't find one.

A faint banging noise from the other end of the hallway startled him. He got up with his back against the wall and peeked around the corner into the hallway. Empty. He inched forward to the first room and pushed the door open. It squeaked so loud he might as well have lit a firecracker to announce his presence. So much for the element of surprise.

But no one rushed forward, and he found the messy bedroom empty. There was that noise again. Turning his head in its direction, ahead of him, he saw a door screen softly banging against the frame in the kitchen.

Had someone gotten out this way? Later, he needed to secure the house first.

The door to the next room stood partially open. Aidan saw a pair of feet sticking out of cheap fabric, and his body temperature dropped. He'd recognize that tacky suit anywhere.

O'Shea's breathing was shallow, but Aidan felt instant relief. He pushed the door all the way open with his foot and swung around the corner with his weapon raised, quickly scanning the medium sized bedroom room: closed door to his left, one open window ahead, black iron bars on the outside. Clothes hung from open drawers, and trinkets and papers lay strewn about a chipped, wooden desk and the floor.

Down on the grungy brown carpet, O'Shea held his chest, dark blood seeping through his shirt. He'd never bothered to put on his vest.

Aidan cursed himself for not being there to back him up, but couldn't allow guilt to sidetrack him. There'd be plenty of time later. He carefully stepped over O'Shea, never taking his eyes off the closed door as he advanced. Holding the gun in his right hand and turning the knob with his left, he pushed it open, finding the filthy Jack and Jill bathroom behind it empty. He crossed it and opened the connecting door to the hallway. No one there. A quick surveillance of the kitchen confirmed the house to be empty.

Aidan rushed back into the bedroom and knelt beside O'Shea, grabbing a shirt off the floor, and pressing it against his chest.

"Backdoor…hurry," O'Shea pressed out between contorted lips.

"MacCaffrey?"

O'Shea managed a nod. "Motherfucker…got the drop on me. Go…get the son of a bitch."

Aidan grabbed his radio and identified himself. "10-31, 10-31, I need a bus, my partner's been shot. Officer in pursuit of armed suspect." He rattled down his position and ended the radio call, then got Franco on the line on his cell phone. "I need you in here *asap*! Last room in the hallway. Apply pressure and don't let go."

He heard Franco swear and ended the call to the pop of a car door slamming outside.

Aidan touched O'Shea's shoulder. "Stay with me, help is on the way."

But O'Shea pushed him off, croaking, "Stop yapping…get him!"

Aiden straightened and raced into the kitchen, gun raised ahead of him. He crossed the small space and stepped into an empty back yard where a crooked gate opened into a back alley.

He took a deep breath, pushed it open, and charged forward in pursuit.

Chapter Thirty-Eight

"Shit," Franco hissed, limping into the house. "Shit, shit, *shit*!"

He couldn't shake the nasty tingle coursing through his body, but Aidan wouldn't have called him in unless absolutely necessary. He crossed the living room and saw Martinez' body on the floor. His stomach lurched, but he pressed on. Time for a change of scene. He'd spent way too much time around corpses lately.

The stink of foul air and rotting food intensified, and Franco held his breath. Wearing the vest over his injured ribs was painful. Heart pounding, he forced himself forward until he found the last bedroom and saw O'Shea lying on the floor, covered in blood. So much blood. He gasped and…

...stands on the sidewalk, his father lying in a dark, wet pool at his tiny feet...

Franco's knees buckled, and he held on to the door frame for support.

Flashlights cutting through darkness turn the scene before him into a vivid, grotesque picture. People stare, talk...blood everywhere. In pools, smears, footprints...stunned, he stands frozen solid, shivering, his wet shorts clinging to his legs.

Franco's breath caught in his throat, and his knuckles clutching the door frame turned white.

Breathe, move—pull yourself together!

He broke through his rigor and stumbled forward. No one else would die on his watch, not if he could help it.

Lightheaded from the sight and smell of blood, he kneeled beside O'Shea, his own injuries protesting in unison. Something hard drove into his knee. O'Shea's blood smeared gun, wedged between him and the cop's body.

"Help is on the way," Franco said through clenched teeth, pressing the soaked shirt against O'Shea's chest. His fingers turned a dark crimson as warm blood pushed out between them. Sour sweat hung in the air, and O'Shea's face looked waxy. Franco gagged, closing his eyes to fight the growing nausea, but O'Shea grabbed his arm. He stared at him, gasping for air, mumbling something that ended in *asshole*.

Franco's jaw tightened. "How about save your strength, insult me later?"

O'Shea coughed, his grip intensifying. "Shut...up. Trying to tell you...I was wrong about your father."

"Oh." His face relaxed. "Next time, lead with that."

O'Shea's eyes fluttered and closed.

"Oh, no, don't you dare die on me, you old bastard." Franco reached for another shirt from the pile and applied more pressure. Blinding pain shot up his arm, but the blood kept coming. Where was Aidan, or the damn paramedics? With one bloody hand he fished his phone from his jeans, but it slipped from his fingers and dropped to the floor.

O'Shea nodded his chin towards his lower body and winced. "My phone... recording."

"What?"

"My phone."

Franco went through O'Shea's pant pockets. "Know I'm enjoying this as little as you do."

All he came up with were a set of keys and a sticky tissue. He dropped them and moved on to the jacket. He pulled out the phone, seeing himself on the screen.

A thought struck, and he turned the camera on O'Shea. "Tell me what happened."

O'Shea panted. "They argued, MacCaffrey shot Martinez. Thought I could...corner him, but he ambushed me." His breathing grew labored. He needed a hospital, *pronto*. Where the hell was Aidan?

"Martinez' phone...find it." O'Shea coughed, and spittle and blood sprayed Franco's face.

He reeled back in horror, and O'Shea's eyes opened wide. "MacCaffrey..."

Franco heard a noise and turned his head to a gun aimed at his face. He froze.

The man holding the weapon stood some eight feet away, sweaty and disheveled, but Franco recognized him from Aidan's photograph. Older now, and heavier, he had tan skin and a buzz cut, the thinning brown hair a third rate dye job. The giveaway: a short-sleeved black shirt, exposing purple discoloration on his elbows.

Unsure what to do with his hands, Franco reflexively opened his fingers, letting the phone slip from his grasp.

"Hand it over." MacCaffrey slightly flicked the barrel of his gun. "Now!" He glanced over his shoulder, then fixed his eyes back on him.

Franco's heart pounded, and he noticed a faint movement next to his leg—O'Shea's fingers, slowly pushing the gun against his knees. Was he kidding? He'd be dead before he ever got his hands on the gun, not to mention he'd never held much less fired one. And with MacCaffrey's piece aimed at his head, the fucking vest wasn't gonna do shit.

The hint of a smirk pulled at MacCaffrey's thin lips, but before he could say anything a thumping sound from the hallway made them turn their heads. MacCaffrey quickly retracted toward the bathroom, his eyes on the door, the gun still aimed at Franco.

"Stop right there, Torrance, or he's dead."

Franco saw Aidan freeze in the hall. For a moment they made eye contact, and with a barely perceptible head shake Franco warned him against making any hasty decisions.

"It's over, MacCaffrey, give yourself up," Aidan said, inching closer. "Drop the gun and I promise we'll find a peaceful solution for this."

"Go fuck yourself, Torrance. Drop your gun and kick it over, or he's done."

Conflict showed all over Aidan's face, but he had to know he wouldn't make it half a step into the room before MacCaffrey would shoot. "Look, Sean, it's over," he said. "We got you on Martinez and Prescott."

"Three, two—"

"All right, all right." Aidan knelt and put the Glock on the floor.

"Kick it over and hit the floor, hands behind your head." Aidan pushed the gun a good distance, but remained in the doorway on his knees. MacCaffrey took a step forward, then kicked the weapon into the bathroom behind him. "Hit the floor, I said, and *you*—phone, now."

Much as Franco strained his ears, he couldn't hear sirens. They'd be dead the moment he handed over the phone. He closed his bloodied fingers around it and slowly raised his hand, desperation and anger clouding his fear. He might die here and now, but he'd do this asshole no favors.

"Go fuck yourself," he snarled, hurling the phone in one swift, painful motion at the open window...and missing it by a foot, shattering the cheap, old glass of the closed pane instead.

MacCaffrey jumped forward and Franco ducked, but Aidan pushed himself up from his kneeling position and slammed into the ex-cop. They stumbled backwards into the wall, and Aidan lunged for MacCaffrey's gun. He struck him repeatedly with one fist while restraining him with the other, but the old cop fought back hard.

O'Shea again pushed his Glock against Franco's leg, and this time he closed his wet fingers around its grip. The weapon was heavier than expected, and Franco steadied his right hand with his left, like he'd seen in movies.

Aidan slammed MacCaffrey's wrist against the wall until he dropped the gun. But MacCaffrey managed to break his other arm free and snatch a lamp from the desk, delivering a stunning blow to Aidan's head.

He reeled back, blinking, and MacCaffrey kicked him hard in the gut, sending him crashing to the floor. In a flash, MacCaffrey snatched up his gun and fired twice. Aidan grunted and dropped.

With an exasperated howl he barely registered as his own, face numb, and heart beating furiously, Franco pointed the Glock at MacCaffrey and pulled the trigger. The recoil caused his hands to buckle hard, sending a painful shock up his arm and through his body. Startled but unhurt, MacCaffrey recovered from his surprise and swung his weapon at him.

Franco fired again and again in quick succession, but MacCaffrey's gun kept rising. Then he suddenly jerked sideways, eyes wide. His torso buckled as another bullet hit home, and a third drew blood from his neck.

Franco pulled the trigger, but the gun's slide locked.

MacCaffrey slumped to his knees, stunned, his eyes locking on Franco's. He swayed, then he slowly lifted his gun. A shot exploded, and MacCaffrey's right cheek evaporated in a spray of blood, bone, and skin. He collapsed forward, and Franco reeled back with a gasp, aware of someone standing in the bathroom.

Sal took a step toward him, one trembling hand gripping an old-fashioned revolver, the other clutching the door frame for balance.

Franco blinked, his stomach lurching in free fall. His lips parted, but no words came out.

"Why couldn't you let it go?" Sal said, not making eye contact.

"What?"

Sal looked at him, the revolver pointing in Franco's direction. "Why couldn't you just let it go?" he said again, harsher.

"I don't..." Franco's mind raced. "Why...are you here?"

Sal's face contorted and Franco inhaled sharply, pieces of an abominable puzzle forming a terrifying image inside his head, one he fought like hell to resist. It couldn't be...yet only one thing explained his uncle's presence here.

Trembling, he choked out, "What did you do?"

"He wasn't supposed to be there," Sal said, as if it explained everything.

Franco felt cold. "What are you talking about?"

"Too late now..."

"*Tell me!*"

Sal's eyes turned glassy. "Frank found out I was working for Lombardi."

Franco stared with his mouth open.

"Small stuff, at first...tipping him off, ripping off the competition. Walker, MacCaffrey, Hannity and I. But we got in too deep and the lines...blurred."

"What are you...I don't understand."

His mouth a thin line, Sal shook his head. "Hannity and I were shaking down Lombardi's competition, that day, but somebody called it in. Walker and MacCaffrey got to the apartment first and warned us. We made it out on the fire escape, but Hannity dropped his gun and it went off. When Frank got to the apartment, the others acted suspicious and he immediately figured something wasn't right. He saw the drugs and cash, found out none of it was booked as evidence, days later. He confronted Walker, who made up a story about Sean having a gambling problem. He promised to make it right, but Frank didn't believe him and decided to follow them." He grimaced, sighed. "That's when he saw us all together, doing business with Lombardi. The next day he tracked me down, furious, and I told him everything. About moonlighting for Lombardi, and driving the final nail in Dad's store so Lombardi could take over the location. Dad would have never allowed that, had he known. But I...just wanted it over, for everyone's sake."

It's my fault he's dead...

Faint sirens grew louder as Franco stared at Sal in horror. "Oh my god... Monday, on the stairs...you were serious..." Except, he'd left out what mattered the most. Franco gasped.

"Spare me that look," Sal snapped. "You have no idea what I went through, the pressure I was under, all the fucking time. No one did. For a moment I honestly thought Frank would at least...understand. Pamela, the hospital bills...there was never enough, and we were drowning. But he demanded I come clean to everyone, then turn myself in." He barked a humorless chuckle. "My own brother. Said I'd brought this on myself, betrayed my family *and* my brothers in blue, and had to take responsibility. Promised to look after the family, the fool. Most of our fucking problems were *because* of him, but suddenly he's playing savior? Romano would have annihilated dad. My way, Lombardi left him and Mom with enough to live decent, and they never knew he was behind it."

"Are you insane?" Franco shouted. "You think you did something noble?"

Sal glared at him. "Just like your father. *So* easy to judge from a place of safety, isn't it?" he nearly shouted. "You weren't there, didn't have the life of your wife and daughter threatened by the Mob. I had one choice, and I made it, thinking, *praying* it would save the family. And I lost Pam and Angie anyway. What, you think your father on his moral high horse would have approved of you and your mess of a life? Carried a flag and walked in your fucking parades? You're a grown man barely scraping by, hanging out with...*freaks* all day. I gave you and your family everything to make up for it, and more. Lombardi wasn't gonna let Frank bring us down. He was dead the moment he threatened to expose us. All I did was come up with a plan."

Franco balled his fists, breathing hard. "All these years, everything you said…all bullshit! You're the reason Dad's case never went anywhere. That's why you gave me the files, because they're useless."

Sal didn't answer and didn't have to. Aidan slowly sat up, and Sal turned his gun on him.

"Don't," Franco said, a chill rattling his body. "Are you…here to kill us?"

"Walker called me to deal with MacCaffrey. When I got here, I saw you run into the house."

Outside, sirens wailed and tires squealed. Hot tears stung Franco's eyes. "So you waited out there the entire time, hoping *he'd* finish us off?"

He couldn't read Sal's expression.

"Just like with Dad," Franco panted, resigned. "Couldn't do it yourself."

"I tried to save you, you ungrateful shit! Walker and MacCaffrey never told me they went after Prescott. I was in the dark until you showed me the letter and had no idea you were involved until I found out from them. I tried to warn you, but did you listen?" Spittle flew from his lips. Shouts permeated the walls and Franco stiffened.

Aidan raised his hand in a calming gesture. "Sal, put down the gun, don't make this worse."

Sal turned his gun back on him. "Stay were you are, both of you."

He took a step into the room, and Aidan said, "What happened to Lombardi and his crew…that was you?"

The walls shuddered as cops charged through the building's main door, shouting. Sal exhaled sharply. "Walker got wind of the FBI's investigation, figured it was our way out. And for thirty years it was." Franco recognized sadness and resolution in Sal's eyes, and his breath caught.

"Drop the gun, drop the gun!" someone yelled from the hallway.

Sal turned and fired at the cops.

Franco jerked forward with a yell, but Aidan grabbed him, flattening him to the ground, bullets tearing through the air. Aidan shouted at the cops to cease fire, identifying himself as police, and something about color of the day.

Aidan's weight pressed sharply against Franco's injuries, and he gasped for air. The shooting stopped, and Aidan rolled off him. Uniformed cops entered the room from both sides, and ahead, Sal lay crumpled in a heap by the bathroom.

Aidan got up, but Franco remained frozen in place.

"Quick, my partner needs medical attention," Aidan said, then crouched over Sal to touch his neck. "Get another bus, I got a pulse."

He placed his fingers against MacCaffrey's neck, but Franco turned his head. Something pulled hard at his insides. What had just happened? He lowered his eyes to the phone lying next to him on the floor. O'Shea's.

In the heat of the moment he'd tossed his own at the window, now lying under a heap of broken glass. He lifted O'Shea's cell and stared at his face on the blood smeared screen. Aidan appeared next to him and pulled a plastic bag from his pocket, and Franco dropped it in.

Someone yelled "clear" before Emergency Medical Technicians rushed in.

Franco pulled himself up on wobbly legs and moved closer to Sal. Two medics were assessing the damage he'd sustained.

"Will he be okay?"

"Too soon to tell," the technician said over his shoulder before glancing at Franco. "You need medical assistance?"

"No." He wanted to reach out and touch Sal and...what, punch him? Strangle him? Give him comfort?

He felt numb, devastated. How could this be? Angela...had she known? After Pam died, they hurt so bad yet both found the strength and love within them to pass on to him, Mom, and Andrea. Trips to the zoo, birthday parties, family dinners, talking and laughing for hours...and now? Franco wanted to throw up and crumble into a ball and cry.

But he swallowed and remained standing, observing everything around him as if through a fog. He lowered his gaze and studied his bloodied hands.

He'd shot a man, something he never believed himself capable of doing. Yet here he was, still standing. Someone pronounced MacCaffrey dead, and the information entered and exited his brain without a single emotion.

Aidan appeared next to him and touched his arm. "Are you okay?"

Franco returned a bleak stare.

"Sal's hurt pretty bad." The man who'd orchestrated his own brother's murder. Franco lacked the words. "The detectives will want to interview us separately," Aidan said. "You should think about getting a lawyer."

His eyes widened.

"You did nothing wrong. You saved our lives and I'll make sure they know it. But you shot someone and there will be an investigation."

Franco stumbled a step back and leaned against the desk.

"You'll be okay. I can't imagine how hard this is for you, but...try to remain calm. Do you know anyone you can call?"

"No...maybe."

A second team of EMTs arrived, and a uniformed officer approached them. "We need you to step out of the room."

Aidan said, "Officer, contact homicide and inform me the minute they're here."

Franco pointed at the shards of broken window. "My phone."

"I'm sorry." The officer eyed Aidan. "I can't let you take anything out of here. It's evidence."

One of the EMTs working on O'Shea waved. "Detective, he's trying to say something. Make it quick, we have to get going."

Aidan walked over and bent down, lifting O'Shea's oxygen mask a few inches. A moment later, the EMTs wheeled O'Shea and Sal out of the room.

Aidan touched Franco's shoulder. "Come on, let's get you outside."

Chapter Thirty-Nine

Exhaustion hit Aidan the moment he stepped out into the front yard, navigating Franco past uniformed cops and medical personnel moving about, his chest burning fiercely where MacCaffrey's bullets had hit the vest. Dark clouds blotted out the sun's rays, dousing everything in an eerie gray light, and the thick air smelled of dirt and asphalt. He checked the time, surprised it was only three in the afternoon.

A few people had gathered, peeking out between patrol cars, ambulances, and firetrucks, their cell phones pointed at the scene before them. Most appeared bored, like they'd seen the same show too many times to feel affected or outraged.

Paramedics loaded O'Shea into the ambulance while beat cops established a perimeter with yellow tape around the house and yard.

Keep moving...finish it. O'Shea's last words before the paramedics wheeled him out.

Aidan rubbed his face and ran a hand through his hair. No time to slow down. Walker was still out there, and if MacCaffrey had managed to tip him off, he had a head start—again.

Aidan steered a catatonic Franco to a paramedic and asked him to take good care of him. Behind him, O'Shea's ambulance sprung to life, sirens ablaze, and Aidan turned, watching it slowly making its way through the crowd blocking the street.

Guilt tore at him. He should have been here to back up O'Shea. He caught a glimpse of Franco, sitting on the ambulance's rear step, staring at a spot between his feet. He couldn't begin to imagine how awful he felt, wished he could talk with him. No time.

Keep moving...finish it.

Worst he could do to O'Shea and Franco right now was lose focus, and fuck up the case. The second medical emergency team loaded Sal into the ambulance.

Franco watched. "Can I ride with him?" he asked, quietly.

Aidan shook his head. "I'm sorry, I can't let you leave. You have to stay for the investigators."

Franco nodded and returned to staring at nothing.

Feeling like shit, Aidan walked away a few steps, trying to gather his thoughts. He pulled out his phone and called Joe Tanner and Mel Bradshaw, O'Shea's buddies from the precinct. It took a while to persuade them, unhappy he gave them so few details about what had happened. But Tanner agreed to go to the hospital and stay with O'Shea, and call with updates about his condition, while Bradshaw headed up to MacCaffrey's place, to keep an eye on things until they obtained a search warrant.

No word to Kaplan for now. Aidan assumed full responsibility and promised to fill them in on everything later, painfully aware he circled dangerously close to ending his career. But after everything that happened, he couldn't risk the entire case, and all their efforts.

Every passing minute tripled his anxiety. He needed to get going, but couldn't do a damn thing until the investigators arrived, provided they cooperated, and let him go.

News crews set up shop and Aidan borrowed someone's baseball cap and moved Franco to a van. He told him to put it on, keep his head down, and not talk to anyone. He didn't want Franco's face on the news, nor his, but he couldn't babysit him, either.

He wiped his forehead and noticed he'd managed to sweat through his clothes. A pair of detectives in their fifties walked up to him, a slim, white man sporting a comb-over in a futile attempt to hide a rapidly disintegrating hairline, and a Black woman with short hair and piercing eyes, both holding out their badges.

"This is Detective Miller, I'm Detective Barton," she said. "Hell of a mess in there, Detective...Torrance, is it?"

Aidan nodded and showed his badge in return. He moved as far away from potentially prying ears before spending the next five minutes talking while they took notes, their foreheads heavily creased pretty much the entire time. They only interrupted twice to ask questions to clarify.

"You keep referring to this fourth man, but you still haven't told us his name," Barton said.

Aidan still didn't want to, but had no choice. "Raymond Lee Walker. He used to—"

Her brows shot up. "I know who Walker is. Are you serious?"

Aidan nodded. "He, MacCaffrey and two others were moonlighting for the Mob back in the 70s and 80s. It ended when they assassinated Lombardi and half his crew. One of them was Franco DiMaso's uncle. He's the guy confessing at the end of the recording, after MacCaffrey shot my partner." Aidan pulled the evidence bag from his pocket. "My partner's phone, it recorded everything."

Barton reached for it, but Aidan pulled back. "I need assurances. This information pertains as much to my homicide investigation as yours."

Barton threw him a sharp glance. "I'm in no mood to play games."

"Nor am I. My partner's life is hanging in the balance, and I won't let his shooting be in vain. Walker has strong ties inside the NYPD, not to mention the city, and is still out there. If he hears MacCaffrey's dead, he'll destroy whatever evidence there still is. We need search warrants on MacCaffrey's and DiMaso's homes, *ASAP*, before we can move on Walker. And get MacCaffrey's cell—"

"Thank you, Detective, we know how to do our job." Barton took a deep breath, her eyes fixed on Aidan's. "Give us a moment."

She and Miller retreated several steps, talking to each other quietly for several minutes. Aidan cursed himself silently. He needed them on his side and couldn't afford to alienate them. His insides clawed at him. How many steps before everything blew up in his face?

They returned and Barton held out her open palm for the phone. "I promise you'll have copies the moment forensics pulls the data."

Aidan nodded, handing her the bag.

"Once we clear it with our supervisor, I'll accompany you to MacCaffrey's residence while Detective Miller will stay behind and process the crime scene until additional units can assist. Mr. DiMaso stays so Miller can interview him at the station."

Expected, but Aidan didn't like it. "This is highly sensitive—"

"No shit," Barton said without malice, "but those are my conditions."

Aidan turned his head to where Franco sat. "He's been through a lot, and he saved our lives."

Barton nodded. "Understood."

While she and Miller began securing warrants for phones and residences for both MacCaffrey and DiMaso, Aidan, realizing he had to bite the bullet sooner or later, called Kaplan.

He informed him of what had happened in as neutral a tone as he could, closing with the accusations against Walker.

Kaplan stayed silent for a few beats after he finished, then he said, "How dare you question my integrity! You and O'Shea held vital information from me because you thought I'd interfere with an investigation over personal relationships?" Kaplan exhaled sharply. "I won't have my loyalty to the department questioned, by you or anyone else, and you better learn this real fucking fast. O'Shea's behavior doesn't surprise me, but I expected more of you. You've proven yourself valuable to the department, but I consider your recent actions a major breach of trust."

Aidan's cheeks stung. "Captain, with all due respect, these guys got this far because they knew how to play the game. It wasn't our intention to disrespect or undermine you. Our intel came at the last moment and we had to make a choice. I stand by my decisions."

O'Shea's, technically, but he wouldn't make him the fall guy. He did find it odd Kaplan's outrage seemed to revolve entirely around his personal status, not the tragedy that had unfolded, or the crimes committed.

"Let me offer you a courtesy you failed to extend to me, *Detective,*" the captain said in a low growl. "I am well aware of certain concerns a federal institution has over a man I respect and believed I knew. I assure you I conducted myself in the most professional manner possible to assist then, and I fully intend to do so now. Hard as that may be. I hoped you knew that about me by now."

Kaplan's words left him stunned. "The FBI knew?"

"If they did, they didn't tell me, their investigation targeted...different allegations against Ray...Mr. Walker, after making his bid for mayor." He sighed. "What you told me is...I pray to God you're wrong. So, you'll do everything by the book, and follow the law to the letter. Obtain any and all necessary warrants and inform me of every frigging step you take before, during, and after. Do I make myself clear?"

"Yes, sir."

"Tomorrow I'm reassigning the case to Detectives Novak and Cole, and you'll assist—"

"Please, Captain—"

"Shut up, Torrance, and be glad I'm not relieving you from your duties right now. Seven years I've run this precinct with a spotless reputation. No one is going to undo this, including you."

Before he could reply, the line went dead.

Chapter Forty

Franco lost all sense of time, first sitting on a sidewalk, then in various police cars, and, finally, a reasonably comfortable chair inside a Brooklyn precinct's interview room. He'd not seen or spoken to Aidan in hours.

I wanted answers for so long...and now that I do, I almost wish I didn't.

He didn't agree with his mother, then, dying to learn the whole truth. Until he almost did. His brain grappled to process all the details. Still so much Sal had not explained, and he wanted to know…or thought he did.

Was he on an operating table fighting for his life? Already dead?

Franco couldn't say if he cared either way. Rage, pain, sadness…even relief crashed over him like tsunami waves, tossing him around, threatening to drag him under.

It's my fault he's dead...

Franco closed his eyes, remembered the torment and guilt in Sal's eyes that day. Had he meant to come clean, but lost his nerve? Was it just another attempt to twist the truth? Fuck with his mind? Or paint himself the tragic victim?

He longed to talk to Gino, Carmine, or Vince…his mother, even though that meant destroying her world all over again. His heart broke at the thought. Maybe saying it all out loud would help make sense of everything, because it sure as shit didn't make sense now.

He'd asked about his phone, but was told it would not be released until after forensics finished examining it. Upon his arrival he requested to make a phone call, half expecting the cops to try and persuade him calling a lawyer would make him appear guilty. But everyone treated him with kindness and compassion, down to the technicians taking blood and gunshot residue samples from his hands and shirt, and photographing his injuries.

Nick didn't pick up, and he left a message. How long ago? Had anyone seen the news, connected the dots, and tried to reach him, worried sick?

Miller brought him a soda and a protein bar, but he barely touched them.

Every time he thought of Sal—his face, the outrageous words pouring from his mouth—Franco felt like throwing up. Had he been so blind? Had there been moments in his life where he should have known? They all believed and trusted Sal, never doubted his grief, his commitment to their family. He even bought him his first camera.

You think your father would have approved of you...?

He'd never know, Sal had robbed him of that. Choking up again, Franco took deep breaths, and swallowed the pain. Not here, with strangers.

At least no one had read him his rights...so far. Baby steps.

The door opened and Franco rubbed his eyes with the back of his hands, wiping them on the ruined shirt. Detective Miller entered the room, followed by a handsome, sharply dressed man with Asian features.

"Tanet Powell, I'm here to represent you," he said, then turned to the detective. "I trust my client and I will have some privacy in here?"

"Yes. Call me when you're ready." Miller turned and closed the door behind him.

Franco shook Powell's hand. "Thank you for coming," he croaked out. "But I'm afraid I have no idea how to pay you."

"Let's not worry about it right now, you have enough to deal with," Powell said, removing his suit jacket and hanging it on the back of the chair. "I'm here as a favor to Nick." His warm smile held something suggestive, and though Franco took issue with Nick's promiscuity when they dated, he now thanked the universe his ex had planted his flag clear across Manhattan.

Tanet Powell sat and placed an iPad with a keyboard on the table between them. "Okay, tell me what happened."

Franco did, and Powell occasionally interrupted to ask a question and make notes. Saying it all out loud *did* help wrap his head around everything, but failed to make it better.

"First of all, I'm very sorry for everything that's happened to you," Powell said, after he finished. "I know you want to cooperative fully, but understand this may open doors to other aspects of your life you might want to keep private."

Franco sighed. "That ship sailed the moment my phone became evidence. I'm sure some poor forensic analyst already has my extensive photo and video library of dicks and asses plastered across their screen, including yours truly's." Tanet Powell flicked a smile. "Nothing left to hide. All I want is for this to be over, and for someone on my side to witness what I have to say…in case things go sideways."

Powell nodded. "After everything you've been through, I don't blame you. I'm here to protect and help you. You're the victim here."

Franco nodded.

"One thing: refrain from calling Detective Torrance by his first name. Better they don't know you're sleeping with him."

Franco blushed. "What? We're not."

Powell pursed his lips, unconvinced. "My apologies, there's something in the way you say his name…anyway, let's not give them the wrong idea, and stick with Detective Torrance. Any questions?"

Franco shook his head.

"All right, take a deep breath. Showtime."

* * *

By the time they finished the interview, it was past nine. Franco told his story twice and Miller asked a ton of questions, many of them the same, but a different way, as if trying to get Franco to trip up. Afterward, Miller told them the DA and Internal Affairs had been notified, and would be conducting their own investigations. He made him sign his statement and released him, advising him to stay available for further questioning. Franco thanked him, then Miller escorted them back to the reception area, where Aidan was waiting on the other end of the room.

Franco stopped and shook Powell's hand. "I can't thank you enough."

"You're welcome. I'm glad I could help." He handed him his business card. "If anyone calls—the cops, DA, IAB, the pope—your first call is to me. Don't talk to anyone. I will reach out to them, make sure they know you're represented. This was only the first of many interviews."

Franco's stomach tightened, but he nodded. "Thank you. I'll figure out how to pay—"

Tanet Powell touched his arm lightly. "Don't concern yourself with that tonight, we will figure it out. Try to get some rest, if you can, and we'll speak tomorrow." He looked over to where Aidan stood, a thin smirk dashing across his lips. He shook Franco's hand and left, nodding at Aidan in passing.

Aidan walked over to Franco, his suit as rumpled as one of O'Shea's. "How are you feeling?"

"Exhausted."

"I'll take you home."

Franco glanced over his shoulder and quietly said, "My place."

"You got it."

They left the station in silence and got into Aidan's unmarked. He started the ignition and pulled out of the precinct's parking lot.

"Did you get him?"

"There's still a lot that has to happen." Aidan glanced at him. "Techs located Martinez' phone and are combing through it. And we discovered over one hundred thousand dollars under MacCaffrey's floor boards, together with half a kilo of coke, a fake passport, and two handguns. Some old notebooks, too, but it'll take a good amount of time to examine everything, see if it relates to the case. He had surveillance photos of Prescott on his hard drive... " Aidan waited a few beats, as if deciding whether or not to continue, "...and you."

Franco blinked and rubbed his prickly arms.

"Nothing incriminating leading to Walker, yet, but I found an old photograph of MacCaffrey as a teenager, with his dad and Lombardi, taken at a barbecue in '70. They were definitely friends. Another team is currently searching your uncle's place...I have to head over there once I drop you off."

Franco stared ahead. "Any word on…how he's doing?"

"He and O'Shea are still in surgery. Do you want me to take you to the hospital?"

Franco shook his head. His eyelids weighed a ton, and he half closed them. "What about you, how much trouble are you in?"

"I'll be okay," Aidan said, but he'd hesitated a second too long for Franco to believe him. He closed his eyes and breathed quietly through his open mouth as they continued in silence.

He didn't realize he'd dozed off until Aidan shook him lightly in his seat, and he recognized The Green Thumb's display window.

Upstairs, Franco turned on the lights and headed straight for his bedroom. Behind him, Aidan's phone rang, and he heard him answer it. The bed beckoned, but Franco fought the urge to drop in and pull the sheets over his head. He stripped, tossed his clothes in the corner, and limped into the bathroom. He barely recognized his reflection in the mirror. For an instant his bruised face reminded him of his father's, the night he died, and his throat closed. Shivering with fatigue, he gingerly unwrapped his bandages and discarded them in the waste bin.

O'Shea's blood had soaked through his clothes and onto his skin, leaving pink traces all over his bruised body. He fought off revulsion and stepped into the glassed shower. The hot water stung fiercely, but he clenched his teeth and endured it. He grabbed a bar of soap and began scrubbing his hands and face ferociously, desperate to get clean.

He thought of O'Shea, and the weeks he'd spent hating him. He didn't want him to die and hoped he'd pull through. And of Sal, whom he'd loved all his life. He didn't know what he wanted for him, or if he cared whether he lived or died.

Enough!

He forced them all from his mind, scrubbing harder. But he still saw blood everywhere, no matter how faint the trace. Exhaustion and grief crushed him, crumbling his protective wall, and he sank to the shower floor, his back against the wall, shaking with sobs.

He wrapped his arms around his chest, squeezing his eyes shut, the water pattering down on his head.

He didn't notice Aidan's presence until he pressed his naked body gently against his. Franco rested his head on Aidan's shoulder, tears flowing freely now. He didn't try to hide them, or keep up appearances.

For once, he simply surrendered, and let them come.

Chapter Forty-One

Wednesday, August 10

Dressed in a faded blue *Star Wars* T-shirt, dark blue shorts and flip flops, Franco enjoyed the sun's warmth on his bare arms and legs as he and Vince entered Prospect Park through Bartel-Pritchard Square. His bruises were healing, but his appearance still left little doubt he was a man who'd been in a fight, and lost—spectacularly. He'd have asked Vince up to his mother's place, where he'd been staying since late Saturday night, but Julie was in no condition for company. And he'd needed the fresh air, and to clear his mind.

"How's Julie?" Vince asked, as if reading his mind.

Franco inhaled deeply, staring ahead. "It's gonna take time." They strolled down one of the park's many paved walkways, traffic from the street mixing with laughter from playing children, and conversations between people passing them. "The first two days were...brutal. She completely shut down. She trusted Sal completely. We all did, and I know part of her blames herself for not seeing it sooner. None of us did." He sighed. "Today she seemed, I don't know, different. Stronger, more resolved. Don't know how she finds the strength, but she refuses to be done in by anything."

"Good for her."

He nodded and glanced at Vince. "Andrea's devastated, she and Sal were very close. It'll be good to get out there, tomorrow, talk face to face."

"How long will you be in Chicago?"

"Four days, and I had to clear it with half of fucking New York first. Mom will stay two weeks. Spending time with Sis and the kids will help her get through this better, I'm sure."

"Any word on Sal?"

Franco clenched his jaw and shook his head. "Still in a medically induced coma. Makes it easier, in a way. Not that I think Mom could face him now, anyway. Or I."

It's my fault he's dead...

No shit.

"You know, I can't stop thinking about that, this entire time, he never said *I'm sorry...*that he knew what he did was wrong. Like he...can justify it all, somehow." His throat closed, and he blinked away the sting in his eyes. They walked in silence for several minutes, sounds of nature muting traffic and honking horns, and from someone's radio somewhere on the lawn, Brenda Russell sang of "New York Bars."

They reached the Prospect Park Bandshell, an open air venue which had been standing there since 1939, and Franco sat on a shaded patch on the open grass. Last June he'd come out here to see Chaka Khan kick off the free Celebrate Brooklyn! festival which took place each year, and had a fantastic time.

Vince said, "You know there were actual benches all the way here, right?"

Franco waved a hand at him, smiling faintly. "Shut up, sit, be one with nature."

Vince lowered himself with an exaggerated groan. "I just figured you'd be more comfortable over—"

"I already have a mother fussing over me." Franco sighed. "Probably helps keeping her mind off everything, but I swear, she's turning into Gino's mom."

"Be glad you have a parent who gives a shit," Vince said, a sad flicker in his eyes. He reached into his backpack and pulled out an older iPhone. "Here, don't know how well it still works, but it's better than nothing."

"Oh, thanks, you're a life saver. Pathetic how lost we are without them. And thank you for coming all the way out here."

"Of course, I'm just glad you're okay. You *are* okay, right? Kinda hard to tell from this mess," he said, waving his hand at Franco's face.

He shot him a look.

"Sorry," Vince chuckled, his cheeks coloring. "Seriously, though, we were all pretty shook when you called Sunday. Hell, we were still digesting what happened at the club."

Franco had called the gang from his mom's to let them know he was okay, and would be staying at her condo for a few days. They'd kept in touch since then, but most days he was too exhausted to talk much after spending all of it being interviewed by the cops, Powell, the DA, and everyone else with questions. Sleep only visited in intervals, and more than once he'd woken soaked in sweat, his heart pounding in his throat.

Vince sighed. "Have you learned anything more?"

"Aidan said a few days ago that news will break soon. They're still gathering evidence, but O'Shea's recording made some lasting impressions."

"You've seen it?"

He shook his head. "Apparently Martinez threatened MacCaffrey by going public, if he tried to make him the fall guy. The cops believe MacCaffrey went to Martinez's home to rid himself of a growing problem." He grimaced, eyeing his hands. "I still can't believe I shot him."

"Better than the other way around," Vince said.

"Too many dead," Franco said and lowered his head. "I never liked O'Shea, but he didn't deserve this. I feel horrible for Aidan."

"Did you talk to him?"

He shook his head. "I called him the moment I heard O'Shea didn't make it, but he's not answering my calls. Or texts. I know he's under a lot of stress, but something's different. He's...I don't know, pulling away." From what, he didn't know. Nothing happened in the shower. "He dropped me off at Mom's after I cleaned up, Saturday night, and that's the last time I saw him. We talked for fifteen minutes yesterday morning, but he sounded aloof, stressed. I can't imagine what must go through his mind. Everyone's gearing up for the shit storm that'll hit the moment they go public." He shuddered, lowering his head. "What worries me is, so far nothing indicates

Walker gave orders, or even knew about what MacCaffrey and Martinez did." That morning, the papers finally mentioned Walker in connection with an ongoing FBI investigation, but nothing about the murders, or the mob.

"Come on, he had to know."

"Try telling a jury. Tragedy of it all is, their convictions could overturn those of dozens of other monsters they put away over the years. There are no real wins here." He grimaced. "My head hurts. Can we talk about something else...*anything* else?"

Vince nodded and shrugged. "Nothing new, here, but Ben and Jerry send their love. Most exciting thing I have to report, and it's real low bar, is, Gino's got a new beau. Some carpenter named Mathew?"

Franco's face brightened up. "Ha, I'm glad he listened to us for once and gave the guy another shot."

Vince cocked a brow. "Really? Listening to him talk it was love at first sight."

"Yeah, right. Terri had to threaten testicular harm before he agreed to go on a second date."

Vince chuckled. "Well, Carmine says getting laid has significantly improved Gino's mood, and he's glad he won't have to euthanize him after all."

Franco chuckled. It turned into a belly laugh and Vince eyed him, amused. "Wasn't that funny."

No, it wasn't, but something inside him gave way, and he couldn't stop laughing. Finally, Vince joined in, and Franco leaned back on the lawn, staring at the blue sky above, savoring the moment.

Chapter Forty-Two

Monday, August 15

Aidan stood in front of O'Shea's casket, dressed in his official uniform, white gloves, and a black band over his gold shield. Few officers had shown up, and he felt bad for Aengus. The man should have retired and enjoyed his pension when he'd had the chance.

Some colleagues offered their sympathies, though Aidan knew few got along with his surly partner. But in times like this they all bled blue, and people showed unity. How far that unity would extend to him would reveal itself soon enough. Some congratulated him on breaking the case, others remained silent, avoiding him. There would always be those who believed cops didn't go after other cops, no matter their crimes.

He felt drained. Interview after interview, interrogations and explanations. Kaplan had reassigned the case to Cole and Novak, as threatened, but for now he got to assist. No word on what would follow after.

This morning's findings completed another piece of the puzzle...provided forensics could do something with what they had found in Sal's safe deposit box. O'Shea would have liked it. Their investigation cracked the case wide open.

But at what cost?

"Detective Torrance, a moment." Kaplan had appeared out of nowhere, dressed in similar fashion, and continued walking to get out of people's earshot.

Aidan followed, and almost bumped into the captain when he abruptly stopped and turned, his eyes like concrete.

"It's no secret O'Shea and I had our differences, but he should have known better. This was completely unnecessary and is a sad waste of life." He indicated the coffin with the slightest of nods. "Novak and Cole can handle things from here on out. As of tomorrow, you're assigned desk duty until further notice."

Aidan clenched his jaw and nodded. "Yes, sir."

"If you ever go behind my back again, I promise you'll curse the day you were born." He inhaled deeply, glanced at O'Shea's casket, and shook his head dismissively. "Senseless waste of life. I hope you still stand by your decisions, Detective. Remember them, next time you stand by your partner's grave. They put him there."

He strode off, leaving Aidan behind. Feeling cold inside, he balled his fists. Kaplan's words hit their mark.

"What was that about?"

Aidan turned, finding Detective Barton standing behind him. Her police uniform fit her snugly.

"It was nothing."

"Looked like you got your ass chewed out, and not the fun way."

Aidan cocked his head defensively, unsure if she was harassing him, but Barton's face showed empathy. She offered her hand. "I'm sorry about your partner."

"Thank you." Aidan relaxed, shaking it. "And for all your help."

"Any time. Probably hard to tell who your friends are, right now. I'd hate to be in your shoes." She pursed her lips. "Any progress?"

"The case has been reassigned." It stung to say it, but no sense sugarcoating it. "But we're getting closer. The samples found under Prescott's nails match Martinez, and we were able to ID him and MacCaffrey off the security camera footage from the apartment. We found a key at DiMaso's home we couldn't assign, at first. Took me four days of calls around town, but I finally matched it to a Chase safe deposit box on Madison. Three revolvers, different makes and models, all in evidence bags dated June 10, 1985, the day Lombardi and his crew were assassinated. Not sure if the techs can pull anything useful from the guns, but seems DiMaso kept them as insurance."

She sighed and shook her head in frustration. "Some cops can't resist temptation, but we can't let them get away with it. Makes the rest of us look bad. What you did took guts...not sure everyone will see it that way, though."

Aidan stared straight ahead.

"If things get too uncomfortable...we're always trying to expand our unit with good police, courageous enough to make the tough calls."

"Thank you," he shook Barton's hand again. "I appreciate it, but I'll be okay."

"I hope so, Detective. See you around."

She left and Aidan glanced at O'Shea's casket. Kaplan was just being a prick, and out for blood, because of his own department's involvement in bringing down his friend. But he was right—Aengus' death could have been avoided.

Nothing he could do about it, except work through the guilt, and take it one step at a time. He sighed and walked out.

Chapter Forty-Three

The elevator doors opened, and Franco, dressed in beige chinos and a dark blue dress shirt, entered the Charles Prescott Foundation reception area, where Derek Brewster waited to greet him. His skin prickled at the cool air, a sharp contrast to the humid ninety degrees outside. But the occasion called for more than shorts and T-shirts.

Brewster smiled warmly and shook his hand. "It is good to see you. You look like you are recuperating well."

Franco nodded. "Getting there." He'd gotten off the plane from Chicago two hours earlier, the visit with his sister's family necessary and exhausting. But in many ways it also made him more resolved and determined each day.

At first, he'd made great efforts to keep it together, and appear strong for everyone else. But something *had* shifted inside him—it wasn't an act, just untapped strength he likely owned all along. For the first time in a long while he had absolute clarity and felt wide awake. No more sitting around, apathetically waiting for life to resolve itself somehow.

"Please follow me," Derek Brewster said, leading the way. He'd shown up at Julie DiMaso's place, last Wednesday, after Vince left, expressing his apologies for everything they endured on his former boss' behalf, and offering his assistance. And he brought up the money.

By the time Franco told his mother about the trust, he knew he had no claim on it. All the struggles and sacrifices over the years were hers alone, and so was the decision what to do with it. The resolution emerged surprisingly fast.

They entered Brewster's office, where he introduced Franco to the foundations' lawyer, Cassandra Mancuso, a tall, well dressed woman in her late forties. They shook hands and settled into the chairs and sofa in the sitting area, the late afternoon sun casting a warm glow through tinted windows.

"Before we start, I'd like to read you a message from my mother," Franco said, pulling a white envelope from his pocket.

"Of course, take your time."

"Dear Mr. Brewster," he read. "When Franco told me about money left by Mr. Prescott, I did not take the news well. No amount of monetary compensation can change the past, or what he did, and I wanted nothing to do with it, least of all for personal gain. But your visit brought me perspective, and I want to thank you for your input. I'm grateful for my two wonderful children. Despite everything, we all prospered in our own ways, over the years, and prevailed as a family. But we all feel the money is best utilized by paying it forward to those less fortunate, and I am grateful for your generosity. May it bring some relief and joy to those in need. I am looking forward to speaking with you when I return."

Franco folded the letter in half and Brewster said, "We are happy to help. But there is still time if you've had a change of heart. The money is legally yours if you want it."

"No, this is the right thing to do," Franco said, echoing his mother's sentiment. The foundation offered to match the amount dollar for dollar in a new trust to benefit low income families who'd lost a parent under tragic circumstances. Distribution of funds would be overseen jointly by Brewster and Julie DiMaso.

Thirty minutes later it was all signed and done. A cool million, come and gone. Derek Brewster took Franco aside. "If there ever is anything you or your family need, please do not hesitate to call me."

"Thank you, we'll manage. You've been most generous."

"Paying your legal fees is the least we can do for you. I'm sure you've heard the news?"

Franco nodded. Hank Porter had finally grown a conscience, and the *Times* reported Domenico Lombardi, last living son of mobster Michele

Lombardi, turned state's evidence to avoid twenty years behind bars, providing detailed information on corruption by city officials, and murders committed by members of the police, on his father's payroll. Clearly, he didn't share his father's honor code.

Walker had been arrested that morning, and charged with several counts of corruption, racketeering, and murder. Franco wondered how many of his high ranking friends would still take his calls now.

"Charles was right, all along," Derek Brewster said, lowering his eyes. "I am ashamed I doubted him. And I'm so sorry...about your uncle."

Franco nodded, lips a thin line. He still battled conflicting emotions about Sal, the fact he hadn't woken a relief. Had it shifted guilt, or been a relief for Brewster, finding out Franco's own family had a hand in the tragedy surrounding his longtime friend?

Part of him still wished he could talk to Aidan, who hadn't returned his calls, but he'd finally stopped trying.

"I'm still afraid to think what this will do to the foundation," Brewster said with a grim expression, shaking his head. "I fear this will get a lot worse before it gets better."

Franco couldn't argue the point.

After a quick change at home, he arrived at the restaurant shortly before seven. It was closed, and he made his way upstairs, hearing music and laughter well before he reached the top landing. "Hopscotch" played in the background as he entered on Carmine's side, the gang busy setting the table, chatting away in the living room.

Gino spotted him first. *"Amore!"* He put down the dishes and rushed over, hugging Franco with a big kiss. "Welcome home."

Carmine hugged him next, then Vince and Terri. "It's so good to finally see you in the flesh," she said, holding on. "How are you, honey?"

"Pooped, but glad to be back."

"How is your mother holding up?"

"Putting up a tough front, but spending time with them is good for her."

Vince said, "So, did you do it?"

"Yep, a fortune come and gone." He flashed a lopsided smile, sighed.

Gino said, "I still think you should have kept it."

"Taking the money isn't gonna bring my dad back."

"Not taking it isn't either."

Franco shook his head. "What, frequently waking up screaming from a misplaced sense of guilt isn't enough? Thanks, but I don't need to see Dad's accusing dead eyes staring up at me from the gutter every time I spend a cent. It's blood money. This way, at least, it's put to good use, and gives mom a new purpose."

"I get it," Carmine said, returning to setting the table. "But it's still a shame."

"I know, but I'm healthy, I always manage to pay my bills, mostly on time, and I have a roof over my head. So I work three jobs to keep afloat, for now—it'll make me tougher, and help me grow. You know, my formative years."

Vince chuckled. "At forty-three?"

The corner of his mouth flicked up. "Point is, I got a lot to be grateful for, and am not stuck in a dreadfully depressing dead-end job. Nick called, said he might be able to throw a gig my way, for one of their emerging, young artists."

"That's fantastic news," Gino beamed, then his face turned serious. "What about your uncle—?"

Carmine waved a hand. "How about we change the subject?"

Gino slapped his forehead. "Shit, my chicken. Be right back." He stormed off, and, from the kitchen, shouted, "Terri, darling, lend me a hand, and Carmine, come get the wine. Everyone else wash up, we're eating in five."

Franco excused himself and headed for the bathroom, closing the door behind him. He washed his hands and caught his reflection in the mirror. He'd definitely looked fresher. Twisted dreams of him shooting MacCaffrey kept him from sleeping through the night. But ever since stepping across the brothers' threshold, a lightness spread inside him. He was home.

Charles, Walker, Sal...Aidan. He had no idea what would come next, what life would throw at him. But he was ready for it, and back in the driver's seat. And much of that he owed to his crazy gang outside, whose love and support propelled him forward.

"*Yo,* dinner's on the table," Gino's voice boomed from the others side of the bathroom door. Franco splashed water on his face and dried off, then joined the others at the table. Gino had prepared a feast of thyme-roasted chicken with red potatoes, mixed vegetables, and freshly baked focaccia bread with rosemary and cherry tomatoes. Vince and Terri passed around plates and Carmine searched through his phone's playlist, settling on Bobby Caldwell's "What You Won't Do for Love." Outside the window the darkening, cloud streaked sky had turned a deep pink.

Everyone sat, Carmine poured wine, and Gino waved his hands. "*Mangia,* everyone, food's getting cold." He turned to Vince. "By the way, I ran into Dan Carmichael."

Vince returned a blank stare.

"Dan—big guy, used to hang out with us at The World, back in the day. Anyway, he was just in Montreal and couldn't stop talking about this gay strip club he visited. Said he spent a fortune in one of the private rooms because the dancers charge twenty bucks a song."

"They sing?" Franco said with a wink.

"Well, *he* might, but for different reasons," Gino said, "Dan's a sweetheart, but let's face it, the poor man has the face of a Shar-Pei and an ass with its own zip code. He works as a consultant in the fraud department of an online dating service now."

Franco stopped his fork midway. "About time someone investigated all those questionable age and dick size claims."

"No, it's a Christian dating site. They mostly deal with con-artists swindling lonely old ladies out of money."

Terri said, "Speaking of old lady, remember our nineteen-year-old intern, Chris? The other day he comes up to me and tells me he picked up this hot chick at a party, and how shocked he was to find out she was forty-five."

Vince reached for the potatoes. "Jesus, woman, what the hell kind of conversations do you have with your interns?"

Terri held up a defensive hand. "Hey, all I said was *hello*."

Carmine said, "Probably his way to tell you he's okay dating a cougar."

"First, I'm not interested, and second, fuck you, I'm thirty-four."

"To a nineteen-year-old that's a certified MILF."

Franco laughed. Hanging with the gang, shooting the breeze and talking trash over a shared meal—man, he'd missed that. They talked about Gino's romance and people they knew, constantly teasing each other as if nothing had happened the past few weeks. And when they called it a night and said goodbye, a little after ten, Franco strolled home, stuffed and elated.

He rounded the corner onto Wooster, and music and laughter drifted up from the other end of the block where a neighborhood art gallery was holding a party. Kenny Loggins' "This Is It" filled the warm night air, and put a little spring in his step.

A Ford stood parked in front of his home. The door opened and Aidan, dressed in jeans, sneakers, and a polo, got out.

Franco felt a jolt of adrenaline and crossed the street, stopping next to the car's hood. "Hey."

"Hey." Aidan averted his eyes, sounding awkward and looking exhausted. "I'm sorry…I should have called."

"No problem. I was having dinner with the gang." Franco's hand brushed against the Ford's cool hood, and he furrowed his forehead. "How long have you been here?"

"I don't…awhile."

Franco had never seen him like this.

Aidan sighed and leveled his eyes at him, his expression pained. "I know it's late…but can we talk?"

"Yeah, sure…of course."

But Aidan just stood there, almost catatonic.

Franco took a step toward him and touched his shoulder, and Aidan slumped forward with a deep sigh. Franco put his arms around him, and they stood in silence amidst the laughter and music from the party echoing through the night. Aidan's cheek felt warm and stubbly against his, and for a moment, everything fell into place. Free of expectations or fears, he smiled, letting the sensation wash over him.

"It's okay," Franco said, and tightened his embrace. "I got you."

Acknowledgements

Thank you, dear reader, for buying my debut—I'm beyond excited to share *Blackout* with you, and hope you enjoyed it! Seven years and countless rewrites and amounts of blood, sweat, and tears later,'getting here' would not have been possible without the love and support from a ton of people:

Thank you, Level Best Books—Harriette Wasserman Sackler, Verena Main Rose, and my wonderful editor Shawn Reilly Simmons—for believing in, and taking a chance on me; my wonderful beta-readers, Connie Miller, Chris Vein, Christopher Read, Michelle Margules, Mark Oliver, Fen Hampson and Gary McIntyre, Darren Hoerner, Winston Gieseke, and Callie Snow, for donating their time and providing valuable feedback. Thank you, Tamara De Vito, for the Italian translations, and to all the writers and teachers I met at crime fiction conventions around the nation who welcomed me with open arms!

I'll always be deeply grateful to all the queer writers who gave or continue to give us wonderful, entertaining, and important stories and queer protagonists, and let an adolescent-me (several decades ago) experience a literary world I wasn't accustomed to—your books made a deep impact, and encouraged me to write my own.

A ginormous *THANK YOU* to superb writers Edwin Hill, James L'Etoile, Gabriel Valjan, and P. J. Vernon, for agreeing to read my manuscript (when most of you didn't know me from a hole in the wall), and supporting me with your wonderful blurbs. Your generosity won't be forgotten.

While I spent a lot of time in New York and spoke with dozens of law enforcement officers across the continent to get the details right, this is a work of fiction—sometimes facts had to stretch to accommodate the story (apologies to the purists). Thank you for taking time out of your hectic schedules to share your knowledge and expertise: NYPD Sergeant Joseph Belladonna, for answering my millions of questions, and being a good friend; retired LAPD detective Ninette Toosbuy of https://www.toosbuyconsulting.com for sharing your incredible knowledge and experience about police procedure, and becoming a fast friend; B Adam Richardson from https://www.writersdetective.com for your insight and help, and everyone who answered my questions online at https://www.facebook.com/groups/WRITERSDETECTIVE and https://www.facebook.com/groups/copsandwriters; Prof. Dr. med. Michael Thali at the Institute of Forensic Medicine (IRM-UZH), Zurich, Switzerland, and author DP Lyle, MD, of http://www.dplylemd.com for answering my various death and drug related questions. Everyone did their best to educate me, and I alone am to blame if I mucked it up.

To my wonderful parents, Ruth and Silvio, and my beautiful sister, Andrea: thank you for your unconditional love and support, and Dad, for having been the kind of father Franco would wish for—I miss you and am sad you didn't get to see me cross the finish line.

Thank you to my friends on both sides of the big pond, those who've been there for years and all the 'new ones' who made my transition to California a warm and welcoming one—I'm very fortunate to have you in my life, and I can't wait to see you again, somewhere, soon.

And for twenty years of laughter, love, tears, passionate/heated conversations, fun vacations, wild parties, hollering at each other over delicious, home-cooked meals (everyone trying to get a word in edgewise, Italian style), and tons of unsolicited advice, THANK YOU, Alfredo Picariello, Andreas Wenzler, and Mauro Picariello (and Flavio Baglivo, who left us much too soon). An ocean may separate us, but you're always in my heart. Now, would it kill you motherf&%*ers to call every once in a while?!?

Mark Gutkowski, you tirelessly championed for my success, kicked my butt when needed, built me up when I doubted myself (*aka*, every five minutes), created a beautiful, kick-ass cover for *Blackout*, and are the best husband and friend I could ever have hoped for. I wouldn't have gotten here without you. *Thank you*, honey, I love you infinity +1!

Playlist

I created a playlist for those who are interested in the music references, or would love to listen to the tracks while reading the book. The most complete list with special edits and remixes is on YouTube:

https://www.youtube.com/playlist?list=PLBwbQDd8EsN3f1T9kX8xGZGMAP7zBSGCe

If you prefer to listen on Spotify (sadly, most special edits are not available there) please go to:

https://open.spotify.com/playlist/3iVe9EdiUozliCAIX7SQ36?si=q7cjMxtDS4m_rB_fljsGBQ

Enjoy, and keep on dancing.

Chapters:

July 13, 1977:

Riders On The Storm, (The Doors), 1971

Chapter 2:

Try It Out, (Gino Soccio), 1981

Chapter 5:

Simplify, (Omar) 2015

Single Life, (Cameo), 1985

Chapter 6:

Pitchdown Disco Boogie Mix, (DJ Osmose) 2013

Don't Let It Go To Your Head, (Jean Carne), 1978

Chapter 7:

Help Me, (Joni Mitchell), 1974

Love Has Fallen On Me, (Chaka Khan), 1978

Chapter 8:

What's In It For Me, (Zalmac) 1982

Everybody , (The Jacksons) 1980, Opolopo Extended Disco Tweak, 2014

Love's Coming At 'Ya, (Melba Moore) 1983, OOOFT! Re-Edit, 2012

Pull Up To The Bumper, (Grace Jones) 1981

Chapter 9:

So You Wanna Be A Star, (Mtume) 1980, BlackLodge Dance Edit, 2010

Chapter 13:

Get It Up For Love, (Ned Doheny) 1976

Who'll Be The Fool Tonight, (Larsen/Feiten Band), 1980

I Apologize, (Larry Carlton), 1978

Pretty Bird, (Terea), 1977

Chapter 14:

Almost Summer Mix, (DJ Supermarkt), 2016

The Memory, (Roy Ayers), 1976

Chapter 17:

Hallelujah, (Leonard Cohen) 1984

Bright Eyes, (Art Garfunkel) 1979

MacArthur Park, (Donna Summer) 1978

The Wind, (Cat Stevens) 1971

Ding Dong The Witch Is Dead, (Herbert Stothart, Wizard of Oz) 1939

Chapter 18:

Sweet Delight, (Dr Packer Edit), (orig. Still got the magic, (Michael Wycoff), 1982)

Cold Blooded, (Rick James) 1983, (Julian Sanza Edit)
Freesia, (Princess Freesia), (Joey Negro Cookie Dough Mix)
Lonely People, (Dr Packer), (Orig: Club Lonely, (Lil' Louis), 1992)

Chapter 26:

Can't Stop The Feeling, (Justin Timberlake), 2016

Chapter 27:

Slow Love, (State Department), 1977

Chapter 30:

Here Comes The Sun, (Nina Simone), 1971 (Francois K. Remix)
(Don't Worry) If There's A Hell Below, We're All Going to Go, (Curtis Mayfield), 1970

Chapter 33:

Fly Me To The Moon, (Frank Sinatra), 1964

Chapter 34:

You Saved My Day, (Cheryl Lynn) 1978, (Joey Negro, Tell The World Mix)

Chapter 41:

New York Bars, (Brenda Russell), 1983

Chapter 43:

Hopscotch, (Gwen Guthrie) 1983, (Larry Levan Instrumental Mix)
What You Won't Do For Love, (Bobby Caldwell) 1978
This Is It, (Kenny Loggins) 1979, (Mad Mat's re-edit)

About the Author

Marco Carocari grew up in Switzerland, where he, over the past fifty-odd years, worked in a hardware store, traveled the globe working for the airlines, and later as an internationally published photographer, and frequently jobbed as a waiter, hotel receptionist, or manager of a professional photo studio. In 2016 he swapped snow-capped mountains, lakes, and lush, green pastures for the charm of the dry California desert, where he lives with his husband. 'Blackout' is his first novel.

For more info, visit http://www.marcocarocari.com

CPSIA information can be obtained
at www.ICGtesting.com
Printed in the USA
BVHW032214230321
603177BV00022B/263